DRAGON LORDS: BOOK FOUR

THE
WARRIOR
PRINCE

By

Michelle M. Pillow

Futuristic Romance

New Concepts   Georgia

Be sure to check out our website for the very best in fiction at fantastic prices!

When you visit our webpage, you can:
* Read excerpts of currently available books
* View cover art of upcoming books and current releases
* Find out more about the talented artists who capture the magic of the writer's imagination on the covers
* Order books from our backlist
* Find out the latest NCP and author news--including any upcoming book signings by your favorite NCP author
* Read author bios and reviews of our books
* Get NCP submission guidelines
* And so much more!

We offer a 20% discount on all new Trade Paperback releases ordered from our website!

Be sure to visit our webpage to find the best deals in e-books and paperbacks! To find out about our new releases as soon as they are available, please be sure to sign up for our newsletter (http://www.newconceptspublishing.com/newsletter.htm) or join our reader group (http://groups.yahoo.com/group/new_concepts_pub/join)!

The newsletter is available by double opt in only and our customer information is *never* shared!

Visit our webpage at:
www.newconceptspublishing.com

New Concepts Publishing, Inc.
5202 Humphreys Rd.
Lake Park, GA 31636

ISBN 1-58608-732-0
2005 © Michelle M. Pillow
Cover art (c) copyright 2005 Eliza Black

NCP books are available at special quantity discounts for bulk purchases for sales promotions, premiums, fund raising, or educational use. For details, write, email, or phone New Concepts Publishing, Inc., 5202 Humphreys Rd., Lake Park, GA 31636; Ph. 229-257-0367, Fax 229-219-1097; orders@newconceptspublishing.com.

First NCP Trade Paperback Printing: April 2006

Other print titles from NCP by Michelle M. Pillow:

Tribes of the Vampire 1: Redeemer of Shadows
Tribes of the Vampire 2: The Jaded Hunter
Ultimate Warriors
Caught
Ghost Cats
Ghost Cats II (In print May 2006)
Emerald Knight (In print May 2006)

Dragon Lords 1: The Barbarian Prince
Dragon Lords 2: The Perfect Prince
Dragon Lords 3: The Dark Prince
Dragon Lords 4: The Warrior Prince

Lords of the Var 1: The Savage King (Continuing the
Dragon Lords series—coming soon to print)

Zhang Dynasty: Seduction of the Phoenix (Continuing the
Dragon Lords and Var series)

Dedication:
To Dan, My Warrior Knight in Colorful Armor

Chapter One

Pia Korbin gasped, sputtering as she jerked back from the blood spraying across her scarred hands. The knife slipped from her fingers to land on top of the man bleeding to death beneath her. Gradually, her drunken mind sobered. His pants were around his ankles, the evidence of his intent lowering as the artery next to his groin bled out onto the snowy black ground.

"You ... ugly ... bitch," the man growled at her, his throat gurgling in pain, his eyes glaring with hatred. Even as she stood above him, she smelled the foulness of his breath. He weakly reached his hand to his bleeding thigh, but then let it fall lifelessly to the side. Those words were the last he ever said.

Pia took a deep breath, looking desperately around from behind the industrial dumpster to the end of the alleyway to make sure no one saw her. Swallowing nervously, she reached down to search the man's pockets, not bothering to check him for a pulse. She knew he was dead. Pulling out an ID card, she froze. It was as she feared. He was the mayor's son.

Behind her, fire burst from the tops of industrial smokestacks. The city of smog, metal and stone was no place to trifle in. She coughed. Even the snow here was as black as death.

Looking down, she knew she'd really done it this time. They wouldn't care that the man had attacked her, thinking to have a bit of morbid sport. On a planet like Rayvic, the mayor's son had every right to take whatever he wanted--including an unwilling woman. They ran their city like the medical mafia ran its mob. One look at her ugly face and they'd kill her--slow and painful like.

Grabbing her knife, she wiped the bloody blade on the man's shirt, grabbed a wad of cash from his pockets, and buried the body beneath a pile of refuse. Taking a deep breath and one last look around, she took off down the alleyway. Daylight would be hitting the cold planet soon.

Then all the goons in the city would be looking for her. She had to get out of there.

Pia sprinted, taking the back streets she'd memorized like the back of her hand. She climbed down to an old, abandoned space dock nestled on the gray shores of the lapping black river. Going to a pile of rubble, she uncovered the personal transport that would take her off the desolate black planet of ice.

* * * *

Two weeks later...

The doctors of Galaxy Brides Corporation eyed the patient before them. The pristine white of their walls matched the white of their jackets and even the white of one doctor's beard. As they searched, they couldn't see the woman's face beneath the heavy fold of her hooded cape, but they'd seen her hand--a wrinkly, scarred mess of variegated flesh.

"Miss Korbin," one of the doctors said delicately. "I've brought a specialist to speak to you. Your blood tests have all come out fine. But we need to see your face to see if we're going to be able to correct it."

Pia lifted her scarred hands. Her hazel eyes were hard as she pulled back the hood. Instantly, she saw the doctors flinch as they took in her face. She refused to show a reaction. It was the same every time--horror, fascination, repulsion, a rush of unasked questions.

One eyelid drooped with a covering of flesh, pulling it down at the corner. The lashes and brow were long since melted away. Her right eye always watered and she dabbed it with a tissue. Part of her hair no longer grew, except in splotchy patches, which she kept cropped short like the rest of her locks. The burns continued down her skull to the left side of her face, burying an ear, over her neck and shoulder, down her arm, to cover over sixty percent of her body. The scars no longer hurt her when she moved and she'd gotten used to their tight feel.

The doctor with the white beard cleared his throat. "Yes, well, Miss Korbin, you're in luck. The burns haven't affected the structural ... integrity of your face."

"So you can fix it?" she asked with emotional detachment.

"Yes," the woman doctor answered. Her eyes strayed to the side, trying not to stare at the patient. "But it will be an expensive procedure. With no Medical Alliance insurance..."

"So long as you agree to sign a contact with Galaxy Brides, it will be covered completely," the bearded doctor said when the lady hesitated. "We have a shipment--forgive me, a load of eager young women just like you going to Qurilixen next week for their Breeding Festival. I can give you a brochure on the planet if you like. I'm told royalty might be there."

"That won't be necessary." Pia had been over all of her options. The Rayvikians were looking for a scarred woman of her description. Soon every lowlife in the galaxy would be trying to collect the price on her head. No, a scarred woman was too easy to see and remember. It wasn't like she could just change her hair color and blend into oblivion. She had to change her face and, thanks to the Medical Alliance jacking up every medical service in the galaxy, this deal was the only way she could afford to do it. "I'll sign right now."

"Wonderful," the doctor said, claiming the company commission for himself. The others looked at him, knowing they were in for a lot of work. "I'll order some uploads brought down for you so you can learn of the Qurilixen while we perform the surgeries. It might take your mind from the procedure."

"Miss Korbin," the lady doctor said pensively. The bearded man walked to the intercom to call for the contracts. "We want you to understand that, because of the nature and advanced age of your scars, it will be a painful procedure. We won't be able to put you out all the way for the entire time."

"It's fine." Her eyes shone forward. "Let's just do it."

"Very good. I'll go set up. If we only have two weeks, we need to get started right away." The bearded doctor smiled. He pushed the intercom again. "Dr. Charles, ready room twelve, please."

Pia nodded. She touched the scars she'd grown used to. There was a strange comfort to their familiar pattern. She was almost afraid of what she would look like underneath them.

"We also need a waver from you so we can document the procedure," the woman doctor said, going to get an electronic clipboard from the wall.

"No," Pia said, stopping her. "I evoke the right of privacy. I don't want anyone knowing I was here. And I don't want any pictures taken of me before, after, or during the procedure."

"But, think of all the people who will be inspired by your story, Miss Korbin," she insisted.

"Don't worry, Miss Korbin, if you don't want pictures there will be no pictures. Our lawyers will even put a privacy clause into your contract if you like. I'm the best in my field, so you have nothing to worry about." The bearded doctor gave the woman doctor a look of displeasure. The compensation for finding brides was great, as there was a shortage of willing women in the galaxy. He didn't want to scare the prospective bride off. "We'll have all your scars removed in no time. Soon it will all be a bad dream. You'll be very pleased, Miss Korbin. I promise."

"All but the gash on my ribcage," Pia said calmly. This doctor knew nothing of bad dreams or the nightmares that could haunt a person even in wake. "Do what you can with the others, but that scar stays."

* * * *

Six weeks later...

Pia stared at the mirror. No matter how much she looked at herself, she didn't recognize the smooth face or wide hazel eyes that stared back at her. The doctors had worked miracles with her. All her burns were gone, her cheek had been reconstructed, and her hair follicles stimulated to grow so she again had a full head of hair. The doctors swore she looked exactly like she would've if she hadn't been burnt.

It was like they scraped off the top layer to reveal what lay beneath. The scars were also gone from her body. Her left breast was made to match the right, both of them lifted and reshaped. She saw muscle definition where before the flesh had been so tight she hadn't been able to see the form beneath it.

Oh, how it had hurt! It was worse than she could've ever imagined. Sometimes her limbs still ached with the memory of it. She'd never complained, not once during those two weeks of surgeries. The doctors had done their job. The Rayvikians would never find her now. How could they? She couldn't pick her own face out of a crowd. When she imagined herself, she still looked as before. In her dreams she was scarred, running away from a stranger that looked like her.

Pia spent most of the voyage alone, getting checkups from the robotic doctor on the flight. She couldn't find common ground with the other women on the ship. They were nice, but they talked of things she knew nothing about-- cosmetics, men, marriage. They all seemed fixated with marrying one of the four Princes rumored to be at the festival.

Thinking of the festival, she frowned. She had to find a husband. Because of her extensive work, she was forced to sign an exclusive contract that said she would go on any voyage Galaxy Brides had until she was married--whether it was this one time or a hundred times. But, in the end, the result was the same, she would be a wife. Until she said 'I do,' she was their property to be shifted around. Pia didn't relish the thought of making more of these trips and she couldn't risk a delivery possibly taking her to Rayvik or one of their affiliated districts.

Besides, she thought, *Qurilixen doesn't sound so bad.*

The planet was inhabited by primitive male types similar to the Viking clans of medieval Earth. They were classified as a warrior class, though they'd been peaceful for nearly a century--aside from petty territorial skirmishes that broke out every fifteen or so years between a few of the rival houses. They kept to themselves, had a simple religion, favored natural comforts to modern technology, and even prepared their own food.

It would be better than being on some high-tech planet run by dimwits. Pia liked the idea of warriors and combat training. She'd be in her element in such a place. She'd have a better chance of finding herself a job.

Qurilixen suffered from blue radiation and over the generations it had altered the men's genetics to produce only strong, large, male, warrior heirs. Maybe once in a thousand births was a Qurilixen female born. Since

Qurilixen women were so rare, Pia wouldn't be surrounded by housewives all day, being forced to plan dinner parties.

Well, she thought with an unamused look around her, *no women but these and others like them.*

Pia was so used to standing off by herself and being rejected that she'd been unwilling to make a move toward friendship with any of the other women. With men, you just had to prove yourself in a fight and they would allow you into their ranks. They treated her just like one of the guys. Women were generally much more fickle.

The spacecraft was outfitted with the best accommodations and services the star system had to offer. Personal droids were assigned to each passenger. There were cooking units in each of their quarters that could materialize almost any culinary desire. Even the doctor Pia had spent all those hours with finishing her treatment had been mechanical.

The women aboard the ship weren't all bad and a few Pia even liked. They were the only company she'd had in the last month of travel, being as they were quarantined from the ship's crew to insure nothing unseemly happened.

The brides were being prepared for the Breeding Festival that night on Qurilixen. It was the one night of darkness on the otherwise light planet and considered the only night the men could choose a mate. It was a primitive ceremony, but Pia thought simple was good. She didn't fancy wearing a large white gown and standing in front of an audience in her new body. She wasn't comfortable in it yet and even missed the protective, familiar comfort of her old scars.

Pia hated to admit it, but she was nervous. She didn't know anything about marriage. From what she'd been told, her parents had been happy before her mother died. As to having children, she knew even less.

Gena, one of the women Pia absolutely couldn't tolerate, laughed. Her voice was abrasive and harsh, as she announced, "Rigan finished her Qurilixen uploads first. It would seem she is most eager to please her new husband."

"Or to be pleased by him," someone added from across the circular room.

Pia rolled her eyes, knowing it wasn't likely she would be chosen for those reasons. Perhaps there would be a nice blind man in need of a wife--a nice blind man who was sterile and couldn't have children.

Well, a girl could always dream.

Pia sat still as the beauty droid worked. She'd refused its services for most of the trip. But now, seeing as it was her best option to get married, she let the robot tend to her. Feeling it pull on her overly long blonde locks, Pia frowned. The miles of hair on her head were going to be the first thing to go.

"I wish I could be so ambitious. I'm afraid I didn't watch a single one of those boring uploads," another woman said.

Pia had used the uploads while in surgery before she'd even boarded the ship. They'd taken her mind off the pain and made her feel more productive. She was sure she knew more about the planet than most of its inhabitants did. Qurilixen was on the outer edge of the Y quadrant. The planet's surface was plagued by a soft green haze of light because it had three suns--two yellow and one blue--and one moon.

"I tried on my gown this afternoon," Gena said, much to Pia's annoyance. She glanced over to see the woman holding her own breasts and closed her eyes so she wouldn't be subject to the scene. Unhampered, Gena continued, "They are gorgeous, but I think I'm going to go get my breasts enhanced again--just a little bigger--and I'm going to have my nipples enlarged. Those Princes won't be able to resist me. Maybe I'll marry all four of them just for fun."

Unable to resist poking holes in the annoying woman's logic, Pia said sarcastically, so everyone could hear, "How will you know who the Princes are? I've heard that all the men wear disguises. You could end up with a royal guard."

"Or a gardener," a brunette offered with a laugh, joining in the fun.

Gena's face fell. Pia closed her eyes to her. Mission accomplished.

"I hear they wear practically nothing at all."

Pia shot Olena Leyton an amused grimace, not liking to be reminded of that little fact. Good thing they couldn't have sex that first night. She was sure she didn't want anyone touching her.

"Except the mask and some fur," Olena finished.

Pia could take no more. She blocked them out of her head as she turned to look into the mirror. Again, the stranger's face was there in place of hers.

When she turned back around, breaking from her own troubled thoughts of getting married, she noticed that most of the women had already left and that her beauty droid was long since finished with her. Nodding kindly at Olena, Pia said nothing as she went back to her suite to get dressed.

Lost in thought, she trailed down the long metal corridor to her room. She startled in surprise to hear the medical droid's voice say, "Miss Korbin, this way. It's time for your last treatment."

Pia stopped walking, embarrassed. Seeing the reserved blue eyes of Nadja on her, she knew the woman had heard. Nadja turned quickly away.

Pia changed her course, glad that the treatments would finally be over with. Slipping her ID card over the wall scanner, the medic room door opened and she stepped inside a machine. Dropping her white cotton robe, she stood naked as the medical droid closed her in. Instantly, a bright green light shot all around her body. The rays tingled on her naked flesh.

Closing her eyes, Pia swallowed nervously. It was almost time to meet her future husband. She just hoped that one of the Qurilixen would want to bring ugly little Pia home with him.

* * * *

Pia's heart stopped in her chest and tears came to her eyes. This was never going to work. She'd spent the last six weeks resigning herself to a Qurilixen husband and now that she saw them, she knew she was going to have to go back and start the journey over again. When the uploads had said large warriors, Pia assumed they were politely meaning fat, potbellied fighters. She couldn't have been more wrong.

Before her were two rows of Qurilixen bachelors. They were large, fighting men. They were warriors. And, to Pia's everlasting horror, they were all in incredible shape and exceptionally handsome. A few had battle scars on their flesh, but nothing so dramatic that it took away from their beauty. If anything, it only added to their dangerous allure.

The Qurilixen were nearly seven feet of pure bone, muscle, and sculpted flesh. She could tell, since they were practically naked. Pia was no out of shape marshmallow, but even she was dwarfed by their thick arms and chests.

Fur loincloths wrapped around their fit waists to leave bare their powerfully built legs and upper bodies. The fire glistened off their smooth, oiled skin. Jewelry clasped around sinewy biceps in golden rings of intricate design. From their solid necks hung crystals bound with leather straps.

Pia knew she looked ridiculous in the outfit the droid had given her to wear. Her shoulders were bared, as the gown only came up to cover her breasts. She could fill the gown out, thanks to the doctors. But the silk and gauze material didn't make her feel beautiful, only self-conscious.

The silk was of the darkest of reds, crimson against her tanned skin. The surgery lasers had given her a soft, all-over bronze color that wouldn't fade. The doctors said it would help protect her sensitive skin from ultraviolet rays--something that would be particularly useful on a planet with three suns.

Pia sighed as a wave of her long hair hit her forehead. Trying to lift her arm, she frowned when she couldn't brush the annoying lock off her face. A belt looped across her back, tapering out to the sides, only to lock onto her wrists instead of heading around the front. The strands wound up to her elbows like chains.

The dress fitted to her waist and hips, only to flare out in strips of material when it reached her upper thighs. The wind whipped the skirt against her legs, chilling her. She might as well have been naked for all the coverage the thing afforded her. On her feet were soft, pretty slippers. She missed her combat boots.

Pia ignored the laughing men behind the bachelors, cracking good-natured jokes about the brides and the lucky grooms. The rowdier men posed, trying their best to playfully gain the brides' attention. The bachelors, however, stayed deadly silent and still, barely smiling as they looked at the women standing on top of the docking plank in a straight, orderly line.

Pia's heart broke as she looked around the wonderful campground. It was perfect, so basic and simple in its untamed, untouched elegance. The colossal trees of the forest were thick, with large leaves that canopied overhead--the shade would be perfect for camping once she got used to the hours of light. She imagined that such a gigantic forest would be great for hunting and fishing, even hiking.

This is a place where she could have gotten lost. It was homey, earthy, and exotic in its smell of burning wood. It was rustic, yet colorful, in its sights. Music played, primal and earthy in the background, hypnotic and enticing at the same time.

In the distance there was a mountain range. Pia squinted, barely able to make it out in the darkening skies. Stars sparkled overhead. The moon was large and gave off a brilliant light. It shone over a valley of pyramid-shaped tents whose walls were lit by torches and whose tops were decorated by waving banners.

Looking back down, Pia swallowed painfully, trying not to feel so disappointed. The bachelors still stood like bronzed Vikings. Maybe the next planet would be just as good, only the men would be ugly and attracted to ugly things.

The Qurilixen all had shoulder length hair. Black leather masks covered each groom's face, hiding them from forehead to upper lip. Their eyes shone bright from the eye slits, like probing liquid metal. Behind them, Pia could see the others were more fully dressed. With such a blatant difference in wardrobe for this ceremony, Pia knew that they would be a sexually charged race. Even now she could see the married couples boldly stroking and touching each other as if it were only natural they did so.

The line slowly moved, jerking her from her thoughts. She dutifully walked down an aisle made up of hot flesh on each side. Her lips curled, though not in pleasure, as she bit the corner of her mouth. She glanced to one side and then the other, knowing full and well no one would look at her for too long with so many other beauties to gaze at. One by one, she saw the men's eyes alight with lust--lust that wasn't for her.

Almost to the end of the line, feeling dejected and ready to go back to the ship and change her clothes, she glanced at one of the warriors toward the end. He was staring at her, his crystal shining from the leather strap on his neck. He was a handsome specimen with light brown hair a little longer than the others and matching brown eyes that seemed to shine. He was taller and had broad shoulders, which bulged with a rocky play of muscles. He didn't smile and there was a commanding nature to his stance.

Pia expected his eyes to move on as everyone else's had. When he continued to stare, she frowned, glancing over her shoulder.

How rude! she thought in growing ire when she turned back to see that he was indeed still watching her.

Taking his look for one of abhorrence, she shot him an angry scowl. She might not be beautiful, but she didn't need this man pointing that fact out to her.

The man bowed his head in her direction. Pia leaned a little away from him as she passed by. Her mouth curled in disgust of his manners. He might be the most handsome of them all, but that didn't give him the right to judge her.

Without a backwards glance, she continued on, following the throng of women to a feasting table. She took a deep breath, glad the worst was over. Now that she'd met with rejection, she could eat, get back to the ship, and prepare for the long flight home. At least the spacecraft wouldn't be full of women for the second leg of the journey. That would be something anyway.

Chapter Two

Zoran of Draig's eyes lit with fire and his mouth suddenly went dry. He could hardly believe his good fortune. The most beautiful woman in line was destined to be his wife. He could see the firm muscles working beneath her shoulders as she walked. Her arms were slender yet strong. She kept amazing care of herself and moved as if she knew how to use her body to full advantage. Her wide hazel eyes looked around without vanity and when she caught his eye, she seemed surprised that he stared.

But how could he not stare at a vision so lovely?

Zoran's lips didn't move to smile. He could barely remember to breathe. Her tanned skin gleamed pleasantly in the firelight and the crimson of her gown was wickedly erotic as it hugged to her very pleasing curves.

She glanced over her shoulder and then back at him. The confusion in her eyes turned to a look of instant annoyance. If not for that hard look directed at him, he would've reached forward and grabbed her. Remembering at the last moment that he needed to bow, he did so.

The woman pulled away from him, her eyes narrowing as she hurried past, almost as if she was afraid he meant to touch her. By the look on her face, she wasn't as pleased with him as he was her. This puzzled him.

Zoran knew he was a handsome, sought after man, even without the title of Prince attached to his name. Whenever he traveled outside his planet, women would vie for his attention. When the prostitutes came to Qurilixen to relieve the men, he was always a hard-fought-for prize between them, having his pick of any of the beauties--sometimes taking two or three. But those wild days were behind him. He was of the age to finally settle down.

He kept an eye on his bride as she walked away. Her athletic legs strode in perfect form and he felt an animalistic growl growing in the back of his throat. His eyes flashed with the glittering of a barbarous gold. His body already craved her and, by the will of the Gods, he would have her.

* * * *

Pia was ready for the night to be over. She stared at the married couples as they laughed and flirted so easily by the firelight. For a moment, she was jealous, wishing she could be one of the beautiful people she saw enjoying their celebration. They laughed and joked like a giant family, a whole community that was bonded in trust and loyalty. She knew what it was like to belong to a family, one you could depend on and go to, one who would fight by your side, no questions asked. She imagined that this place would be like that for someone who belonged in it.

The brides had been directed to long wooden tables where a large buffet had been spread beneath a canopy. It was a veritable feast of roasted two-horned pigs, blocks of Qurilixen blue bread with whipped cheese, strange fruit, and crusted pastries. Pia didn't eat and she didn't drink what they offered. She just wasn't in the mood. As soon as she got back to the spacecraft she planned on a nice, long massage and a bottomless cup of green tea.

The Qurilixen men wore simple tunic shirts and breeches. Servants carried pitchers full of a strange berry wine. Pia's attention was caught as Olena, at her side, eagerly waved one of the servants over. The man's light blond hair fell over his shoulders as he bowed. Olena held up her goblet, barely giving him a second glance.

Pia did notice him however. He was dressed plainly like the others, but Pia knew well the use of a disguise. Clothes didn't create a person. They did, however, conceal a person. If you watched close enough, the real person's nature would always shine through.

She frowned, seeing how the servant's large hands shook when he poured. They were callused along the side ridge of his palm. This man wielded a sword, probably a heavy blade used typically by foot soldiers. Narrowing her eyes, she studied his movements. He was light on his feet as he walked away, but hadn't been so graceful when he took Olena's goblet from her hand. It had been almost as if he were trying not to grip it too hard.

"He makes for a peculiar servant," Pia mused thoughtfully to herself. She suspiciously watched him as he moved down the table. His eyes didn't travel to the goblets and he seemed more preoccupied with the married couples out by the bonfire pit than with the brides. Bumping into another servant, he mumbled an apology, spilling his wine as he walked down the platform.

"They make for a peculiar race," Olena mumbled.

Pia glanced at the woman, surprised to hear her answer. She hadn't realized she spoke out loud. Forcing herself to laugh softly, she nodded in agreement. "Do you believe this whole deal?"

"What are you doing here anyway?" Olena asked curiously. "You hardly seem like the type to get trapped into coming."

"Free benefits," Pia said, her words enigmatic. She could tell Olena meant no insult. Pia's eyes shadowed for a moment as she watched the blond man slipping away into the dark forest. Absently, she glanced at Olena, seeing the woman was about to speak. Quietly, Pia stopped her, moving to stand. "I think I'm going to follow that servant. He's up to something."

Before she could get up, she looked down the dining platform. Pia quickly sat back down. The grooms were before them, walking up to the table. She'd have to stay put and leave to follow the servant in a moment. What else was she going to spend the night doing? Besides, it would be nice to explore a little before getting cooped on the ship for another month.

Leaning back, with the plan of waiting out the brides and grooms leaving, she suddenly looked up. Before her loomed the rude stranger who had stared at her in line. She crossed her arms over her chest, showing she wasn't amused by his joke.

Sure, that's right, pick on the ugly girl. Ha, ha, ha, very funny. You are so hilarious, Pia fumed inwardly. Even her thoughts came out sarcastic. Her brow lifted as she waited for him to take his best shot.

"I'm Zoran," the large warrior stated. His voice was softened with the accent of his people. Though the words were gentle, he didn't smile as he studied her.

His tone was seductive in its low pitch, but Pia refused to be affected by it. She was too angry. Her brow lifted higher, as if to say, *So? That concerns me how?*

Zoran's brows knitted beneath his mask. She wasn't moving. Drawing near, he placed his palms on the table and softly ordered her, "Come."

"Come?" she mused, the word more a mockery of him than an actual question.

Pia slowly stood and looked him over with a barely contained snarl. Zoran was surprised when she didn't swing for his head. She looked like she wanted to. To his further astonishment, she said nothing as she came around the table to better face him.

Pia was livid. It was real funny of this guy. He couldn't find a wife so he'd come to play games with her. What? Were all his friends watching in the distance? Did he lose the bet? Draw the short straw? Was he going to lead her to the wrong tent and leave her there as a cruel joke on someone else? Was he going to toy with her and then refuse to let her choose him as husband? Or, worst of all, did he think she would fall readily into his oversized arms and he'd get a free night of sport?

Standing, hands on hips, she looked him over and sighed.

"Well?" Pia demanded through tight lips. "Lead the way."

Zoran wondered if she was perhaps nervous. Seeing her aggravation, he knew better. At a loss for words and unable to speak them even if he could think of what to say to her, he nodded his head and began to walk. Hesitantly, he looked over his shoulder to see if she followed. She did, but she didn't seem to be enjoying herself.

Pia watched the quiet stranger carefully, her eyes scanning the crowd. Other brides were being led forward-- some by hand, some not. She saw Olena behind her being carried over a man's shoulder, a look of amusement on her pale face. Turning her attention back to the barbarian Zoran, she eyed him critically, looking for faults.

He was too big, too muscled, too much hair, too tan, too built, too ... naked, too incredibly graceful when he walked, too handsome of body with skin she could imagine touching, too firm, especially in the backside as it stirred beneath the fur loincloth. Pia gulped. What was she doing?

Her frown deepened and she let loose an aggravated sigh. Zoran glanced at her, but held quiet as he continued on. Stopping at a red tent, he moved to open the flap for her.

"Come," he said.

Pia stopped to eye him warily. She lifted her hand to push back the blonde strands that blew across her face, constantly taken aback by them, but her arm was trapped by the belt.

When she didn't step forward, but only continued to stare, Zoran stepped closer. He repeated his word louder, his tone growing hard as if he was stating a direct order, "Come."

"After you," Pia answered, doing her best not to look at the glowing crystal snuggled into the depths of his incredibly admirable chest. An ache moved its way into her stomach.

Oh, great! To top off the perfectly dreadful night, she was going to get sick as well.

Zoran forced a shrug and led the way in. Inside, he was confused. Outside, he gave nothing away. When he turned, he almost expected her not to be there. Not that she could have escaped. If she'd tried to run, he would've gone after her.

Pia followed him inside his tent and glanced around. She really had no choice. If she took off too quickly and this man protested, she'd void the contract with Galaxy Brides.

Within the tent, the red earth floor was covered completely in soft furs. In the middle, beneath the center point of the pyramid, there was a low bed with more furs and pillows. It sat about a half foot off the ground.

In one corner of the red tent was a low table with giant pillows on the floor. It was laden with chocolates and fruit. In the next corner was a steaming bathtub with perfumes and oils. In the third corner, she saw a bondage table with straps and whips.

Zoran watched her reaction carefully. She gave nothing away. She wasn't even shocked as her eyes moved past the bondage table. Without flinching, she went to the low food table and studied it.

"Ah," she murmured to herself. Zoran tensed as she picked up a knife. To his relief, she didn't wield it at him, but turned it on the belt around her waist. With a deft flick, she cut the straps and stretched out her freed arms.

Pia studied the blade for a moment. It would be too dull to slice through her hair.

More's the pity, she thought, putting the blade down.

Zoran watched as she took the straps from her wrists. Then, grabbing the curls that flowed beautifully down her back, she made quick work of the mass. She tied it into a makeshift bun at her nape to keep the locks off her shoulders. Muscles moved temptingly beneath her skin.

Zoran's darkening eyes grew with heat, the rest of his body simmering. Her stunningly tanned flesh glowed in the firelight coming from the torches affixed along the tent walls. He wished to tie her, just like that, with her hands trapped above her head so he could have his way, taking his time as he thoroughly explored the long line of her back.

Closing his eyes, he pictured it vividly. He'd take his knife, cutting the slinky material from her skin. He would peel it back to see the tender peaks and hollows of her body. She'd tremble for him. She'd pant as she tried to remain calm. Once naked, his eyes would study her as his hands tested her response. She would grow hot. She would beg. Her mouth would part in beautiful, soft moans. He'd kiss her and they'd make love just like that, with her long legs wrapped about his waist as he thrust...

Nearly moaning with the agony of it, he opened his eyes.

Pia turned and again stretched her arms, completely unaware of his thoughts. When she looked at him, the pleasant expression caused by the simple act of freeing herself from her hair was lost. She scowled and sighed. Placing her hands on her hips, she studied him.

After a long, tense moment, she asked quietly, "Is this some kind of a joke?"

Zoran's stomach lurched, only to tighten. She was disappointed by him? She didn't think he was worthy? As the Captain of the Guards, he'd proved himself to the entire kingdom that he was the worthiest fighter in the land. He led armies, won battles and tournaments. But here was the woman destiny had chosen for him and she didn't think he was good enough for her. The bitterness of it stung like a blow to the gut. She continued to look him up and down in disdain.

Slowly, he shook his head in denial. No, this was no joke. He found nothing funny about it at all.

Pia ignored his silent answer. "What is it? Someone outside listening?"

Again, he shook his head.

"I know we aren't getting married, so you can drop the act." Turning, she plucked a piece of fruit off the table and stuck it in her mouth. Her mouth full, she said, "I'm contracted to go along with this. That's the only reason I followed you here. I know you're up to something. So you might as well get it over with or give me permission to leave. I'm starving and I want to go back to my suite and drink some green tea."

When he moved, it was with slow purpose. He passed by her, moving to pull a pillow out from the low table for her to sit. She eyed him despairingly.

"I'd just as soon eat on the ship," she said, frowning.

He motioned for her to be seated.

"All right," she sighed. Her eyes gave away her suspicion, but her curiosity was strong. If she ran away from him too soon, Galaxy Brides could try to call her on her contract. She couldn't afford to pay them for the surgeries and she wouldn't risk them sending out a bulletin with her before and after pictures on it. They claimed they didn't take any, but Pia didn't trust that lady doctor.

Pia had no choice but to wait this prank out. She couldn't risk letting the Rayvikians find her. To do so would be a horrific death sentence.

Zoran sat across from her, leaning back on his heels. Pia eyed him resignedly and waited. When she didn't move, he motioned to the fruit. She took up a piece and bit into it. Chewing thoughtfully, she took another bite and then another to finish the piece off.

Zoran watched her in silence. She seemed completely unaware of the effect she was having on him, as she placed fruit in her mouth and licked absently at her fingers. Every once in awhile she'd sigh as if she were bored. He poured her wine and handed it to her. She took it and sipped dutifully, though he noticed she didn't swallow it.

Pia hated wine. The smell of it made her sick to her stomach. Holding her breath, she pretended to politely drink and set the glass down. She took more fruit, her stomach beginning to stir with delight at finally being fed.

Eating a few more pieces, she nodded her head at him. "Well, thanks for the snack. It's been real ... entertaining."

He didn't miss the sarcasm. She didn't try to hide it.

Zoran lowered his head. He whipped his arm over the table so he could gracefully stalk forward on all fours. Pia watched him, wondering what he was up to. Seeing the look on his face, she stiffened. Her mind told her to stand, that whatever he planned boded ill for her. But she couldn't move.

A trance fell over her, growing with each pulsing beat of the glowing crystal necklace. Firelight gleamed off the gold bracelet on his arm. She'd been trying to feign disinterest in him as she ate, but her eyes hungrily sought to study him. It was torture to want him and know he couldn't possibly want her.

Pia parted her lips in breath. He didn't stop until he'd crawled completely to her. His brown eyes bore unflinchingly forward, trying to claim her soul as they explored her. In that moment, she felt him connecting to her. It was strange. It was almost like she knew him and that he wasn't a stranger at all. But how could she know him? She'd never been to this quadrant before.

Zoran settled his hands on either side of her thighs. He trapped her without touching. His eyes dipped to her lips, still moist with juice.

Pia's eyes widened as his closed. She swallowed nervously, pressing her lips shut and pulling them tight against her teeth as he neared her with a kiss. The first brush of him sent a shockwave over her spine. She trembled violently, feeling the rough texture of his tongue as he licked over her bottom lip.

Pia didn't return his peculiar kiss. Zoran took his time, licking the fruit juice from her. He traced the seam of her mouth with his tongue, prying her lips easily apart as he pushed deeper.

Zoran felt her breath deepen, detected the heady scent of her fragrant longing. His probing met with the barrier of her teeth. He moved to suck her bottom lip into his mouth. A jolt washed over them both at the intimate act. She stubbornly refused to allow him entrance.

Pia was frozen with shock. She didn't know what to do. It felt wet and wrong, yet so incredibly right. Her head lightened, nearly swooning with pleasure. His lips pressed closer, trying to get hers to move. She didn't know how, had never kissed a man. To her amazement, she realized the doctors had repaired not only her skin, but her nerve endings as well. Her mouth tingled with feelings. Before, her whole left side had been dead to the lightest of touches.

Zoran worked forward, his kiss forcing her to lean back. He didn't look at her. She couldn't stop staring at him. She couldn't believe it was happening. Then, the dark demons of her past reared their ugly heads and she pushed his shoulder violently to stop him.

"That's enough," she said. Her whole body ached in protest of the broken contact. The ache had begun to grow, spinning its web within her stomach. Her words were not as strong as she would've liked, as she said, "You've had your fun. Now point me in the direction of my ship."

He shook his head. Her hand was still on his shoulder, trying to hold him back from her precarious position. It would be so easy to pull him back to her or push him firmly away. She wanted to pull him close. Zoran leaned over to nip playfully at her wrist. Pia snapped it from him as if he'd tried to sting her.

"Come to the bed," he urged her. His eyes shifted and flashed with danger.

"No!" she practically screamed. She scrambled back on her feet to get away from him. She should've known that was all he wanted from her.

Zoran stood, hopping up in one swift movement to tower above her.

"Stay back," she commanded, her eyes glowing with hazel fire. "I'm not a prostitute! I'll not whore for you."

That stopped him.

With a scowl, she looked around the tent. Then, storming to the front flap, she was surprised when he was there to block her way. She gasped. She hadn't heard him move.

He lifted his hand to block the opening.

Pia stared at him hard, ordering, "Move."

Zoran didn't budge. His jaw lifted. If this were a test to see what he would do, he would show her he was worthy of keeping her. He would prove to her that she'd never find a better husband than he. The crystal had decided. It glowed as proof of their match and his body lit with the fire of her taste. They couldn't fight their fates. It had been written before they were even born.

"I said move," she growled fiercely. "Your game isn't going to work. I'm not staying here and sleeping with you. Now move it!"

He shook his head. Pia hesitated and her brows narrowed.

"Don't make me hurt you," she warned.

Zoran grinned. He couldn't help it.

Pia was enraged. Was he laughing at her? Her eyes dipped for a moment and she swung her fist, upper-cutting square into his jaw. The force of the hit took him by surprise and he stumbled back. Her plan had worked. The smile was gone.

Pia dipped from the tent, shaking out her fist, without a moment to lose. Soon, she was storming around the sides of the red pyramid, looking for his eavesdropping friends. She found the pathways to be empty.

With a frustrated sigh, she looked all around, even at the sky. She noticed the moon still shone bright and blue. What was going on here?

Pia was glad for the air. It cooled her fiery skin. His touch still lingered on her mouth and she was sure she would still feel it in the months to come. She wasn't stupid. She could guess that her body was awakening to him. But why him? Why now? It had never bothered to stir with longing before. What had those doctors done to her?

"Come."

Pia trembled in fear despite herself. She heard the rough growl before she'd even heard him approach. As she spun on the backs of her heels to face him, she didn't let her fear show. Her father had taught her that confidence was half the battle.

Zoran eyed the frustrating woman with narrowed eyes. His chest heaved in controlled anger. The woman actually hit him!

He watched her, secretly stirred by her boldness. Her blonde hair glistened in the blue moonlight as did her hazel eyes. As his body fought to control his anger, another passion threatened him. It rose fiercely beneath the fur of his loincloth, ready to do battle, ready to conquer. She had spirit and fire and a wealth of passion. It called to him.

Pia eyed the warrior and then turned her back on him. Just to irritate him, she began to walk away. Zoran's voice left his throat in another growl. He sprung forward. She tried to duck from his grasp, but he'd been ready for that. He caught her as she spun away and pulled her hard to his chest.

Pia swallowed in panic. She looked up at his serious brown eyes shining through the mask. Her heart hammered in her chest at the nearness. No one had ever willingly held her so close. She couldn't speak.

The folds of his hard muscles pressed into her, boldly pushing into the full length of her body. But it was the hot press from under his loincloth that stopped her from screaming. Her hips lurched in hesitant response.

"Your name," Zoran said quietly, liking the softer feel of her skin against him. She smelled like fresh fruit on a warm spring day. He reeled with passion. It flowed into his feverish blood.

"Pia," she answered truthfully, momentarily stunned. "Pia Korbin."

Zoran took a step and then another. He allowed her to feel his desire for her as he moved. Before she realized it, he'd walked her back to the tent opening and was ushering her inside. He kept his large arms wrapped around her, trapping her to him, but not hurting. She felt his chest muscles working as he moved, muscles that could lift her with ease, throw her, crush her, touch her, control her to his will.

Insanity threatened to fog her brain. She wanted to be kissed. She wanted to be touched with affection and longing. She wanted to be held. She wanted it to be his lips and his hands and his body that did it. But he was so handsome, even with his face covered. He couldn't possibly want her.

Pia knew that she didn't affect him as he affected her. His heart was steady and sure. His breath was too calm and she was panting like a dog in heat.

Zoran desired her like he had no other woman before her. Her eyes flickered, becoming soft and feminine. Her chest heaved hot, panting breaths against him. Her breasts rose and fell beneath his gaze, tempting his mouth. Her lips parted as he pulled her closer.

Suddenly, he tried to kiss her. Pia panicked, thinking he meant to head-butt her. She dipped her face to the side, whacking him in the cheek with her forehead. Zoran let her go with a start. He was so sure he saw her desire for him, yet she refused.

Pia stumbled back. She tried to smirk but her body was too disturbed to make the look last. "You want some more? You want to get beat up by a girl?"

Zoran glared. Now she was taunting him?

"Choose," he said, desperate to get his own say in. If she wanted to fight with him, fine. Let her face his sharp tongue as well. No more attacking when he couldn't defend himself against her.

"Choose?" she blinked in surprise, her voice turned as soft as falling snow. She stared at him with a look akin to horror, as if he might carry the plague. Her body shook in fear and hope. Did he just ask her to marry him?

Chapter Three

"What in the--?" Pia began roughly, coming to her senses the moment she saw a smile beginning to curl on his lips.

"Choose." Zoran's smile faded as he took a step forward in warning. His face turned red. He clenched his fists in anger. Oh, but this was an aggravating wench the Gods had sent him! Surely his brothers weren't given such headaches. They were all probably cozying up on their beds, talking and kissing. Not him, he'd gotten the shrew of the bunch.

"No," she howled in horror.

"Choose!"

"I can't marry you!" she shouted back, incredulous. Her eyes shot daggers at him. "Are you mad?"

Zoran darted forward. His naked chest glistened as his bare feet stepped over the floor. Pia ducked and backed away. His eyes narrowed. He came for her again. She'd got one punch in with the element of surprise and thought she could do it again.

With lightening speed, she kicked. Bringing her whole body around as she jumped for his head. Zoran's fingers snapped onto her ankle with one hand, effectively stopping her foot from striking. Pia landed awkwardly on the ground. As he held her leg in the air, she straightened, rotating her hip as she jerked her leg, trying to set herself free.

"Tsk, tsk, tsk," he held her ankle tight, not letting go. To his pleasure, the position lifted her skirt and he saw the cotton lines of her underwear. Unconsciously, he licked his lips. "Choose."

"No!" Pia was mortified. Bringing her free foot forward, she flung her body back. Zoran had no choice but to let her go as she backflipped out of his arms. It was a foolish move on her part. If he'd restrained her, he'd have broken her ankle. Still, as she landed, he was impressed.

Pia landed neatly, bouncing the cramp out of her liberated leg. Daringly, she looked at him. A light entered her eyes.

To Zoran's amazement, he realized she was enjoying herself. Her eyes sparkled in a way that he hadn't seen all night.

"Choose," he said calmly.

"No," she repeated. In that one instant, it became a game. Challenge lit in their mutual gazes. Pia relaxed, now on familiar territory. Fighting she could easily do.

Zoran never envisioned he'd be sparring on his wedding night. He never imagined his bride would be so well trained. With a little polishing, she would make a fine soldier, not that he intended on letting her fight in battle. That had been the old way. But, after many men lost their wives and the population dwindled for a generation, they'd changed tradition for the sake of their race. Besides, he planned on keeping his family safe. It was the man's job to protect.

Pia darted forward, using her arms in swift blows to attack him. He blocked her easily, returning moves only to have them opposed by her maneuvering. He didn't turn the full force of his energy on her, not wanting to hurt her. But, as the leader in him naturally moved to test her skill, he was impressed beyond words.

Zoran's hand knocked a bruising blow into her arm. Pia flinched but didn't stop for an instant as she regained her footing. She didn't whine in pain or call a time out as he'd seen younger soldiers do at such a hit. He nodded at her pleased.

"Choose."

"No."

They sparred around the room, kicking and punching, circling and gauging. Zoran watched her chest heave, delighting in the flushed color coming to her neck and cheeks. Her eyes sparkled like stars.

Trapping her to his chest, as her punch went long, he held her backside to his fur-covered arousal. Nipping her delicate ear, he murmured, "Choose."

Little ripples of odd sensations prickled her skin. Pia bucked away and gasped, "No."

The fight continued. Pia struck at him, amazed at the grace with which the big man moved. He blocked all her best moves, but, to her credit, she was blocking most of his. Her blood rushed through her body. Sweat glistened on his.

Pia became very aroused by his power as he stood up to her. Not many men could.

Kicking suddenly, her foot landed in his ribs. He grunted as he fell to the side onto the fur bed. Pia stopped, her breath heaving as she looked at him. Her muscles were loosened for the first time in a long time. She'd practiced and exercised by herself, but it wasn't the same as having a live sparring partner.

Pia eyed him warily, hands on hips as she caught her breath. He didn't move. His eyes were closed.

Wryly, she frowned. "Well that was disappointing. You're not much of a warrior, are you?"

When he didn't rise to the bait, she came forward in fear that she'd killed him. She slowly pushed his shoulders back and leaned her cheek over to his mouth to feel his breath. She placed her hand over his heart. It beat steady. To her surprise, he licked her cheek just as his hand grabbed her palm to his chest. Pia gasped and tried to pull back. He was faking it!

Zoran wasn't wasting such a good plan and he definitely wasn't absorbing a blow like that for nothing. He instantly wound his arm around her, rolling her over. Her body was trapped beneath the solid form of his. Pia's eyes widened. He ground his hips intimately into her. Lust fired through her rushing blood, spreading quickly.

This time when he kissed her, she didn't refuse. Pia's mouth moved naturally against him without thought. No man had ever taken her down, by ploy or by force. That this man could do so excited her to the point that she forgot who she was.

Zoran was pleased that her passion matched his own. He pressed into her, receiving her kiss. She became gentle as she touched him, soothing the many places she had moments before tired to strike.

She forgot her insecurities as her hand explored his sweaty body, gliding over the ridges of his flesh. She moaned. His weight forced her legs to part for him. His kiss deepened, sucking her breath from her chest. Soon he was pulling her clothes from her, baring her chest.

Wickedly, he eyed her. His breath came in pants, as he moved to taste her flesh. She shivered beneath his hands.

Pressing his mouth against her throat, he rumbled, "Choose."

"No," came her instant answer, but she didn't stop touching him. She didn't push his kiss away.

Zoran's growl echoed over her, reverberating along her flesh with pleasure. He kissed his way down her body, taking a ripe nipple into his mouth. It was the most intimate touch she'd ever experienced and her body exploded with pleasure as she discovered nerve endings she'd never realized she had. His teeth bit lightly and his tongue soothed the ache.

"Ah," she moaned, almost afraid to feel what he did to her. Yet, she was powerless to stop it.

Zoran's body was on fire. The blood rushed in his veins from their sparring, stirred feverishly by the taste and smell of her. She desired him. Her scent filled his head. She pressed into his hard body. However, he couldn't finish claiming her this night. The council would know if they came together completely. She would be taken away from him and he'd be alone.

Just awhile longer, he thought, suckling deeply at her breast. His groan of pleasure joined hers.

Pulling up, his chest heaving to catch breath--breath that had been steady during their fight but now panted like he'd run five miles full out. Looking into the passion-hazed depths of her stubborn eyes, he said, "Choose."

"No," she gasped as he pressed his arousal into her. The promise of gratification flooded her limbs at the intimacy.

Zoran grabbed her hand in his. Moving her fingers to the side of his head, he forced her to pry the mask from his face, not seeming to notice when she pulled out a few strands of his hair. His hair spilled over her as it was released. He let her hand go. Pia clutched the mask, looking at him in amazement. She gasped to see the excitement he held for her. He frightened her.

Zoran had strong, proud features. He had the face of a devil--a wickedly handsome devil--and he was looking at her without repulsion. His nostrils flared. His lids narrowed possessively.

"You chose," he said, lowering to taste her throat. Groaning against her, he announced, "You are mine."

* * * *

"My King," the blond servant, who Pia had been so keen on following, said. He'd seen the look on the woman's face. She didn't trust him. Good thing the other Draig fools did. He'd made his way from her, through the forest of colossal trees. The torches didn't reach this part of the grounds, but the moon shone bright to light the way in a blue glow. He didn't need light. He smelled where he was going.

Stopping suddenly, the man stuck his hand over his heart and bowed. He was dressed as a servant, but his eyes looked around with the cunning of a spy. "All the Princes have found brides."

He watched King Attor come forward. He knew the man's nostrils flared in disgust. He had to wear the Draig scent so they wouldn't discover him. The King stayed back, avoiding being downwind.

"Very good," the blond King answered, smiling a cruel smile. "Let us wait until they are bonded completely. Only then can we assure the end of their line. Once those Draigs lose their mates they will be done. The new Princesses will die, starting with the oldest son's bride. The line of the Draig rule will be ended and the Var will once more be the only force in this land."

The warrior-servant smiled, thinking of the blonde Princess who'd been curious about him. It would be a shame to kill her. She was beautiful. But, once bonded to Prince Zoran, she would never choose another man for her mate. Not that he had any qualms about forcing her to choose.

King Attor of Var rolled his neck on the shoulders as he shifted into a more natural form. Hair grew to cover his face and body, claws formed on his hands. His mouth elongated, gnashing with sharpened fangs. When he looked back, it was through the eyes of a wild cat. His voice crackled in slow tones in the back of his throat. Growling, he ordered, "Go."

The spy took off into the trees, not shifting for fear it would unmask his scent. He'd been in the Draig household for almost a year now, smelling them, eating their food. And, *Sacred Cats*, he was ready for the torment to be over.

* * * *

Zoran's words rolled over Pia in complete possession. The mask was still clutched firmly in her fingers. She was amazed he wanted her so badly, that he would force her hand in removing the mask. She carried it over the flesh of his back as she moved to touch him. She continued to boil close to the brink of losing her inhibitions.

Zoran knew he had to slow down before he became mindless. Leaning back on his arms, he studied her. Pia blinked in surprise when he stopped his kisses. Taking a strand of her long blonde hair, he brushed it off of her face. He trailed his fingers over her lush lips. Lightly, without thinking, he murmured honestly, "You're so beautiful, Pia."

Pia froze. It was the worst thing he could have said. All desire left her limbs in a mad rush as she perceived his words to be a placating lie. Slowly, she blinked.

Zoran felt the instant change in her.

"Get off me."

Zoran pulled back, confused by her hard tone. What happened? Why was she suddenly so angry?

"Get off," she said. "Or I'll scream so loud the entire encampment will know of my displeasure."

Zoran had no choice but to pull back. Her breasts were still bare, the peaks a little red from his enthusiastic treatment of them.

Pia grabbed a piece of fur from the bed and pulled it over her chest. Making quick work, she tucked it around her shoulder in a makeshift shirt.

"You forced me to remove the mask," she said, not looking at him. She picked it off the floor and threw it at him. He caught it to his chest. "Put it back on."

Zoran scowled. He didn't obey. Instead, he went to a torch and lit it on fire.

Pia gasped going after him to stop him. In her haste, the mask dropped from his fingers and landed on his arm. His eyes glowed instantly with golden slivers as his skin hardened in defense. Pia gasped, confused.

Zoran pulled back from her. He turned around before she could see the beginnings of his shift. It wouldn't do to give her more reason to reject him.

When he turned back around, she was trying to stomp out the fire with her slippered foot. It did no good. The mask was destroyed. Angry, she looked up at him.

Placing her hand on her hips, she demanded, "Let me see your arm."

"It's fine," he grumbled.

"You're burnt." Although her words spoke of concern, her features expressed annoyance.

"It's fine," Zoran answered uncomfortably, not used to being coddled.

Pia huffed. Going to him, she grabbed his arm and lifted it to the light. It was fine. The flesh was unharmed.

"How?" she questioned in awe. "I saw ... I felt you jolt."

"I was trying to stay your attack," he lied. In truth, his arm had shifted with the hard armor of his changing just in time to save his skin.

"Oh," Pia breathed. Realizing she held his arm and was standing a little too close, she dropped it with a harsh push and stepped back. Recapturing her outrage, she asked, "Now what, you dolt? You ruined the mask."

"Now you are my bride," Zoran said, commandingly. He placed his strong hands on his hips, daring her to deny his claim to her.

"I'm not!" Pia debated. Her heart beat erratically as she looked at him. "You forced my hand."

"Prove it," he said with an aggravating smirk pulling at his expression.

Oh, but he was handsome. Pia shivered.

"If you like," he continued. "I can take it up with your corporation. I'm sure they will see things my way."

"You bastard! You can't do this to me!"

"I already have," he answered, liking this game of domination. He went to the table and poured himself some wine. She glared at him as if he were insane when he lifted her goblet to her in offering.

"I hate wine," she ground out.

Zoran shrugged, having guessed as much. Her lips didn't taste of it when he'd kissed her and he knew she hadn't drunk it.

"Why do you do this? What could you possibly have to gain in marrying me?"

Zoran tried not to flinch at her obvious displeasure in him. Setting the wine goblet down, he turned to her. His body hadn't cooled as easily as hers.

"Are you just a monster? Is that it?" Pia was thoroughly confused. Throwing up her hands, she said, "For you must be a sadist to make me stay here."

Zoran's jaw hardened and his eyes became dark. "Being my wife brings you pain?"

Pia gulped. Well, truthfully, it thrilled her on a baser level, which in turn terrified her, which in turn made her angry because she shouldn't let him get to her, which in turn irritated her because she shouldn't have cared enough in the first place.

Zoran came forward, swiftly taking her up in his arms. She didn't answer fast enough for him. Touching her cheek, he said, "Maybe I should show you the pleasure of belonging to me."

"I'm not property," she stated, jerking her face from him. She wanted his anger back. She needed it. She couldn't fight this gentleness.

"No," he agreed, to her greater distress. "You're not. But you are mine, just as I am yours."

"I don't want you," she lied.

"Not yet," he answered quickly, purposefully mistaking her words for a challenge. "But give me a chance. I'll make you beg for me."

"I don't beg, Zoran." Pia's words lacked heat as she struggled to be free. He held tight. His soft accented words combined with the thrilling strength of his body was doing something to her head, making her weak-kneed and pliable.

"Your lips don't," Zoran agreed, knowing she would never ask him for what she so obviously wanted. "But your body does. I can smell it on you."

"You smell me," she grimaced. "Then let me go and I'll take a bath."

"You will bathe for me?" Zoran asked, grinning. He was enjoying himself way more than he should've been.

"Oh," Pia harrumphed sarcastically, rolling her eyes. "Please."

"Please?" Zoran asked softly, moving forward as if to nuzzle her neck. Her arms were trapped to her sides so she couldn't punch him, but it didn't stop her from trying to head-butt him. He pulled back just in time.

"So much passion," he mused in a low sultry voice that gave her chills.

"Not for you."

"You have a sharp tongue, don't you, wife?" Zoran continued in a murmur.

Pia saw approval in him and wondered at it. He leaned as if to kiss her. She tried to bite him.

Zoran snapped his head back, smiling. "I bite back."

"Try it and you're dead."

"It's not good to threaten your life mate. If I die you will be alone."

"If you're my life mate, your life must be very short indeed." Wiggling for good measure, Pia didn't succeed in setting herself free. He was too strong. "And make no mistake, you can be replaced."

Zoran almost groaned in agony when she rubbed against his already potent erection. It was the wrong tactic if she wanted him to let her go. He opened his mouth to rebut, but her words stopped him.

"Why do you want me as a wife?" Pia asked. There was no vulnerability in the hard question. "Why would you want a wife that doesn't want you?"

"Quit saying that you don't want me. I can smell the fragrance--"

"Finish that and I promise to knock your teeth out of your head," she warned.

"Are you ashamed?" he asked, surprised by the swift, maiden-like defense.

"Ashamed? The only thing I'm ashamed of is finding myself here with yo--u, *ahhh*."

Zoran swooped in for the kiss, delighting in the soft feminine sound of her answering moan.

Pia froze. She melted instantly at the expert movement of his lips. His skill was too much for her innocence. She forgot the battle as she softened into his arms.

Zoran broke free, seeing her dazed eyes staring back at him in wide wonder. This was more like it. Her mouth was still parted, as if she could still feel his lips. He smiled in manly satisfaction.

"Tell me how one so beautiful gained so much fire." His eyes couldn't stop looking at the fine structure of her face.

Pia's mouth snapped shut and her face dropped into a mask of ice. She tore from his arms with a burst of force.

"Mock me again an--" she began in warning, pointing at him.

Zoran blinked, confused. He lifted his hands to stop her words. "I know, you'll kill me or maim me in some impossible way."

"I'll do it," Pia said, angered that he didn't think she could.

"I'm sure you'd try," Zoran admitted. A small devilish part of him looked forward to the idea.

Pia adjusted her fur shirt. Her eyes were hot pools of lava as she tried to ignore him. He thought her captivating in her tirade. To his delight, he saw the curve of her breast peek from beneath the fur before she righted it.

"Go away," she said. "I want to take a bath."

"I can't," he shrugged, settling down on the fur and turning toward the tub with the obvious intent to watch her. "This is my tent and I cannot leave."

"What if I set it on fire? Could you leave then?" Pia asked with a smirk. The idea had some merit.

"It won't burn. See how the torches touch it," Zoran mused, absently. He was too busy imagining the different positions he could take her in.

Zoran sat near to where Pia stood. Lifting his hand, he touched her leg playfully and tried to run his palm up beneath the seam of her red gown. She swatted at him and stepped away.

"Are you always this impossible?" she huffed. He grinned.

Pia moved to tug at the big piece of fur beneath him. After a mighty struggle, he lifted his backside and let her have it. As she moved, his hand lifted, pulling the end of her fur shirt. With a jerk, her breasts fell bare and he smiled with pure delight. She gasped, hiding beneath the fur coverlet.

"You brute," she mumbled.

His smile widened.

Curiously, he watched her as she kept her strong back to him. Taking the coverlet, she draped it on two torch sconces and made a wall between him and the tub. Then, ducking behind the fur, she eyed it for holes.

"You'd better keep back if you value your manhood," she said.

"This does not please me," Zoran yelled, just to be irritating.

"I don't really care." Pia shrugged out of her tattered red wedding dress. She stepped into the warm bath and almost sighed in relief as she sunk into its depths.

"Can I join you?" Zoran called, hearing her splash. His body was on fire and he knew it wouldn't be a good idea.

"I'll have to drown you." Closing her eyes, Pia rolled her neck on the edge.

"May I wash you, then?" he tried, his voice dipping.

"Pain," Pia growled in dark response. "Death and pain."

Zoran smirked, hearing her yawn. Their little foreplay workout had taken a lot out of her. Glancing down at his enthusiastic erection, he sighed. Too bad it couldn't take anything out of him.

"So you admit you're staying?" Zoran asked. The imaginary gremlin on his shoulder made him say it.

"I have no choice." Pia moved to lather her arms. If he turned her into the corporation, the Rayvikians would find her. Besides, she liked this planet and its culture. The only thing she didn't like was her husband. But, hey, no life could be perfect. If anything, she'd have someone to spar with and to aggravate. The imaginary gremlin on her shoulder winked at her and grinned.

Zoran frowned at her dejected words. Coming to sit on the other side of the fur, he gave her privacy. He looked at the fur curtain, but couldn't see through it.

"I'll make you a good husband, Pia," Zoran said seriously, all teasing gone from his tone. His arm reached around the fur barrier and his wrist draped onto the side of the bath so that his hand dipped into the water.

Pia jumped hearing his voice so near to her. She tensed, ready to strike. When his head didn't follow behind it, she relaxed. Absently, his finger swirled in the surface.

"That remains to be seen," Pia answered after a moment, not giving an inch. She looked at the fur, glad her voice didn't waver. Tears entered unbidden into her eyes.

"We will have strong sons," Zoran said softly, thinking more of making them than of having them. "I'll give you a strong family that will make you proud."

She watched his powerful fingers thoughtfully rippling the water, tempted to reach her foot to them so she could feel his light touch on her leg. She refused to move, content to stare at him. Her eyes became mesmerized by the undulation he caused on the water.

"I don't know that I want children," Pia said truthfully. The idea made her heart nearly explode in her chest with panic. "I'm not the nurturing type, Zoran."

Zoran trembled at her words. He drew his fingers back, flicking the water off of them as his arm once again disappeared behind the curtain. He wanted children desperately, many fine warrior sons that would make them both proud. He decided not to press the issue. There would be plenty of time for that.

Pia's hair was pulled back in the bun and she left it, refusing to wash the locks. Twirling a wayward piece thoughtfully, she asked, "Do you have a sharp knife?"

"I have several," he mused quietly.

"I meant here, now, with you."

"No, why?" He almost chuckled. Was she going to try and skewer him?

"No reason, really. I just wanted to cut off this hair. The corporation made me grow it out and it's too heavy."

Zoran balked. He pulled back the fur to see if she was serious.

"Get out!" Pia screamed at him, trying to cover her body with her hands. Curling into a ball, she glared at him.

Zoran ignored her. He looked at her beautiful golden locks and, like a most typical male, declared, "You are not cutting your hair!"

Pia's eyebrow shot up. Oh, she was definitely shaving her head now, if only to aggravate him.

"You have no say in it," she laughed, irritating him further. Her hazel eyes danced with delight. "I'll do whatever I please. It's my hair."

"Why would you purposefully disfigure yourself?" he asked in surprise. "Do you seek to shame yourself, shame us?"

"It's just hair, Zoran," she shrugged. "Now go away so I can get dressed."

In aggravation he dropped the fur back down and said, "We will discuss it later."

Pia heard him stand and stalk away. She smiled. He was definitely upset.

"There's nothing to discuss," she answered, her tone flippant. "I'll do whatever I wish."

A low grumble in the Qurilixen tongue was her only reply.

Chapter Four

The torches were beginning to dim when Pia took the fur coverlet from the sconces and pulled it around her naked body. Zoran lay on the bed, his ankles crossed and his hands threaded behind his head. He looked thoughtfully at her and gave her a slight, interested smile.

"Any chance you are planning on spending the night outside this tent?" she asked dryly.

Zoran grinned. He wasn't going anywhere.

"Any chance you're going to share that blanket with me?" he questioned instead. His eyes lit with meaning as they dipped over the fur.

"Not on your life." She came down next to him, though far enough that he couldn't touch her without making an effort.

"What if I said I was cold?"

"Sorry," she answered without a moment's consideration. She turned her back on him, snuggling into the warmth. Giving a contented sigh, she said, "I'd have to tell you to quit being a baby."

"I'd share with you."

Pia stiffened. His voice had drifted closer though she hadn't felt him move. The bed hadn't shifted under his weight. She closed her eyes, concentrating on him while pretending to fall asleep.

Gradually, she felt the light caress of a hand on her hip, running softly up her side over the fur. Her arms were buried beneath the blanket so he didn't meet with flesh. Slowly, he worked his fingers into the bun in her hair, loosening the strands and combing them out with his fingers. Pia shivered, starting not to mind her hair for the first time since growing it. When she didn't scream, Zoran grew bolder, edging closer so that his body wrapped next to hers.

Pia felt a tender kiss on her neck. His face buried into her locks, breathing deeply.

"I want to make love to you," he said boldly. "I've wanted to since the moment I first saw you."

Pia scrunched up her nose in disbelief. Some men would say anything.

Zoran's hand discovered an opening in the fur and dipped in to find the heat of her bare stomach. He kissed her again, nudging the fur down over her arm. Pia couldn't move, could barely breathe. She tensed against his expertly searching caress. Since first walking into his tent, she'd felt a wondrous fog tempting her. It now threatened her tired mind and she didn't fight him as hard as she should have.

Zoran's fingers bumped the long scar on her ribs. He trailed it down and found the navel buried in her flat stomach. He dipped his hand lower only to pause on her stomach. She tensed beneath his hand. He knew she didn't sleep. She was holding her breath too tightly.

"Turn around," he urged against her long neck. "Let me kiss you."

Pia didn't move. His kisses dotted insistently behind her small ear.

"I want to look at you," he murmured, his voice husky with desire.

To his amazement, her voice skeptical, she asked, "Why?"

Why? He pulled back. Was she serious?

"Because it would give me pleasure." He massaged her stomach in agonizingly little circles. Her skin felt so good, so soft against his callused palm.

Pia did turn, but it wasn't to receive his kisses. "Do you think you're funny?"

Pia grabbed his hand and threw it back. What had she been thinking, marrying a complete stranger? Oh, right, it was either this man or being skinned alive.

At least being skinned had a definite ending, she thought, wondering what it was going to be like living out the rest of her days with this gigantic frustration next to her.

"Pia...?" Zoran was confused.

"You want to see?" Pia fumed, tearing and kicking out of her blanket. She was completely naked except for her underwear. "Now will you leave me the hell alone? Huh?"

Zoran's eyes unabashedly roamed her skin. Aside from the long gash on her ribs, she was smooth and tanned. He itched to explore her, his hand lifting to touch her. His mouth went dry. She was gorgeous.

"Have you had enough of a laugh, Zoran? Or do you want more?" Pia grabbed her underwear, tugged them off, and threw them. Outrage blazed in her heated gaze. "Is that enough? Have you seen enough?"

Pia didn't stop there. She tore up from the bed, holding her hands out to the side before twirling in one angry circle. Her hair whipped erotically around her shoulders.

Zoran's body lurched with molten desire. His eyes swept to the part between her thighs, enjoying the performance. The hair between them was trimmed short and instantly drew his attention. Unconsciously, he sat up, a smile beginning to line his masculine lips.

Pia mistook the look for amusement. Her lips trembled and her eyes pooled with moisture. Quivering, she snatched up the fur and wrapped it around her arms. Her movements jerky, she stomped around the bed and lay down on the opposite side.

Zoran frowned. Rolling over, he was undaunted as he reached out to touch her. She jerked her arm away and scooted to the outermost edge of the low bed.

"Pia," he began.

This time she scooted so far she nearly fell off. Zoran lurched forward and grabbed her hip, holding her up. Forcibly dragging her into his embrace, he turned her face to his. He stroked her skin. Her wide hazel eyes stared back at him. They were the loveliest shade of brown and green, perfectly combined.

Pia was torn. The way he had looked at her, the smile on his face, it had tore at her soul to have him see her. He was so handsome. Even if he seemed pleased with her now, even if she could believe his touch wasn't meant in ridicule, in the morning it would be different. He would be ashamed of her. How could he not be? She was ashamed of herself.

The crystal glowed softly between them, drawing his lips forward to kiss her pain away. His mouth was gentle. His hands were searching, as he slowly peeled the fur aside to find her flesh.

Zoran wouldn't make the mistake of calling her beautiful again. But she was beautiful. So beautiful that it was inconceivable that she didn't know it. So, he just assumed that she did know and had been hurt because of it.

He stroked down her neck, happily feeling her racing pulse. He glided his fingers through the valley of her breasts and down her stomach. When turned, moving to cup her between the thighs, she jolted.

"*Ahhh*," she moaned, trying to close her legs to him. It was too late. He had his hand there and had no intention of moving it away.

"Sh," he whispered into her mouth, keeping her dazed with his soft kiss. "Don't think, Pia. Just feel me. Just feel my hand. I'm not going to hurt you."

To his relief, her fingers lifted to his shoulder and lay still, tentatively holding him to her, but poised so she could push at any moment.

His words were soothing, as if taming a wild animal. "Close your eyes."

She obeyed.

"You are my wife," he stated, so there would be no mistake. "I'll look at you. I'll have you look at me. Do you understand?"

Weakly, she nodded. The power of him transferred into her, connecting them so she felt his longing for her.

"I'll kiss you, Pia," he murmured, deepening his kiss slightly before pulling back to whisper his words against her panting mouth. He lifted his hand from her thigh to touch her neck. "And I'll touch you."

Pia moaned when he moved his hand down to her breasts, circling his thumb around her sensitive nub. He was so commanding, everything about him whispering of power and strength. Pia had never been a woman who could be easily controlled, but this warrior did something to her.

"I'll touch you here." Zoran caressed the other breast in his palm, taking his time.

Pia's hand clutched absently at him. She felt as if she were falling through clouds. She kept her eyes shut, not wanting to break the spell he wove.

"And I'll most definitely," he continued, trailing his hand back to her thighs, "be touching you here."

As Zoran said the word 'here,' he let his finger slip into her moistened folds. Pia's hips jerked. Inside he groaned with satisfaction, outside he kept his voice calm. It wouldn't do for this wild mare to buck him off quite yet. He had every intention of taming her.

"Zoran," she cried as his stroke deepened. Her back arched.

Zoran took the sound into him, relishing it. It pleased him greatly to hear his name calling forth on her lips.

"Do you understand what I have told you?" Zoran's voice left no doubt that he was in control of their situation and that he was in control of her. He stroked her a little deeper, staying on the outer rim of her sex. Her hips tentatively moved against him.

"Yes," she breathed.

"Yes, what?" he insisted, not wanting to mistake her pleasure for an honest answer.

"Yes, I understand," she moaned loudly, biting her lip. The ache that started when she first looked at his glistening tanned body grew, until she finally realized the hot blaze was her desire--stirred and put there by him.

Zoran's erection begged for freedom. Pia convulsed tightly around him. The warrior in him couldn't resist as he explored her, probing deep. She was so snug, as if it had been a long time since she'd been with a man.

"Take the fur from my hips," Zoran instructed her. Again he stroked her, dipping ever so slightly deeper inside her moist cavern. "Look at me, Pia. Look at your husband. I want you to touch me, feel how I am. Feel what I'll touch you here with."

Pia trembled, pulling at the fur loincloth. It fell to the side. She hesitated, her hand stopping near his stomach.

"Touch me," Zoran demanded, needing more than anything to feel her hands on him. He closed his eyes so she couldn't see their shifting. He growled. "Lower."

Pia's hand dipped lower.

"Lower," he insisted. "Take me in your hand."

Pia's hand journeyed down at the heated request. He tensed as if in pain. When her hand bumped the tip of his hot erection, she jerked back in surprise.

"Argh," Zoran growled. Removing his hand from her, he guided her fingers to grip around him. He urged her to stroke him. All the time he continued to ply kisses on her face. "Just like that. Oh yeah, Pia, just like that."

Zoran's hand moved back to touch her and his mind was numb to anything but release. He slid his finger once more inside her. Gulping, he shook. She was moving her fingers as he taught her.

"You're so tight." His voice was a tortured rumble to the flesh of her throat. His hot breath panted beneath her ear. "Have you been with a man?"

Pia innocently shook her head, past the point of lying or caring.

The admission was more than he could take. The conqueror in him needed to lay claim to her. The sweet smell of her, the taste of her mouth, it was all blessed insanity. Maybe she'd been right, maybe he was mad. He didn't care.

Before Zoran could stop himself, he was above her, opening her thighs, poising to drive into her. Pia stiffened in fear, but her body was singing so sweetly. A moan escaped her followed by a ragged pant. She wanted him. She wanted his touch. Her body arched in virtuous offering, trusting him completely.

Zoran brought himself to her, felt her moist fire calling to him. Suddenly, he got a hard jolt to his chest. The crystal was fading fast. He looked at Pia's face.

Pia's wide eyes stared at him. Her chest heaved. She felt the sensation, too.

With a grimace, Zoran pulled away from her. He couldn't take her. Not tonight. The crystal would fade and the council elders would know. She would be sent away and he would have to live out his many years all alone.

Pia saw his look as he pulled away. Her body was poised, open to him. Immediately, she recoiled, curling into a humiliated ball. He couldn't pretend. He couldn't force himself to do it. Silent tears poured bitterly down her cheeks. She held perfectly still.

"I can't." Zoran was nearly mindless with the agony of denial. "Not yet."

Pia nodded, believing to understand. She couldn't speak. He'd given it a valiant effort, but could she really blame him? Even as she hurt, she forgave him. She knew what she was. She wasn't pretty. She wasn't anything. She felt Zoran wasn't a mean man, she saw it in the tender way he'd looked at her. He'd tried. She would give him that.

"It's fine," she said softly. "I know."

Zoran took the fur and put it tenderly over her lean shoulders. The sight of her naked back was pure torture. His hand actually trembled as he drew it away.

Pia took a deep breath, knowing he couldn't look at her anymore. She lay quietly for a long time, barely breathing as she tried not to move. As she felt his even breath, Pia didn't turn around to look at him. She was unable to sleep throughout the long night. Her body ached too badly. Never had being ugly hurt so much. Her tears were silent and she sucked them inside, burying her pain. Even in his sleep, Zoran didn't touch her again.

* * * *

Morning came slowly to the planet of Qurilixen and Pia was awake to watch the sunlight as it crept in from the tent flap. Slowly, she stretched her arms, pushing quietly forward as she suppressed a yawn.

Her tired eyes glanced over to Zoran and she felt a little resentful at him for the ache in her loins that wouldn't go away. Taking the fur coverlet with her, she walked over to the table. Her stomach churned with hunger and she picked up a couple pieces of fruit and ate them. Eyeing the feast, she wished there was something else besides chocolate and cream sauce--and, lest she forget, the disgusting wine.

Suddenly, she heard a quiet shuffling at the door. Her arms stiffened. Was this it? Were his friends coming after all to have their peek at her? She swallowed, angrily crossing over to the tent flap.

The servant on the other side startled in surprise to see her enraged face. Pia blinked as the young man recoiled from her in shock.

"My lady," he mumbled to Pia with an awkward bow. "Your clothes for the ceremony today. King Llyr and Queen Mede request your presence."

"Ah, thanks," she answered, taking the bundle from him. The man bowed his head, but scurried away from her. Pia glanced down at the black and red clothing she'd been given. The dark material was of a fine quality with red stitching that suspiciously matched the tent walls.

Frowning, she carried them inside. Zoran was still sleeping, so she went back to the table and laid the clothes out on a cushion seat. She found a tunic shirt and breeches, obviously made to fit Zoran. There was a pair of leather boots in the stack, also his. On his tunic shirt, a red dragon was embroidered with fine hand-stitching.

The second outfit was a long dress. Pia frowned. If she was going to be staying, it was time for their little custom of women in dresses to change. The gown was finely made, but very heavy. The black material would fit tightly to her body. Red trim parted the front to show more red beneath the split in the floor length skirt and a red dragon was embroidered on the center of the chest to match his. There was also a hairpiece. Looking at its ribbons and straps, Pia frowned. She had no way of knowing how to work that contraption.

Eyeing Zoran, she grinned. The servant handed her the clothes, so it was only right she got first pick. Dropping the fur around her ankles, she slipped his tunic shirt over her head. It was a bit large, but with a roll of the sleeves, it worked just fine. Next, she pulled on his breeches and tucked the waist, before making herself a belt out of the hair piece. She rolled the legs up and smiled. There, much better than a dress. His boots were too large so she decided to go barefoot.

Now, didn't the servant say something about her presence being requested by royalty? Oh, that's right. She had to go before them with Zoran to proclaim her marriage. The imaginary gremlin on her shoulder did a little jig of mischievous pleasure.

Going over to Zoran, she knelt down and touched his shoulder to shake him awake.

"Zoran," she said softly, waking him gently.

Her imaginary gremlin giggled.

Instantly, Zoran's eyes were open. Seeing her face, surrounded by the waves of her blonde hair, he smiled.

"The King and Queen wish to see us. I'll be right outside." Pia stood before he could react and was out of the tent.

Zoran sat up, scratching his stomach. Seeing a pile of clothes on the bed beside him, he absently grabbed them to tug them on. Blinking as tried to move the shirt, he realized it wasn't a shirt at all but Pia's dress. Frowning, he saw his boots on the floor and none of his other clothing.

"Pia," he began, keeping his fur loincloth on as he crossed to the tent's opening. His armband sparkled in the sunlight as he ducked his head outside. His little bride was nowhere to be seen. *"Pia!"*

* * * *

Pia smiled and kept walking, hearing Zoran yell her name. A light bounce entered her step. Heading toward the campgrounds, she ignored the other tents. Soon, she was where the giant bonfire had burned so brightly the night before. Its flames were low, almost out.

Grinning like she didn't have a care in the world, she ignored the stares of awe she received. Somehow the adverse attention was comfortingly familiar to her. She was at ease under the obvious scrutiny and wonder.

Pia saw the platform in the front of the crowd. Councilmen stood to the side of the royal couple, who were seated in the middle. King Llyr and Queen Mede's crowned heads shone pleasantly. They were dressed in matching purple tunics.

Seeing her attention, the King stopped in mid-sentence and bowed his head regally at her. His eyes clouded in confusion as he took in her attire. Soon all the council was staring at her too. Pia slowly stepped up the stairs and curtsied in her oversized breeches. Her bare feet poked out and she tapped her toes absently on the wooden planks.

"Where is Zoran?" the Queen asked, after taking in the woman's masculine attire.

Pia smiled and gave an impish shrug. Her voice clear, she said, "In bed. I guess he overslept."

The crowd laughed. The King gulped in discontentment. The Queen stiffened, her brow knitting ever so slightly in worry.

Pia's smile wavered at the sound of amusement. She expected to be funny, but the sound of the crowd's laughter was growing on mocking. She glanced behind her at them and then back to the King and Queen. The crowd grew quieter, edging closer to hear anything she might say. "I was told I was to come and--"

"Excuse me," Zoran announced, giving a quick wave to the crowd. They cheered him like he was a hero, even as they laughed in good humor. He stepped arrogantly up behind his naughty wife.

Pia shut her eyes, suppressing the grin that tried to spread over her features as she heard the crowd reel in amusement. She wondered if he wore the dress.

Zoran, still wearing his fur loincloth, bowed to his parents. The King's eyebrows shot up and Zoran shrugged dismissingly.

"We will be back to report in just a moment," Zoran announced clearly. The crowd laughed louder, enjoying the great comedy of the morning event.

Pia finally got the courage to look at him. He was eyeing his tunic on her. With a grunt, he threw her over his shoulder. Pia screamed, her shout of displeasure causing the crowd to fall in on itself. The laughter grew by leaps and bounds.

King Llyr looked at his wife. Mede's eyes widened and she tossed her hand. She shook her head, at a loss for words.

Zoran didn't say a thing as he carried Pia back to his tent. Even under the tunic, he felt the slender press of her hips to his shoulder. If he turned his head, he could take a playful bite of her tender hip. It was hard, but he refrained.

Before Pia knew what was happening, he dropped her to the ground and stripped the tunic off of her back in one swift movement. His eyes gleamed as he looked at her naked breasts. Pia frowned, turning to hide them from him. Zoran instantly pulled the loose breeches from her hips to bare her backside.

Pia gasped in outrage. She would've run, but he grabbed her to him, causing her to shudder. He was naked and pressed intimately against her backside. The hard length of morning arousal burned into her flesh.

"I'll have to punish you publicly for that stunt, wife," he said darkly into her ear before biting the tip. She trembled. His nearness was stirring and heating her blood. "It's a matter of honor."

"Do and I won't finish the ceremony," she swore, forcing her tone hard to hide her body's reaction to him.

"Oh, you'll finish it wife," he promised, bending his knees and nestling himself to press hard fire into her very firm derrière. "Then, we're going back to my home and we're finishing what we started last night."

"I would rather die." She was frightened by the power in him. Pia had seen his anger, barely constrained beneath his simmering surface. "I'm not going back out there with you and I'm not putting on that dress. I hate dresses. I want my own clothes."

"Either you put that dress on, or so help me I'll drag you out there naked," he swore. Zoran set her away from him. Despite his affectionate caresses, he was furious.

When Pia peeked over at him, his face was red with contained anger. She shivered and hurriedly put on the dress. Zoran took the tunic for himself.

"Come," Zoran ordered, as he pulled on his last boot. He dared a glance at her. Pia stood insolently in her black dress slippers, hating her outfit. She looked positively miserable in it. Her jealous eyes looked at his feet and he saw her jaw stiffen.

"No." Pia was outraged as she thought of what public humiliation he might plan. Suddenly, she saw that thin ties were in his hands. "I don't want to and you can't make me."

Zoran leapt, pouncing on her as he tackled her to the bed amidst her screams of protest. Within seconds, he had her bound and gagged. She cursed him, a muffled sound full of fire and vinegar. He ignored her, smiling down at her with a terribly aggravating sweetness.

"You must be punished," he said by way of an explanation. "I'll not have my reputation destroyed because you hate dresses. I'll not be humiliated by my wife."

Zoran threw her over his shoulder and carted her out of the tent. Pia tried to kick and jerk. Zoran was glad he'd gagged her, for her words were heated as she muffled curses to his head. Her arm hit into his temple, trying to strike him any way she could. His head leaned to the side, out of her wrath's way.

Time had passed in quiet murmuring at the platform, as they waited for Prince Zoran to return with his bride. The crowd was most anxious to see what he would do with her, and they were not disappointed. A tittering laughter resumed amongst them.

Zoran came through their depths carrying his bride. To their merriment, they saw she wore the gown he'd ordered for her, a gag, and ties around her wrists and ankles. A smile shone widely on his face. He waved politely to acknowledge the crowd before turning around to wink at his mother. She shook her head in maternal disapproval. The King chuckled despite himself, causing the Queen to turn her look on him.

Pia glared at the crowd. They laughed back and pointed.

Her hair bounced and flew as Zoran took the stairs as if she were no heavier than a leaf. Then, with a firm toss, he set her down before the watching Qurilixen.

"Queen Mede. King Llyr. May I present Lady Pia of the Earthen people," Zoran introduced loudly, twirling her about to face them. To much merriment, Pia tried to bounce away across the platform. Zoran grabbed one of her ties to keep her still. Her body jerked to a stop and she growled.

The Queen waved her hand regally for him to proceed, at a loss for words.

Slowly, Zoran reined his bride back to his side, twirling the tie in one hand. Pia growled and shot him daggers with her eyes. He winked merrily back at her causing a long, muffled string of curses to be thrown at his head.

"Allow me to help you," he murmured gallantly to Pia.

Zoran smiled as he took the crystal from his neck and dropped it on the ground. Then, lifting his angry bride up, he brought her tied feet down on top of it and forced her to smash it.

A fog lifted from Pia's brain as the crystal smashed. She grew dizzy, falling over to the side. Her eyes blinked as the full force of the sleepless night came over her. Her body ached worse from Zoran's denied touch. She shivered, swaying on her feet.

The Queen looked at the King, who just shrugged his shoulders and motioned for her to continue.

"Welcome to the family of Draig, Lady Pia. I hope you will enjoy your new home," the Queen stated weakly.

Pia nodded at her the best she could. Suddenly, her head couldn't control itself as it spun into circles. With a weak moan, she blacked out. Zoran caught her up in his arms and held her by his side.

"She says thank you, Queen," Zoran said with a grin. "Now, if you would excuse us?"

"Certainly," Queen Mede said, still shaking her head at her wayward son. Out of all her boys, Zoran was the most stubborn. But he also had a lot to prove. Being the leader of the soldiers, he couldn't have his honor or his position called into question--especially not by a woman.

With little effort, Zoran picked up his bride into his arms and took her from the platform. Her eyes were closed and her bound wrists bounced limply on her chest as he walked. He nodded to the crowd. They nodded back, smiling at their leader and his audacious cunning. Zoran carried the motionless Pia to the front gate in the side of the mountain palace and into his wing of the castle home.

Chapter Five

Pia's eyes popped open with a start, her fists automatically balling in outrage. She swung at the air, causing a great laugh of delight to echo over the bedroom. Her chest heaving with her unspent anger, she pushed herself up on the soft mattress. Her hands were no longer tied and the gag was out of her mouth.

"Where...?" she began, glancing around the bedroom.

There were white, paper thin sliding doors with decorative wooden boxes over the sides. It looked heavily influenced by the Japanese style of ancient Earth. Light shone through from the other room. The bed was low to the ground, covered in fur. There were potted plants on either side of a long dresser. Through a cracked sliding door to her side, Pia saw a walk-in closet. A large dome overhead let the sunlight in, though it was tinted to give the room a soft, comfortable haze. Two swords hung on the wall as decoration, dragons emblazoned on the hilts.

On the bed was a black dragon head emblem on a sea of deep red material. Its color was as dark as blood. The fierce creature stared at her for a moment. She shivered. Then, hearing the laughter lessen to a chuckle, she turned.

Her eyes met with a gaze she didn't readily recognize. The woman's movements followed her startled ones. It was her reflection staring back at her through a circular mirror atop the dresser.

"You're in our home," came the belated answer to her question.

Zoran had been watching her beautiful confusion as she blinked herself awake. At the sound of his voice, her eyes narrowed in on him and she tried to jump up. The gown tangled her feet and she fell back on the bed, kicking and fighting the long skirt as she tried to be free of them.

"It's only a dress, Pia," Zoran mused wryly, unable to help egging her on. "It's not attacking you."

"As soon ... as I get ... out ... of ... this...," she threatened, fighting all the harder. With a huff, she finally managed to work her way off the bed. Her chest heaving, she opened her mouth to finish. He held up his hands to stop her.

"I know, you will behead me, skewer me ... yeah, yeah, yeah." Zoran yawned, though he was nowhere near bored with her. He loved her fire, her passionate anger. It was a good complement to his title as a warrior leader. It would serve his honor well to have a fiery woman at his side--so long as he alone could tame her.

"You keep it up," she warned, her voice growing.

"So much talk, so little action." He shook his head.

"Ah," Pia gasped in open-mouthed outrage. Instantly, she lunged at him. The skirts tangled her feet and she tripped. Zoran caught her up in his embrace, subduing her easily.

"Ah, Pia, you didn't need an excuse to fall into my arms. I'll open them willingly for you," Zoran murmured annoyingly in her hair. He got the response he expected. She tried to slug him. He dodged her shaky blow.

"I'd tear your arms from you before I'd fall into them," Pia said, trying to kick. To her satisfaction, she hit his shin and he frowned, letting her go. She stumbled away from him, out of breath. "I want to call the royal council! It's my right to do so."

Zoran froze. She was serious. His jaw tightened, as he inquired, "On what grounds?"

"On the grounds that you forced me to marry you," she said, a smile coming to her face. She swiped at her nose, regaining some of her composure as she sniffed. "I did my research before coming here. You can't force a bride to choose you. It has to be her free will. It wasn't my free will. I told you no and you forced me to take off your mask. When I told you to put it back on, you burned it."

His face turned red. He said nothing.

"And then, this morning," she lied. "I was going to go tell the council that I didn't choose you, but then you kidnapped me..."

His brow rose dangerously on his forehead.

"Fine, you *apprehended* me, tied me up, and forced me to stomp on the crystal. I would say I have a pretty strong case and plenty of witnesses. I want to speak to the royal council--*now!*"

A bitter look lined Zoran's lips as he took a menacing step toward her. "Did you happen to research, *wife*, that the royal council is particularly busy this time of year with important matters of this kingdom? Did you also happen to discover that marriage disputes can only be claimed after a full year of marriage has been achieved and whereas the bride can prove that nothing of a sexual nature happened between the married couple for that full year? Furthermore, a decision usually takes another year to be reached, considering the royal council will not always agree and the dissolution of a marriage is a very serious matter to us. So I would say, you have at least two years as my wife, and that's only if I don't contest the divorce. And I'll contest. Believe me, wife, you're stuck whether you like it or not."

"I don't care if it takes five years. I'm not staying married to you."

"I felt how you melted in my arms, Pia," Zoran murmured in a tone that sent chills over her spine. He came closer. His brown eyes held her. His knuckles stroking her face. "Do you think you could resist me every night for five years and never succumb?"

Pia shivered. To her shame, she didn't move away from him. Already a fire blazed from his touch and she knew she couldn't--not if he looked at her like that. She'd relent in less than a week.

"I'll get my own place. I'll find a job and support myself. I won't even see you."

"What job?" Zoran asked with an amused grin. Inside he boiled.

"I'll join your military," Pia announced, pleased with herself until she saw his look. He stayed his hand on her cheek, not moving and yet not leaving her soft skin. "Soldiers usually get free room and board."

Zoran grinned like a fool. If she joined the military, she would be under his command, even more so than now. He didn't let her in on the joke, as he said, "Women are rarely allowed to fight in the military--especially wives. Only widows can join."

Her eyes rounded, as if to say, *that could be arranged.*

"Don't even think it," he said, his hand fisting next to her cheek. "I would snap your neck in an instant if you so much as tried."

Pia backed down, finally managing to get the strength to pull away from his disarmingly gentle fingers. She scowled. "Then I'll pray to every one of your Gods for your death in battle."

Zoran sprang forward with a rage that took Pia completely off guard. His eyes glowed with a fire all their own, as he gripped her shoulders. His nails dug into her flesh and she wheezed in fear despite herself.

"If you ever say anything like that again, wife, I'll punish you. So help me, I might get transferred to guard duty in the lowest of underground prisons where I'll never again see the light of day, but I'll not put up with your blasphemous manner." Zoran shook her before tossing her away from him. With an angry growl, he strode out of the bedroom. Slamming the thin door, he said, "I'm going to work."

Pia shivered watching him leave. It didn't take long before she heard the up and down slide of a door. Her knees weakened in fear. She'd seen the devil in that handsome gaze of his and, so help her, she liked it.

* * * *

Zoran's home was a splendid exercise in simplicity. The bedroom Pia woke up in was off the front hall. The doors separating the one level of rooms were paper thin and had no locks on them. They slid soundlessly with a single push of the finger.

The walls were wooden planks of straight lines. A floor of matching wood was placed together in an intricate pattern of long cut strips. In the center of which, in the front hall, was fashioned the impression a giant dragon. The dragon sat before a heavy oak door that Pia couldn't get to open.

From the front hall, a single step down was the only room divider. She came to an open living room with a marble fireplace. There were straight lines carved into the plain surface and another dragon head in the center top. A step back up took her to a dining room, complete with low table and cushioned floor seats. A bowl with a single ball inside it decorated the middle as a centerpiece.

A tapestry hung on the far wall, just behind the table. It was red with the depiction of a black forest. If she had to venture a guess, she would say it was the forest she'd seen at the festival. In the middle was a noble phoenix.

"I'm surprised it's not another dragon," she mused wryly, moving on.

The kitchen was much of the same--plain and of wood. The cabinets were miniature copies of the doors, sliding to the side instead of swinging open. Pia laughed seeing a dragon inlaid on the countertop.

As she crossed back into the dining room she noticed that a chandelier hung beneath a giant dome. The crystal shards reflected the light, brightening the room. A thick curtain was affixed to the dome.

Finding another door, Pia slid it open. It was a bathroom with a natural hot spring bubbling in the side, made of the red stone of the planet's surface. A wooden sauna was next to it, a pull switch for steam on the side. On the opposite wall was a shower stall with a wooden half door and bench seats made of red stone. There was also a vanity, a sink, a toilet, sliding cabinet drawers, and a top dome of smaller proportions.

Next to the bathroom, Pia was amazed to discover an exercise area. It was a long, flat floor with a higher ceiling. Weapons hung on the wall for ease of use. Arranged on the floor was a punching bag, a wooden pegged contraption with many arms fashioned into spikes, a post with gashes taken from it with a sword, and a mat rolled into the corner. Pia shivered in excitement.

"This room alone would be worth staying married for," she mumbled to herself. Almost reluctantly, she turned around and forced her legs to move away. She still had the dress on and couldn't possibly work out in the heavy skirt.

Getting an idea, she went back to the bedroom and began rummaging through the closet. She smiled, seeing her bags on the floor. She wouldn't have to steal Zoran's clothes after all. In no time she was in a pair of comfortable charcoal pants, a navy T-shirt and light boots. Going to the fireplace, she tossed the dress on top of the wood and left it. She would've started a fire, but she couldn't figure out how to make it work.

Dusting her hands, she nodded in satisfaction. Her stomach growled reminding her she was hungry.

"First I eat," she said absently to herself, making her way back to the kitchen. A great big smile came to her face as she thought of aggravating Zoran. "Then I find scissors and do something about this mess of hair."

* * * *

Zoran spent the first day of his marriage training the soldiers in swamp warfare. It was a grueling affair as the swamp mud was hard to walk in without shifting into Draig form. Many of the men were stupefied by the surprise workout. Though Prince Zoran was known for springing a training drill at any hour of the day or night, they hadn't expected him to show up the first day of his marriage.

Many of them had celebrated late the night before, believing that this day of all days would be safe to sleep in. They couldn't have been more wrong. Zoran worked them to the bone, pushing them, yelling them into action until their bodies could take no more and they literally crawled their way back to the barracks that evening.

Zoran smiled grimly at the irritable men. His crossed arms were splattered with muck, though not as bad as the soldiers were. "I warned you when you began this training to be prepared for anything."

The men grumbled as they stopped in their departure to look at him. There was respect in their tired eyes. They knew Prince Zoran was the greatest warrior amongst them and, after today, his dedication would never be questioned.

"As a warrior, you can never be caught off guard. You can never slack in your duty. If you do," Zoran stopped and pointed down the valley where the quiet village lay. Lowering his voice to a deadly growl of warning, he let his eyes shift yellow. "If you do, they die."

The men nodded in serious understanding.

"Now go eat," he hollered, uncrossing his arms and jumping down from his post. "You did yourselves proud today."

With his gruff praise, their exhausted shoulders rode a little higher. Zoran made his way wearily back to the castle's front gate. The guard saluted him as he passed and Zoran motioned dutifully back.

His body was covered in drying sweat. He'd worked himself the hardest of all. Every muscle in his back ached. But it had been worth it, if for only a brief moment of peace. Pia never strayed far from his thoughts, though as a trained warrior, he didn't let her distract him from his obligations to the men he commanded.

Now that the drills were over, he frowned. The closer he stepped to his home, the more his anger renewed itself inside him. Oh, but she was an aggravating wench! One minute he wanted to kiss her in rough mind-altering passion, the next he wanted to strangle every last breath from her beautifully formed body. He wanted to tie her up and throw her into Crystal Lake. Hell, he wanted to tie her up and throw her onto his bed.

That thought in mind, he quickened his pace. The oak door to his home slid up with a stern voice command. Stepping inside, he felt it shut automatically behind him. Stopping, he sniffed the air, looking around. All was deadly still. He took a step forward.

"Pia?" he called softly, listening for her to stir. There was no answer. He stepped forward, frowning to see the gown he'd bought her in the barren fireplace.

"Uh," he heard her voice groan. "Got it."

He frowned. She was in the bathroom. Stepping up to the door, he took a single finger and pushed it open. His eyes rounded in a mix of horror and utter disbelief. He had to blink several times to make sure he wasn't hallucinating.

Pia jumped at the sound of the door. Lowering her hands from her hair, she pointed the knife at him and darkly asked, "You ever hear of knocking?"

"What are you doing to your hair?" Zoran demanded, unable to take his eyes away. Half of Pia's locks were still firmly attached to her head. The other half was sprinkled over the sink and floor in long discarded curls.

Pia turned back to the stranger in the mirror and smiled. If she hadn't been sure about her new haircut before, she was now. She grinned happily, lifting the knife to her longer side.

Willfully, and to his dismay, she grabbed a heavy chunk and sliced through it, cutting it off at about chin length. Then, lifting her handful of severed tresses, she wiggled the mass insolently through her fingers, sprinkling them before him like falling leaves.

"Do you mind?" she asked. "I was in here first and I could use a little privacy. If I mess this up, I'll have to cut it shorter to get it even."

"Why?" he breathed through his shock. Her hair had been the crowning glory to her wonderful features. Any woman in the kingdom would've given their freedom for her golden locks and here she was hacking them off. "Why do you disobey me? I told you not to cut it."

Pia just laughed and continued to slice and saw at her hair.

"Why would you purposefully disfigure yourself?" Zoran asked despairingly. "Do you seek to humiliate me?"

That made Pia mad. She lowered her hands to the countertop. "Humiliate you? My hair has nothing to do with you."

"Everything you do has something to do with me. I'm your husband. Our honors are interlinked. Only women who are shamed cut their hair," Zoran said darkly. He swallowed, again looking at the floor in disbelief. All that spun gold lay around their feet. He had the strange urge to gather it up and glue it back to her head.

Pia shrugged. Her little, naughty, naughty gremlin nodded its head in approval, urging her on. "Well, I would say it's very fitting then."

Pia lifted her hand and defiantly took off the last chunk with a heavy whack of his knife, which she'd taken off the wall in the exercise room. Zoran flinched. Pia made a show of examining the evenness of the new length and continued speaking, unhampered by his darkening features.

"For I find I'm very shamed to be married to you. Maybe you should divorce me before I *humiliate* you any further." Pia gripped the last of her hair and tossed it at him. "But if you want it so badly, here. I give it to you."

"Argh," Zoran growled hotly, brushing the soft strands from his arms. He turned to storm away, before suddenly whirling around to face her. Angrily, his face worked and he held out his hand. "My knife, wife."

Pia glanced down at her fingers. Then, slowly, as if it was no big deal and he was overreacting, she turned the hilt and placed it in his hand. Zoran's fingers gripped around the blade and he jerked it back from her.

Pia followed him as he stormed out of the bathroom. "Don't you think you are overreacting just a little bit? Really, Zoran. It's just hair. It grows back."

Zoran again saw his gift to her in the fireplace. He swallowed, too angry to face her.

"Zoran?" Pia asked, seeing his rigid back and the hard profile of his turned face. Still amazed and unsure how it happened, she thought of how handsome her husband was. He looked at her dress. Instantly, she wished she hadn't of tossed it aside like that. She almost went to retrieve it when his words stopped her.

"If you wish to insult me and throw my gifts back at me, wife," Zoran growled under his breath. He was chillingly calm as anger radiated from every one of his pours. "Do it right."

He turned to her. Pia froze at his hard look.

Boldly, he shouted, "Fire!"

Pia jerked at the sudden sound. The fireplace lit and the beautiful gown that she suddenly wished she'd saved went up in flames. She gasped. His eyes roamed over her short hair in what she took as a look of disgust. It would seem her hair was the only thing pleasing he had found about her. With it gone he couldn't bring himself to want his ugly wife.

Zoran studied her face. No matter what she did to herself, she would never be able to hide her beauty from him. It was in her hazel eyes, her steady gaze. It was in the fiery way she challenged him with words and her luscious body. He wanted her even more, now that she continued to defy him. It was strange that his passions could be ignited to such scorching depths by her disobedience and blatant insubordination.

Confused, Zoran turned his back on her, as he headed to the bedroom. "I'm taking a bath and going to bed. I have to get up early tomorrow to go to work."

"But, you just got off."

Zoran glanced over his shoulder and said, "I should think you would be pleased to be rid of me."

He disappeared into the bedroom.

"I am!" she yelled belatedly.

Zoran came back out holding a robe in one hand and a blanket and pillow in the other. Pushing the blanket and pillow at her with barely a glance, he said, "If you have no wish to share my bed, then you will find somewhere else to sleep. Might I suggest the couch? The fire seems to be burning quite bright as of now."

Pia gasped as he went into the bathroom and shut the door. Seconds later, she was still standing there as she heard him step into the natural hot spring. A loud moan escaped him and she would've sworn he did it just to irritate her.

Looking at the couch set before the marble fireplace, she threw the pillow angrily onto its cushioned red depths. She wrapped the blanket around her shoulders and sat down. A pout formed on her face without her realizing it, as she stared at the burning gown, watching the last of the red dragon disappear into ash.

Chapter Six

Zoran was up with the dawn. His wife had spent the entire night on the couch. Although he wasn't surprised, he was disappointed, as was his body that dreamt of her defiantly naked form in a myriad of different, lecherous ways.

"Faster!" Zoran yelled, pushing the men through the waist deep swamp mud. He'd decided that one day of grueling exercise wasn't enough to purge him. Lifting his sword arm high into the air, he motioned to the side. Instantly, the men ducked down and began crawling through the muck. It was slow going in this part of the swamplands. The mud weighted their human forms down and kept them from moving with precise speed.

"Attack position!" Zoran commanded.

The men hollered, shooting up from the swamp. Muck flew everywhere as their dirty swords lifted high in the air.

"Attack!" he shouted with a growl.

Zoran watched as the warriors plunged forward as fast as they could. The target, a battalion Zoran had ordered hidden within the trees, suddenly emerged to fight the muddy swarm. Metal clanged against metal as the heavily muddied hoard fought the outnumbered men.

Zoran hung back, watching the outcome of the fight. He crossed his arms over his chest, picking out the victors of the battle. The victors would get to go back early. The losers would have to spend three extra hours with him doing swamp drills.

Zoran thought suddenly of Pia and frowned. Maybe he'd better make it five extra hours.

* * * *

"Ugh!" Pia gasped, eyeing Zoran as he came in. He was covered in a grayish-brown muck and stunk to high heaven. She wrinkled her nose.

Zoran said nothing as he slipped out of his boots and left them by the door.

"What do they have you guarding anyway? A sewer?" she asked, waving her hand in his general direction as if it could keep the smell at bay.

"I spent the day in the swamps," Zoran said, rolling his neck.

"Oh." Pia wished he would elaborate. She'd just spent the entire day trapped in his house with nothing to do. She'd done a freestyle workout, taken a bath, and ate some leftover rice looking stuff from the refrigerator. That had use up about three of the twelve hours since she woke up.

Zoran eyed her tanned features. She'd pulled her hair back into a small ponytail at the nape of her neck and the sides fell forward to frame her face. As he watched her, she tucked the sides behind her ears.

Zoran was weary from the two grueling days, though he was much better off than the men were. He'd have to reward them with a lighter workout tomorrow morning. He should give them a day of rest, but he needed an excuse to leave the house. He couldn't sit in her cold presence for a day and not strangle her.

"I ate the rice in the refrigerator," she said at last, when he didn't look away.

"Fine," he grunted, heading barefoot toward the bathroom to clean up.

Pia gasped, seeing his arm. It was bleeding. Looking for any kind of adventure, even a second hand one, she jumped over the back of the couch and went to him. "Did something happen? Was there an attack?"

"Just an accident," Zoran said, wondering at her sudden concern. He didn't miss the light of excitement in her hazel gaze when she asked it. She eyed his blood with almost a longing.

"What happened? Was anyone hurt?"

It was as he'd said. It was an accident. One of the men lost his footing on a high perch. When Zoran caught him, the man's knife had nicked his shoulder.

"No," he answered.

"Oh." Pia bit her lip. Suddenly, she realized she was standing close to him and he really did reek like putrid swamp. She took a step back. "Maybe you should take a shower."

"I had planned on it," Zoran chuckled, despite himself. He couldn't help teasing, "Is your inquisition over then, my bloodthirsty wife?"

Pia frowned. "Well, what do you expect? You trapped me in this house all day with nothing to do. That," she pointed at the front door, "contraption won't let me pass no matter how many different languages I yell at it."

"That's because it's not programmed to your voice," Zoran answered quietly. Honestly, in his ire, he'd forgotten about her being stuck in the house all day.

"Obviously," she said sarcastically, crossing her hands over her chest with a sigh.

The motion pushed up her breasts and Zoran, being a healthy man of recently denied passions, looked unabashedly at them. Pia glanced back around to him. Seeing his heated gaze, she screamed and automatically moved to slap him.

Zoran caught her hand in his muddied grip. Her wrist slid along his palm. His eyes lit with promise.

Pia tried to slap him with her other hand. He caught that one too.

"Come bathe with me," Zoran invited. His tone dipped as he made a show of ogling her breasts. There was nothing she could do to stop him.

"I already had a bath," Pia said, wishing her voice were more forceful. "I don't need another."

At that, Zoran smiled. Pulling her forward into his arms, he crushed himself to her cotton pants and white T-shirt. Mud plastered their clothing together as if they wore nothing at all. Pia shrieked in dismay. Her eyes narrowed angrily.

"You need one now," Zoran said, leaning down to catch her lips with his. She turned her head and he hit her cheek with his mouth. He pulled back disappointed. "One kiss, wife, and I promise to let you go."

"Let me go and I promise not to beat the ever-living sh--" Pia's gaze shot daggers, but her words were cut off with his swift mouth. He pressed his lips firmly to hers in a dry kiss. She froze, wide-eyed, not knowing what to do. As suddenly as he began the kiss, he ended it with a loud smack of his lips to hers. Zoran let her go, seeming very pleased with himself.

"Now that wasn't so hard, was it?" he mocked.

"You're right," she answered carefully. She made a great show of looking him over before wrinkling her nose in disgust. "It was nothing at all."

Zoran's grin turned sour. "Well, as long as I have no effect on you, you should have no problem helping me out of these clothes."

Pia saw the challenge. He was daring her to run away in fear. She wouldn't give him the satisfaction.

"No problem at all," she tossed back lightly, turning to walk into the bathroom first. "It's not like looking at you would do anything to me anyway."

"Oh," he said, following her. "Then you wouldn't mind helping me wash up, would you? I couldn't tell how deep my cut was. It may need to be bandaged."

Pia wasn't so quick to respond.

"No," she squeaked at last. "No problem at all. It will be like washing the dishes."

"Good."

"Fine."

"Fine," he mimicked, his voice dipping ever so slightly.

Pia's jaw stiffened, as she ground out, "I'll start the shower."

"Fine," Zoran repeated. When she turned her back on him, he just grinned.

"Ah...?" Pia looked at the shower for a handle. There was none. She looked for a spout. There wasn't one of those either.

"Here," Zoran said from behind her. He came close to her back and waved his hand in front of one of the tiles. It read his palm and automatically went to his preference settings.

Pia watched as little doors opened in some of the tiles. Water sprayed out at waist level and at shoulder level. One spout came down from the ceiling and rained softly overhead.

"Would you mind helping me with my shirt?" Zoran asked, his tone sultry.

Pia lifted her jaw. She couldn't force herself to do it.

"You should get in just like that," she said. "That way you can rinse most of the smell off your clothes. Besides, that blood looks dry and if I rip it off of there, it might start bleeding again."

Zoran smiled, knowing that she was stalling. Stepping into the shower, he let the warm water hit over him without shutting the door. He turned around to look at her and placed his hands on either side of the shower. There was enough room for her to join him.

"What about your clothes?" he asked, his accent rolling thick over her. She shivered. He directed a pointed look at her white shirt. It was stained from where he'd touched her with his chest. When she hesitated, he mocked, "You're not scared of me, are you?"

"No," Pia said with a feminine gasp. She boldly stepped in before him.

Zoran's eyes lit with delight when he saw what the water did to her white shirt. Of course, he was too much of a gentleman to point it out to her. He hid his smirk.

Leaning forward, he purposefully came close to her as he leaned to pull the door shut behind her. Pia jolted at the sound.

How did I get myself into this? she thought, briefly closing her eyes.

"Are you all right?" Zoran asked, seeing her sway lightly on her feet.

"It's just this stuff smells awful," she lied. In truth, it was the way the water made his clothing cling to his muscular flesh that made her nearly swoon. The material adhered to his every muscular curve, lifting and shifting with each breath he took. Scowling at him, she commanded, "Move, let me rinse off."

Zoran was only too happy to comply, as he sat down on the stone bench in the corner. He leaned back, crossing his arms over his chest.

Pia turned her back to him. She had no idea how the wet material of her pants clung to her backside, outlining every lush curve, or else she'd never have done it. She pulled out her shirt, letting the stream of water beat against it until all the mud was gone, leaving a faint stain. Then turning, she took out her hair and leaned back to get it wet, raising her hands to push the shorter locks from her face.

Zoran's body tensed. It was clear she had no idea how the thin shirt was displaying her naked chest underneath. When her hands lifted to her head, it pushed her breast up and out.

Her darker nipples shone through the transparent barrier. His fingers twitched. His shaft became achingly erect.

He knew she'd scream if he touched her, but he wondered what she'd do if he touched himself. The water hit upon her flesh. He blinked, his mouth suddenly dry. Her darker nipples budded against her wet, clinging shirt--hard, erotic. His mouth bit at the air, almost tempted to....

"What are you doing?" Pia demanded. Her wide eyes had found his and she was staring at him like he had just developed boils.

"My jaw hurts," he lied, reaching up to rub his chin as he flexed. "I got punched."

"Punched?"

"There's nothing to tell, so retract your fangs, my bloodthirsty ruffian," Zoran mused. Gently, he added, "Now move so I can rinse off."

Pia stepped aside. She eyed his sleeve. "Here, try to lift your arm."

Zoran watched her, as her tone became most business like. She worked her hand beneath his sleeve, the fingers gliding over the ridges of his muscles as she lifted the material carefully up from the wound. Zoran thought with wonder that she had an amazingly delicate touch for someone with such a wicked right hook.

"There," she murmured, pulling it free. "Lift up."

Zoran lifted his arms, letting her work his tunic off his chest. He tossed it outside the shower stall. She leaned to the side, taking his rigid bicep and moving it to the water to rinse it off.

Probing the wound with her fingertip, Pia said more to herself than to him, "It's not so bad. I've had much worse."

Zoran's injured arm flexed beneath her hand as he moved to touch her face. His broad shoulders dwarfed her in size.

Pia looked up at him, momentarily surprised by the contact. The large shower didn't seem so big with him looming close to her. She swallowed nervously.

Zoran drew his hand down to the bottom of her shirt. His eyes narrowed slightly. He longed to see her, to touch her, to drink the water off her parted lips. Lifting the edge of her shirt, he kept his gaze steady.

Lightly, his fingers spread across her stomach to her side. He found the long, jagged scar puckered by her ribs.

"Like this one?" he murmured. His tone was so close, so intimate.

Pia blinked, transfixed by him. Leaning forward, he gently kissed her. He slid his fingers along her long scar, moving up one side of it and down the other.

Zoran's head angled down, persuading her to fall against the waterspout buried in the tile. Water rushed over her back onto his fingers. His lips were wet as they glided over hers. He opened his mouth wider, trying to consume part of her as he deepened his intent. He dipped his tongue forward, drawing a taste. He moaned into her, letting her hear his desire for her.

Pia trembled. She tried to touch him but held back, too afraid. When he pulled his lips away, she wanted to follow them and urge him on.

Zoran swallowed. She hadn't really kissed him back, only allowed him to take his taste of her. Her wide eyes stared at him through the thick set of her lashes and he felt her quivering beneath his fingers. He had to remind himself that she was innocent, pure. It wasn't hard looking down into her hesitant eyes.

Zoran's body lurched with rough ideas, with bold and fiery longing. However, he couldn't just back her up into the shower wall and have his way. He had to be gentle. It took a lot of effort to hold back. Warriors weren't exactly known for their gentleness and he was one of the best.

"How did this happen?" Zoran asked softly, keeping his forehead drawn close. The water beat its hard, steady rhythm around them.

Pia stiffened, remembering herself at the question. Closing her eyes, she felt shame. She knew what she looked like, even before the fire scarred her body. Before the accident, she'd been a gangly teenager. Now, she was a gangly, ugly woman. How could he even look at her like that? How could he kiss her with such sweetness?

Even though she still stood before him, Zoran could tell she'd pulled away from him mentally. Little droplets of water sprinkled her down turned lashes. Her breath deepened and she edged away. When she opened her eyes, she was no longer looking at him.

"It was a gift," Pia said, her voice coming out a quiet whisper. She turned and his hand was forced from her waist. She quietly stepped out of the shower, shutting the door behind her.

Zoran sighed, watching her trail out of the bathroom in her wet clothes. She didn't look back. The water hit his body as he leaned his forehead against the side. He could still feel her softness under his hands and against his lips. Letting her walk out was the hardest thing he'd ever done.

At moments, when she looked at him, he thought she wanted him. Then, an instant later, it was as if she felt nothing at all. He couldn't figure her out. All he knew was she was driving him mad every waking moment and tormenting him every sleeping one.

"Cold," he mumbled to the shower. The shower instantly sprayed cold water onto his heated body. It didn't help. "Freezing."

* * * *

Pia looked at her naked body in the bedroom mirror. Her skin was damp from the shower. Her short hair clung to her face and she pushed it back. She tried her best to be objective, but she didn't see anything worth looking at.

Touching the long scar on her side, her finger traced over the wet path Zoran had made around it. She couldn't see why he picked her in marriage. Sure, her skin was improved thanks to the doctors. But now she was back to being the unattractive girl all the boys on her father's military base had made fun of. Her face was narrower, but her eyes were the same wide hazel. Her body had filled out, but she was still too muscled and too skinny.

Pia shrugged, having long ago learned to live with her imperfections. Not wanting to get caught naked by Zoran, she hurried to the closet and grabbed some sweat pants and a T-shirt. Eyeing her bra, which she was still trying to get used to, she threaded it on under her shirt.

Zoran came into the bedroom, a towel around his naked waist, to the sight of Pia struggling underneath her shirt. A smile lit his face at the scene. She was too adorable.

"Do you need rescuing?" Zoran asked with a good-natured grin. He held the towel to his waist. He still ached with fire for her, but the freezing water had finally cooled him enough so he could think straight.

Pia jumped slightly at his voice, but didn't turn to look at him. Grumpily, she said, "I'll ... ah ... never understand ... ugh ... the need ... oh ... for these stupid contraptions ... ah, got it."

With a heavy sigh, she turned to him and rolled her eyes as she weaved her arm though her sleeves. Seeing he was standing in the towel, she hurriedly forced her eyes away. "Sorry, I didn't think that you'd be out so quickly. I'll get out of here."

"Actually," Zoran murmured in his low spine-tingling voice. As the cold had taken effect, his head cleared enough to remember how she relaxed a little when taking care of him. He'd dug at his shoulder while in the shower to get the gash to bleed. "If you wouldn't mind, I'd appreciate it if you'd take a second look at my arm. It started bleeding again."

"Oh," Pia said, instantly coming forward to look at it.

"It doesn't hurt, but I have to work tomorrow--"

"Again?"

"I work every day, Pia." Zoran would've sworn she looked dejected by the news. Could it be that she actually missed him during the day?

"Well, no, that's fine," she said, realizing what she sounded like. "My father was the same way, so it's perfectly fine. I mean I understand. It's just..."

"What?" His voice again dipped and he watched her breath catch slightly in her throat.

"You're too tall, come sit on the bed so I can see what I'm doing," Pia said, changing the subject with ease. Zoran nodded.

Lifting his hand, he gave her a bandage he'd brought with him. As he sat down, she took an edge of the bandage and tried to wipe the blood from his wound. She was firm but gentle in the task.

Studying the gash, she said, "You got hit with a knife blade, huh?"

Zoran's brows furrowed. Wasn't it obvious? Slowly, he said, "Yes."

"The blade depth isn't bad, too shallow for a sword unless it was done on purpose with the tip." Pia bit the corner of her lip, trying to figure it out. "The angle is strange. Was the man taller than you?"

"No," said Zoran watching her eyes carefully. She was concentrating on the wound.

"I know," Pia smiled brightly, as if she just achieved victory. "The man fell, you reached to catch him and his blade nicked you."

Zoran's eyes widened in surprise, as he asked, "How did you guess?"

Pia shrugged, growing slightly embarrassed. "It's just this game we used to play. It's not hard. You just have to be observant and logic your way backwards. Then you'll see how it happened."

"Guessing at knife wounds was a game you used to play?" Zoran watched her face for changes. Her features became completely blank. "Where exactly did you grow up? In a prison complex?"

Pia froze. This conversation was getting too personal and she didn't want to go there. Her eyes dipped down over him, realizing how intimate the situation had become. He was sitting before her on the bed with only a towel between his naked body and her. Gulping, she made quick work of wrapping up his arm.

"You shouldn't have any problems with this," she said. "I know it might itch, but don't scratch at it anymore. That's why it was bleeding."

Zoran gave her an idle grin.

"There, you'll be fine." Pia tied off the end and turned to leave.

"Wait." Zoran reached out to grab her hand. Pia blinked in surprise, turning around to study him. There was a lot he wanted to say to her. She could see it in his eyes, but he held back. "Is there anything you need? You seemed ... concerned that I was going to be working."

"Oh, no, it's fine," she answered. His brow rose in disbelief. "Well, it's just I'm not used to being trapped in a house all day and there isn't a lot of food in the kitchen. I don't wish to be a burden and, since I don't plan on staying married to you, I'm more than willing to get a job to pay my own way until we can get this mess fixed...."

Pia let her voice die off. His face had darkened with her effortless denial of their marriage.

"Pia," Zoran said. His jaw was very tight and worked against his flesh as he tried not to yell at her. He took a deep breath, standing to tower over her. "I'll only tell you this one more time. You are my wife and that's the end of it. If you need something I'll provide it for you. If you need food, I'll buy it. If you desire new clothes, I'll buy them. If you want to leave the house, I'll take off early tomorrow and show you around so you don't get lost. But, make no mistake. This is your new home. I'm your husband and there will be no divorce."

"That's what you say," Pia said. There was a distinct finality to his words and she felt like she was a soldier being given a command. She wrinkled her nose in distaste. "I'm sorry, but I'll convene the royal council. It's nothing personal--"

"Nothing personal?" he bellowed in disbelief. "You talk of divorcing me and you say it's nothing personal?"

"Zoran," she began, trying to keep her tone soft, though there was a definite edge to her words. "You are a very nice man and you will make someone very happy--"

"You have no grounds for divorce," he declared, cutting into her placating speech with a slash of his angry hand. "To even bring it up to the council will dishonor us both. I can provide for you. I can give you sons. What will be your reason?"

"I..." Pia hesitated. How could she explain when she wasn't sure herself? *I'm scared of you and how you look at me. I think you're too handsome and strong and I want a wimpy husband who doesn't have such a striking voice or a devilishly wicked grin. I want a man who can't give me children because I'm scared of being touched or looked at.*

"Well?"

"I," she tried again. Her eyes dotted with moisture.

"Out with it!" Zoran yelled, waving his hand through the air.

"You are just impossible!" Pia screamed at him instead. "You're nothing but a big baby who has to have his way! You don't want me, you're just mad because I don't want you! Well, get over yourself! I'm getting a divorce and there is nothing you can say or do to stop me!"

Pia stormed away.

"What about your contract?" he asked, as a last effort.

Pia stiffened, stopping in the doorway.

"I received a copy of it," he said. In fact, he'd requested it. The way she'd referred to it in the tent, he'd been most curious to know what the corporation had on her to make her follow him regardless of how she felt at the time. It'd been clear she wanted to leave the tent, but was too scared to.

Pia's breath deepened with long pants of air. She couldn't look at him.

"You'll owe them a lot of money if you leave me."

"I can pay it back," she lied, her voice a trembling whisper.

"If you could have, you wouldn't be here," he said.

"I can go on another trip," she said, feeling suddenly trapped. "I can find a different husband to settle my obligation to Galaxy Brides."

"Maybe you should read the fine print," Zoran said. "Since I chose you, you can't leave unless the wedding isn't finished. If you leave me and I complain, you will have to pay them back for breach of contract."

Pia spun to him in horror. Her eyes were round and her voice was an inaudible murmur, as she asked, "Why would you do that?"

"Because you are my wife." His jaw was stiff. It was a shallow victory, but he'd take it. Lowering his tone, his eyes were still hard, as he stated, "You belong with me."

"I have no choice, do I?" Pia asked, though she didn't expect or receive an answer. "You're serious."

"Very."

Pia gasped for breath. She looked completely stricken. Her lips trembled and her eyes became moist. The tears didn't fall.

Zoran was sorry that it had come to this. He'd never wanted to force her hand, but if she kept speaking of divorcing him someone would eventually overhear it. It would dishonor him and his family. The divorce would never be granted. As a Prince, one of the votes was his and he would never allow it. But, the shame of going through the trial would undermine his authority with the men and embarrass everyone involved.

Pia slowly nodded at him. She felt numb. Sighing in resignation, she said, "You win, Zoran. You win. There will be no divorce."

As she turned to leave him, Zoran didn't feel like he'd won anything. Her shoulders held back, proud. She didn't cry or pout over her fate. She handled it with dignity.

"Pia," he called, not knowing what he could say to bridge the gap between them. He only hoped that time would mend it. She stopped, waiting. "Thanks for looking after my arm."

At that, he heard her give a short, humorless laugh. "What else is a wife for?"

Chapter Seven

Zoran left his home with the dawn. Pia was fast asleep on the couch, curled into a ball beneath the blanket. He felt terrible for forcing her hand, but was proud of how well she accepted her fate. She didn't cry or whine. She honored herself well.

Standing, arms crossed, he shouted commands to the young soldiers. He couldn't slack in his duties. But as hard as he'd pushed the men lately, he could call off early in the day and give them a break. He wanted to extend a peace offering to Pia, maybe get her out of the house for a little bit.

Seeing one of his brothers, Olek, striding toward the field, Zoran gave a wry chuckle of self-amusement. His brothers had been most lax in their training since getting married. Ualan had joined him for a little bit during the swamp battles, but other than that the Princes had been scarce.

Olek's features were drawn into a tight scowl and he stormed as if he were being chased by demons. When Olek's troubled eyes lifted from the surrounding village, he nodded solemnly at his commander brother. Zoran smiled a devilish smile in return and sternly nodded back. He knew just what his little brother needed.

Lifting his arm to the men, he motioned to Olek and yelled, "First wave, attack!"

Olek blinked in surprise, but a healthy grin came to his features as he swung his sword up from his waist. Zoran watched in brotherly mischief as the whole of his first battalion rushed forward and tackled the bravely fighting Olek to the ground.

* * * *

"Here."

Pia looked up from where she lounged on the low cushion next to the short table in surprise. She'd been flipping through a weapons manual she'd found, looking at the pictures, though she couldn't understand the words. Her mind had drifted some time ago and she didn't hear him come in.

Zoran stood before her, sweaty from work, but not covered in swamp muck. In his extended hand he held a bunch of flowers. He'd pulled them up by the roots and red dirt still clung to them.

Pia eyed him and his wilting flowers unenthusiastically. "You're off early."

"I thought," he began. "Here, take these. I'm trying to ... ugh."

Pia blinked. It really was a sweet effort, one he didn't seem all that comfortable making. She would've laughed if he didn't look so pained.

Standing, Pia set the manual aside and took the flowers.

"Ah, thanks," she mumbled. "I guess I should get them in some water."

Zoran rolled his eyes at himself and smacked the side of his temple, as she turned to walk the sorry bouquet to the kitchen. He'd known it was a stupid idea when Olek suggested it. Olek seemed so sure his own wife liked plants from the forest and assumed that maybe all Earth women did.

Following her to the kitchen, Zoran watched as she grabbed a knife and cut off the roots. She then filled a goblet with water and stuck the flowers in it. As she swept the roots into the trash, he said, "Come on. I got you some things."

Pia eyed him suspiciously.

"Just," he frowned and grumbled, waving her forward. "Come on."

Pia followed him to the main hall. She hadn't noticed until now that there was a bunch of packages on the floor.

"What's all this?" she asked.

"I thought, well, you looked like you might need some stuff. So I went shopping for you."

"Okay," Pia allowed carefully, wondering what in the galaxy he thought she needed. Aside from something to do during the day and food in the kitchen, she couldn't think of a thing.

Zoran leaned over and picked up the largest bag, handing it to her. "I got you some clothes. I know they aren't what you're used to, but it's our fashion. I got the most comfortable stuff I could find."

Zoran had gone to the dressmaker, grabbing a random woman off the street who appeared to be about Pia's size. The woman was shocked beyond belief to have the overlarge Captain of the Guards, and a Prince at that, grab her and yank her into the dressmaker's shop. But, after realizing what the big bad warrior was trying to do, she took pity on him and helped him out. She even went so far as to make him a list of everything he should consider getting. Zoran had gotten most of the items off her list--at least the ones he could understand. For the life of him he couldn't figure out what a mascara and a blush tinter were. When he'd asked the baker, the man had just shrugged.

Zoran then ordered the old dressmaker to give him everything she had that a wife might have need of. She'd only been too happy to comply, insisting that he bring his wife back to the shop so she could measure her for a dress. Instead, Zoran told her to send one of her assistants to the house to take the measurements. He hated to admit that he was still disturbed by her hair and not ready to bring her out in public. Not that he thought she wasn't ravishing, but that the rest of his people would assume he did it to shame and humiliate her. The Qurilixen would never believe that a woman had purposefully done it her herself.

The seamstress' helper would be arriving any minute. Zoran had picked out a few dress designs and materials he liked. Then, he'd given leeway to the woman to make Pia whatever else she saw fit before leaving the shop.

Pia hesitated. No one had ever gotten her anything like this before. No one had ever brought her flowers. She didn't care how sorry they looked. To her they were the most beautiful flowers in the galaxy.

Zoran frowned when she didn't speak. "You aren't pleased."

"No," she rushed. "It's fine. There's just so much of it. I don't need all this."

"I can't take it back," he lied. "So you might as well go through it and pick out what you want."

Pia nodded. She took the bag and sat with it on the front hall floor. Carefully reaching in, she dug out several pairs of cotton slacks. The material was soft and flowing and reminded her of pajama pants. They came in all colors, most predominately black. One even had a red dragon embroidered on the front hip. She smiled. Maybe that could be her new formal wear.

Zoran saw her smile and relaxed some. "So you're not going to throw them in the fireplace?"

Pia blinked, not knowing he was teasing. "I'm sorry about that. I shouldn't have done it."

"It's fine. Forget it."

Pia nodded, still feeling guilty.

Zoran lifted a couple bags and began walking to the kitchen. "I'll put the groceries away. The rest is yours, go ahead and put them wherever you see fit."

Pia swallowed nervously. Without him watching her, she dug into the sack with shaking fingers. She found several cotton shirts with built in support. Reaching to scratch where her bra rubbed her side, she sighed in excitement. These shirts would be so much more comfortable.

Pia heard Zoran rummaging around in the kitchen. She leaned back, trying to get a peek at him. She couldn't see him from her place on the floor.

In one of the smaller bags was a bunch of perfumes. She wondered if he'd even tested them or if he simply walked along and plucked them randomly into a bag. She smelled a couple. Most were exotic flower blends and not bad. One, a very decorative bottle encrusted with fake gems, was awful and she capped it immediately.

"You'll be decoration," she said to the offending fragrance, setting it apart from the others.

There were socks, leather boots, and a low pair of shoes perfect for exercising. Lifting them up, she slipped the low shoes onto her bare feet. They fit perfectly.

"I thought you could use those if you wanted to work on your kicks," he said from behind her.

Pia was in too good of a mood to take offence. It was just like Christmas--or what she imagined Christmas would've felt like. "There's nothing wrong with my kicks. I got you, didn't I?"

They both instantly remembered their little fight in the tent. Zoran's eyes lit with the memory. Pia turned quickly away to hide her mortified blush.

"I let you hit me," he said. "I took it easy on you, you know, because you're a girl."

Pia's mouth dropped open at his presumption. "Hey, I've been in a lot of fights. I can hold my own."

"I'm sure with a weaker, less skilled opponent, you could," Zoran said, provoking her on purpose. She was lovely when she was fired up.

"Are you saying I couldn't take you down?" she asked, hands on hips. "I'll have you know that I've taken down creatures twice your size."

"Have you?" he smirked, not believing her.

"Yeah," she stated. "I have. In fact, once in the Sollure System I took on two Yehtis from--"

"Yehtis are slow, cumbersome creatures," Zoran broke in, dismissing her words away with a toss of his hand. "Anyone with half a brain could outwit them."

"I was thirteen," she said darkly.

All right, Zoran thought. *That's impressive.*

"You could have just gotten lucky." Not letting her see his admiration, he continued to goad her. "It doesn't mean that you don't need to work on your moves."

"My *moves* are just fine," she said, outraged. "I'll take on any man you put in front of me!"

"Is that so?" he asked, taking a step forward.

"Yeah, that's so!"

Zoran stepped directly in front of her, crossing his arms over his chest. "All right, then."

Pia blinked up at him.

"Well?" he questioned, with an arrogant raise of his brow. "You said you could take down any man I put in front of you. So, what are you waiting for? Take me down."

Pia narrowed her eyes. Instantly, her hand darted out for his neck and she turned to sweep him down over her hip. Zoran ducked out of her way and grabbed her from behind as she spun. Pulling her hard to his chest, he said, "I'm sorry, were you not ready? Would you like to try again?"

Pia grumbled darkly as he let her go. Backing up, she eyed him. Coming forward, she faked a kick and punched toward his jaw. He dodged her fist, lifting his hand to catch it in his large palm.

Pia flinched, as he squeezed her fist lightly in his grasp, showing her how easily he could have broken her hand without really hurting her. She jerked her hand away from him with a loud growl of frustration. Zoran smiled. "Are you done playing around?"

Pia shook out her hand and circled around him. Zoran lowered his arm to his side and didn't move to watch her. He had to give her credit, she wasn't bad. He listened to her steps carefully, anticipating her attack.

"Ow," Pia cried out breathlessly, as if in pain.

Zoran instantly turned to check on her. It was a mistake. She grabbed his arm in mid turn and bucked him over her knee. He landed on his back with a thud and she jumped on top of him, pinning down his arms with her knees.

Smiling victoriously, she said, "You military guys are all the same. It doesn't matter who you are, if you hear a womanly cry for help you're all over it." She shook her head, her short hair brushing up against her jaw. "I'm sorely disappointed, Zoran."

Zoran grinned. He was anything but disappointed. He could've gotten out of her hold if he wanted to, but the view was too great to disrupt. He had an eyeful of her breasts right above his face and if he were to lean his head in he could nuzzle her inner thigh. To bad she wouldn't take her clothes off. This game would be much more entertaining if they were naked.

"Do you give up?" she asked.

"And relinquish this view?" he said playfully, giving a meaningful nod to her chest. He licked his lips. "Never."

Pia gasped, instantly trying to stand. Zoran pushed up from the floor, bending straight over so she straddled his lap. Then, whipping his legs straight to the sides and around on the floor, he pinned her down with his body, fitting himself between her thighs.

Pia gasped to feel his swift grace. His flexible gladiator body pressed into hers.

"Though, this view isn't bad either," he smirked naughtily. Looking down at her breasts beneath his face, he asked, "Do you mind if I just take a closer look?

"Ah!" Pia's mouth fell open in outrage.

He took the opportunity to place a swift kiss on her mouth. Her body jolted in shock beneath him. She squeezed his waist with her legs, trying to get him to back off.

"Get off me, you gigantic oaf!" she screamed. "Don't you dare touch me!"

Zoran chuckled and rolled to the side. She shot to her feet. Suddenly, a knock sounded on the door. Pia blinked looking down at her husband who was lying on his back, eyeing her from the floor.

"That would be the man here to take your measurements," he answered her unasked question. Bucking his feet into the air, he hopped to standing with little effort. He winked at Pia as he passed by. "I know you hate it, but you do need to have a few formal dresses for special occasions."

Pia was too weak to answer, as she watched the graceful way his body moved and flexed. It was strange to see large man so nimble, yet overwhelmingly powerful and strong. The way he could so easily overtake her did something to her insides. She watched him, her mouth dry, as he went to answer the door. It was as if he had no idea the effect he had on her. Her heart hammered in her chest, pounding wildly. She was severely shaken.

In the tent, when they'd fought, he hadn't moved as swiftly and surely as he had just now. Pia realized that he'd held back that night. He'd let her think she had him matched. Now, watching his body with new appreciation, she understood that he was trained well beyond her years of experience. She might get a few lucky shots in, but in the end he would always be able to defeat her. A small part of her wanted to beg him to train her. The other parts of her beat that small part up.

Zoran glanced back at her. He narrowed his eyes wondering at her dumbfounded look. With no reason to think otherwise, he assumed the look meant she didn't want to be fitted for formal gowns.

Pia tried to hide her thoughts from her warrior husband. She looked over Zoran's shoulder. A man stood in the doorway, looking at her with a look akin to horror. She blushed, suddenly realizing he must have heard them from outside the hall.

"*Draea Anwealda,*" the dressmaker's assistant said, turning to address Prince Zoran with a slight bow. The man made a compassionate face, glancing back at Pia's hair. The man motioned to her again with a look of pity, asking

Zoran their shared language, "Should I leave? Is the Princess in exile?"

Zoran should've known it was coming. He glanced back at Pia, knowing he would have to face a rampage of rumors the next day.

"No," Zoran answered the man in kind. "She isn't disfigured."

Pia watched as the man motioned to her and then to his own longer locks. She self-consciously touched her hair as she watched him. When he looked at her again, it was as if he felt sorry for her. The man shook his head sadly.

"What?" Pia asked, looking at Zoran to translate the man's words. "What's he saying?"

Zoran frowned, but answered honestly, "He wants to know why I have disfigured you and if he should leave your presence. He thinks you might be in exile."

"What did you tell him?" she asked unenthusiastically. Suddenly, she began growing extremely self-conscious. Annoying Zoran with her haircut was one thing, but eliciting pitying looks from outsiders was another completely. She didn't wish to be pitied. She hated those 'oh, that poor thing' looks people sometimes gave her when they'd seen her scarred face. That's what this man's expression reminded her of.

"That you weren't disfigured," Zoran answered.

Pia eyed the man, scowling. He continued to stare at her. She stiffened. Her jaw lifted regally and she stared back. The man blinked, looking away first. It was a grim victory.

Zoran said something to the man. The assistant rushed forward. Zoran nodded at his wife, going to the kitchen and leaving them alone. Lifting her arm, the assistant ran his measuring tape over her stiff body. He finished quickly, without looking directly at her again, and turned to leave. The door slid shut behind him.

"Please tell me not everyone is going to react like that," she said darkly.

"Like what?" Zoran asked. He pretended not to know what she spoke of, as he came out of the kitchen wiping crumbs from his mouth.

"Never mind." Hands on hips, she looked over the packages. "Where do you want me to put this stuff? The closet or dresser?"

"It's up to you," Zoran answered. "I cleared out the right side of the dresser and half the closet for you before the festival."

The comment struck Pia as odd. It made her realize how much he'd actually planned on getting married. Was that why he picked her? Because he'd already set his mind to finding a bride and wouldn't change it? Was she like the only girl left and he had to take her?

"Ah, thanks," she mumbled, for lack of anything better to say. To hide her nervousness, she picked up the bags and carried them to the bedroom. Within minutes, she had everything in its place. Then, going back to the hall, she took the perfumes and went to the bathroom.

Zoran was in the hot spring when she walked in and she jumped in surprise.

"Ah, sorry," she said in distress. "I didn't realize ... that ... you..."

She threw the bag on the counter a little too hard. The bottles clanked as she began her retreat, trying to keep her eyes diverted from his naked body.

Zoran laughed, completely unashamed. "Pia--"

The slamming door cut off his words.

* * * *

The next morning, Pia was lying on the couch, lazing away the morning hours when she heard the door slide up. Zoran was gone when she awoke, not that she expected him to be home.

Not moving, her heart skipped. Her eyes turned to the door, waiting for him to come through.

"Hello?"

Pia froze. That wasn't Zoran. Sitting forward, Pia tried to smooth back her hair. Queen Mede was standing in the front hall. She looked very formal in her gown a regal dark blue.

"Zoran...?" the Queen began.

Pia stood from the couch, wishing she'd taken the time to change from her cotton shirts and slacks. She felt very out of place standing before royalty. She had no idea what to say.

Mede's eyes found the quiet Pia. The smile faded from her features into a look akin to horror.

"So it's true," the Queen said, coming forward. She lifted her hands as if to touch Pia's shortened hair before drawing back. She shook her head sadly. "Zoran's disfigured you."

Pia stiffened.

The Queen frowned at the look the woman gave her. "Do you know who I am, dear?"

"Oh," she breathed. Thinking the Queen thought her rude, she quickly moved into a curtsey. "Yes, of course, Queen Mede. I'm sorry, you took me off guard. Please, come in."

Mede looked at her daughter-by-marriage and frowned. It was clear Pia didn't know she was a Princess or her new daughter. The Queen nodded royally. It wasn't her place to intervene. She knew her son would tell her about it when the time was right.

"Zoran is, um, well, he's working. I don't know where but I do know he was on guard duty at the swamps earlier this week if that helps," Pia said nervously. The Queen was staring at her hair and she didn't dare glare at her as she had the seamstress' assistant.

"I was actually looking for you, dear," the Queen said politely.

Zoran? A guard on swamp duty? Mede thought. It was hard, but she managed not to laugh. This woman really had no idea what sort of man she'd married.

"Oh?" Pia asked, fidgeting.

"It was reported what he did to you." The Queen motioned to her hair. "I know that he had to do something to cover that little stunt you pulled the morning of the festival, but I never thought it would be this."

Pia paled.

"Which I might add, the King and I were thoroughly amused by," Mede said with a good-natured chuckle. Pia only stiffened more. "Lord Zoran is a tough man. We were glad to see he's met his match."

"Lord Zoran?" Pia asked. She wasn't so sure she was Zoran's match, but she didn't correct the woman. Her knees weakened a little. "He's titled?"

The Queen cocked her head to the side and didn't know how to answer. "I'm told our culture is complicated for someone new to it. I'm sure Zoran will explain it to you if you ask him."

Pia smiled, though she wasn't so sure.

Mede's eyes turned over her again. She looked mournfully at the woman before her. "I just had to see for myself that the rumors were true. I'm terribly sorry about your disfigurement."

The last thing Pia wanted was the Queen stopping by to pay her condolences for her shorn locks. She didn't need the woman's pity. She didn't want it.

This is getting ridiculous! Maybe I should've had a funeral for it, Pia thought wryly, *so everyone could pay my hair their respects.*

Pia touched her blonde locks. She unconsciously turned her mouth down into a frown. "I don't see it as a punishment. Actually, all that weight on my head was the punishment. I like it short."

"You're right to look at the positive," the Queen said, giving the brave girl a bright smile. She nodded proudly at her in encouragement. Mede was glad to see that her spirit wasn't broken by her son's actions. She'd known grown women who cried and went into exile while waiting for their hair to grow back. In their society it wasn't just the loss of hair, it was the loss of honor it represented that shamed them. "It's only hair and luckily it will grow back someday."

Pia thought of her scars. She'd hate to see what these vain people would've done about those.

Mede, seeing the woman wasn't going to encourage her to stay, smiled kindly and said through her disappointment, "I'll give Zoran an earful that's for sure. In the meantime, I have some beautiful headdresses I'll send you."

"Thank you," Pia said, still at a loss.

The Queen looked like she wanted to say something more, but drew back. Pia's nature wasn't exactly open to friendship.

"Well, I should be going," Mede said, heading toward the front door. Pia slowly followed behind her. "Tell Lord Zoran I stopped by and I wish for him to call on me as soon as it's convenient."

"Please, don't bother on my behalf," Pia said solemnly.

"No, no, of course not," the Queen mumbled. There was an uncomfortable silence between them, before she said, "There are other matters I need him to tend to."

Pia nodded and tried to smile. The Queen left and she was relieved. She shook her head, more annoyed by the visit than anything else.

Chapter Eight

"Father," Zoran called, leaning his head into the King's royal offices. His father looked up from his desk and waved him in. Zoran crossed with natural grace and stealth over the plush carpet and took a seat across from the King. His back was at rigid attention as he looked at his father expectantly.

"Zoran," the King stated. He finished writing on a document and turned his full attention to his son. Reaching over, he grabbed a stack of papers that needed Zoran's attention and handed them over. "How are the men shaping up?"

"Fine," Zoran answered, knowing that wasn't the reason his father had asked to see him. He put the documents on his lap, aware that he would be required to read over them later. "I've pushed them hard these past few days. We have a few weaknesses but I'm working it out. A few of the men show great promise."

"Glad to hear it," the King said. He rested his chin on his folded hands and studied his most stubborn son. Zoran was a good man and an excellent leader. Leaning back, he pressed his lips together in thought. "Yusef stopped by last night."

"Is everything well at the Outpost?" Zoran asked, concerned.

The King sniffed wryly to himself. "Militarily speaking."

Zoran watched his father expectantly.

"Yusef's bride is in chastisement," the King said. His voice was controlled. "She took a blade to his ... anyhow. I decreed that the chastisement stands until he releases her. Officially, I need your agreement on the matter and then it will be settled."

Zoran tried not to laugh. He failed miserably. Chuckling, he got out, "Agreed."

"Ah, wipe that smile off your face," the disgruntled King ordered, waving his hand. Zoran wasn't worried by the fatherly tone. "Your marriage is giving us just as much of a

THE WARRIOR PRINCE

headache. You know I had to listen to your mother for nearly three hours this morning. It seems she took it upon herself to visit Pia."

Zoran's face gave nothing away. His heart tightened in his chest and his stomach rolled into knots. Had Pia tried to divorce him despite her contract?

"I honestly don't know what to do with you boys," the King admitted wearily. "I'm planning on having a celebration in about a week to coronate the Princesses. But it seems only Olek's bride is aware she's a Princess and, apparently, Nadja is none too thrilled with the fact. Yusef's wife is in chastisement and even he admits he doesn't know her real name. Ualan's wife, Morrigan, has declared herself a slave and can't leave his home. And then, I have to hear it from your mother that you disfigured your own wife."

Zoran felt his heart beat again and he almost sighed with the relief of it. Pia hadn't tried to divorce him.

"I don't know what you're smiling about," the King said, seeing Zoran's lips tilt slightly, though the look on his son's stern face could hardly be called a smile by most standards.

"I didn't cut her hair," Zoran said quietly. "She did it to herself."

The King blinked in disbelief. "Regardless of her disfigurement, I need your wife at the coronation. Now, I have excused Yusef's bride from attending. Since she's in chastisement and will undoubtedly not repent, your mother has agreed to spread the word that this nameless woman is ill and in recovery. Enough people have seen the medic going to the Outpost these last several days to validate the story."

Zoran frowned. A week to turn his bride around and tell her she was a Princess? He wondered how Pia would take the news. Laughing to himself, he wondered which she'd hate worse--the fact she was a Princess or the fact she'd have to spend an evening in a formal gown.

"Can't the coronation be set back?" Zoran asked. "There's no reason to have it so soon."

"There have been rumors that the brides have not been seen within the castle and that all four marriages are in ruin," the King allowed. His look said that he was well aware that the rumors weren't completely unfounded. "If anything, we need to keep up the appearances of being a united family. You are all mated, my son. If the people feel that our line is ending because each of you had an unlucky marriage and cannot produce heirs, there could be panic."

Zoran nodded, understanding what his father said. If the people felt their line was too weak to continue ruling, they would overthrow them. It wouldn't matter how much they liked and respected the royal family, or how long they'd ruled.

"Olek and I have spoken on the matter," King Llyr stated, "and we feel that a quick coronation with healthy, accounted for brides is just the thing to stop this threat to our house."

Olek was the Draig ambassador and had to meet with the neighboring kingdom of Var on a regular basis. Zoran didn't envy his brother's job, for he'd much rather fight the Var in battle than talk on a regular basis to their forked tongued nobles.

"And, if one of you boys can manage to breed before next week...." The King let his words trail off as he looked pointedly at Zoran. His son didn't move and he frowned in disappointment. All four Princes knew how much their parents wanted grandsons.

"Olek has been to meet with King Attor and feels that he grows restless. I fear the Var will try to invade. It's quite possible they have spies within our walls already," the King continued. Zoran listened in his customary silence, his face giving none of his thoughts away. "This matter with the brides needs to be resolved so we can focus on what's important."

"I'll work the men twice as hard," Zoran said, seriously. "If battle comes we will be prepared. The Var will not make it past the outlands."

"Fine." The King wasn't worried. Zoran was the best at what he did. He was invincible. "I have already invited King Attor to the coronation to prove to the entire kingdom we're not scared of him."

"I'll personally see to the security," Zoran said. As Captain it was his duty.

"No, I'll have Yusef keep an eye on him since he'll be free that night." King Llyr stood and leaned over his desk to stare down his son. "I'm ordering you as your King to get your house in order by the coronation. I want to see happy brides. I want to see dancing and singing and merriment. Hellfire, I want to see some inappropriate kissing and groping as well. A little scandal in that direction would do this matter a world of good and would stop the wagging tongues. I want your bride completely besotted with you."

Zoran's jaw flexed. It was an order from his King and he couldn't refuse. Zoran could just imagine if he kissed Pia in public. She'd no doubt take him and his army of warriors on. Standing, he nodded his head and said the only thing he could. "It will be done."

"Good," the King bellowed, smiling widely. He had full confidence in his son's abilities. Zoran's prowess with the female sex was legendary amongst his men. He walked Zoran to the door. As he ushered him out, Llyr said, "And no more of this disfiguring nonsense. If you have to, put the biggest damned headdress you can find over her head to hide it."

* * * *

Pia looked over the edge of the couch to where Zoran sat cross-legged at the low dining table on a floor cushion. His hands were threaded through his hair as he read some papers he'd brought home with him. He was unusually quiet and it was driving her to distraction. She was bored-- really, really, really bored. She'd even started biting her nails, a habit she had never had before this day.

"The Queen came by," she said to break his concentration. It didn't get as big of a reaction as she'd expected.

Zoran knitted his brow, glancing over with only his eyes before turning back to the page. "I heard."

"Oh, did you go see her then? Because she wanted me to tell you to go and see her," Pia said, turning to kneel on the cushions so she could better study him. She laid her arms over the back of the couch, resting her chin on her hands as she waited for him to answer. He read a few more lines before speaking.

"I'll take care of it," Zoran answered, without bothering to look at her again. He continued to read and Pia watched him in silence.

"Are we nobility?" Zoran made a great show of sighing. "The Queen called you Lord Zoran and said I should ask you to explain it to me."

Zoran chuckled quietly at that so she couldn't see. Trust his mother to try and help things along. He knew it was irritating the Queen that she couldn't openly go to her new daughters and proclaim their relation. No doubt she had grand feminine plans in store for all the new brides.

"I'm trying to get this done, Pia. Do you mind if we talk about it later?" he asked, giving her his most serious face. The truth was he wasn't sure he wanted to tell her. He had no idea how she would react. If she were happy, he would worry that she would start looking at him for his title and not himself. If she were mad about it, he would worry that she wouldn't get over it in a week's time.

"Oh, sorry," Pia mumbled. With a loud sigh, she sunk back into the couch and absently kicked her feet at the cushions.

Zoran looked over at the couch. Her foot was lifted over the back, swinging in loud boredom. He tried not to smile. She'd been trying to get his attention ever since he walked in the door. Ignoring her wasn't a tactic he would've thought of before now. It was working beautifully.

"Pia?" he sighed, forcing exasperation.

Her head popped back up from behind the couch, expectant.

"Can you do that a little quieter?" he asked, with a meaningful nod at her still dangling foot.

"Sorry," she huffed, scrunching up her face. As she lay back down, he heard her mumble, "You try spending all day in this stupid house and see if you don't get a little stir crazy."

Pia would never tell him, but earlier that day she'd been so bored that she tried on all his formal tunics and pretended to fight with one of his swords. The sad thing was the imaginary creature she fought against won the battle. Though, her dramatic performance in the death scene was quite good, if she did think so herself.

Pia quietly got up from the couch and wandered around the house. Slowly, she circled her way closer to him, going into the kitchen before slithering out to loom behind his back. She raised up on her toes, trying to read over his shoulder to see if he was almost finished.

"Argh, woman," Zoran said, spinning around to look at her. He leaned a hand on the floor behind him to support his weight. She was beautiful. Even without her little noises, she would've been distracting him with her presence. Every time he tired to read a line, he'd start imagining her naked body on the page and what he'd do to her if she'd only let him. Already, he'd started the same paragraph five times. "What is it you want?"

"I wanted to ask you something," she said. "Are you still busy?"

Zoran's eyebrow rose on his forehead. A lecherous smile came to his lips as he looked purposefully over her body.

Pia blushed, denying instantly, "Not that!"

Zoran watched the heat that came to her features. He shrugged. Was he busy? He looked back at the stack of royal documents needing his attention.

"I need your permission for something," she rushed to keep his attention on her and not the paperwork.

That intrigued him. Zoran slowly turned to study her again.

Pia idly made her way past him to sit across the table. She crossed her legs as she lowered herself onto the surprisingly comfortable cushion. Her eyes drifted to his documents, seeing a dragon on the top of the page--his dragon.

Pia swallowed, thinking he would deny her if she asked him what she wanted to. So, instead, she lifted her finger to ruffle the side of his stack and inquired, "What are all these, anyway?"

"Work," came the short answer. Pia gave a light grimace at him and drew her hands to her lap.

Zoran's body tensed. Oh, how he wanted nothing more at the moment than to crawl over the table and kiss the incredibly erotic pout off her face.

"Well?" he probed, feigning an annoyance he didn't feel. He enjoyed their little games.

"Any chance you'd just give me permission without knowing?" Pia asked. His expression said that it wasn't likely. She shivered, very drawn to the handsomeness of his eyes. Every time she thought of them, she got chills. "All right, I want..."

Zoran smiled, growing unbelievably aroused by the way her mouth moved when she talked. His stomach tightened and his leg muscles were ready to pounce at the slightest command from his brain.

Swallowing, Pia was completely unaware of the effect she had on him. However, she was all too aware of the effect his presence was having on her. Easily, she could recall the look and feel of his chest. Considering her words carefully, they still came out all wrong. "I want to touch your weapon."

His grin grew, as did his desire. Slowly, he stood. Pia followed suit. A soft look of hope came to her innocent features. His manly 'weapon' stirred to eager attention. What exactly was she asking him? To his disappointment, her next statement answered that question. It wasn't the answer his taut body wanted.

"Just the throwing knives," Pia hastened, seeing his look and mistaking it for displeasure. She came forward to lay a pleading hand on his arm. "I wasn't allowed to bring my set on the ship and had to leave them behind."

In truth, Pia had to sell the antique set to get to the Galaxy Bride's corporation headquarters to see the doctors.

"Please," she begged. She bounced in jittery excitement. "It's been making me crazy staring at them all day and not being able to do anything. I'll go mad without something to keep me busy."

"Knives?" he mused, just to be sure his body's disappointment was founded. His hand lifted to stroke her cheek. She blinked in surprise at the touch, almost startled, and he drew away.

"It's polite to ask before taking," Pia explained. "Otherwise I wouldn't have bugged you about it. My father..."

She stopped suddenly.

Zoran saw the look on her face and frowned. Something in her eyes wavered, but she lifted her chin proudly and didn't continue. He smelled her pain as well as felt it inside of his chest as she mentioned the man.

"Give me a kiss," Zoran said instead, a grin curling his devilishly handsome mouth.

Pia's brows furrowed.

"Just one."

Pia swallowed and didn't move. His eyes were staring boldly into hers. Her mouth pressed shut and she denied him. With a shake of her head, she said, "Don't change the subject."

"Can I at least kiss you?" he murmured seductively, drawing closer still.

"Please," Pia said, staring at his full mouth. Then, shaking herself, she added, "I'll take good care of them."

"I can't supervise you just now," Zoran answered at last, sighing in disappointment. He glanced back at the documents. His father would expect their return the next morning. Zoran doubted the King would take any excuse short of him impregnating Pia with a grandson. Since that wasn't going to be happening, he knew he should get back to work. "But I'll show them to you later."

Pia wrinkled her nose at him and grumbled, "I don't need supervision, tyrant. I know what I'm doing."

"I don't want you hurting yourself." He crossed his arms in a very commanding way that was full of authority and power, as he looked down at her. "I keep all my weapons very sharp and ready for battle. Maybe I could get you a child's set to begin with."

The offer had been genuine. Pia was genuinely ticked off. Her face turned a bright shade of angry red. Her mouth fell open at the audacity.

"Yeah, you do that and I'll shove that child's set right up your stubborn--"

"Pia," he warned.

Her mouth snapped shut and she glared at him in consideration. Suddenly, she smiled agreeably, "Husband?"

Now Zoran was worried.

"Is this my house, too?" she asked, her voice sweet.

Stiffly, he nodded, very afraid.

"Fine, if you are going to be a tyrant, so will I. Where I come from a wife runs the household and if I have to get used to your culture, you have to get used to mine. And I'll make you as crazy as you make me. You are to pick up after yourself. No more leaving laundry on the floor, no more dirty boots in the front hall. You'll rinse your own

swamp mud out of the shower. That was really very gross--
"

"Pia," Zoran interjected. He'd noticed with no small amount of husbandly pleasure that she was picking up after him.

"Huh?"

"Are you finished? I really need to get back to work." His eyes were devouring her face. He kind of liked her giving him commands.

"Zoran, what part of this are you not understanding? I'm going crazy in this house," she cried. "Please, please, please, let me go outside."

"Open," he yelled at the door. Pia turned her eyes to the front door. It slid open. He waved at it. "Have fun, try not to get lost."

Zoran sat back down at the table, pretending to ignore her.

Pia glared at his down turned head. "You know what I mean. Program my voice into it so I can leave during the day."

"And what will you do?" he asked. To the door, he called, "Shut!"

"I'm going to get a job," Pia answered, carefully. She drew her finger in absent circles around the table. "You're gone all day so it's not like you'd even notice."

"You don't need to work." Zoran didn't like the idea of her being able to support herself. He didn't want her getting any ideas in her head about leaving him again. He studied her carefully, wondering at her forlorn expression. Was she pouting about his absence? Did she actually miss him during the day as he did her? Rationally, he added, "We don't need the money."

"Oh, but I do need to work," she rushed. "I've never been as useless as I have been these last several days. If you're not going to let me divorce you, then you have got to give just a little. Otherwise, you will have a neurotic mess on your hands and not a wife."

"And what exactly are you going to do?" Zoran asked, standing once more and stalking forward to tower next to her. To his delight, she shivered and inched back from him in nervousness. He couldn't take much more of this. His hands were itching to touch her. His mouth throbbed with the need to kiss her.

"I--I don't want to tell you," she said, backing further away from his looming body. "You'll only laugh at me."

Zoran grew worried.

"I'm going to talk to the dressmaker," she lied. "I'm pretty handy with a ... needle."

"Really?" Zoran mused. Sewing wasn't too bad. It could have been much worse. "I'll speak to the seamstress tomorrow for you. I don't think she's looking for an apprentice, but it doesn't hurt to ask."

Pia scowled. She had no intention of speaking to the seamstress. The only thing she'd ever stitched up was her own hide. "Never mind, I would've rather done it myself."

"She doesn't speak your language."

His logical tone frustrated Pia even more. This conversation wasn't going as she'd hoped. All she wanted was to use his knives and to go outside to do it.

Zoran turned back to his documents. Giving her an expectant look, he asked, "Was there anything else?"

Pia glowered hotly at him and stalked away.

Chapter Nine

Pia smiled, watching the slight spark as she hit two wires together. The front door slid up. It had only taken an hour for her to find the controls in the wall and reprogram the door. The hole she'd dug in the side wall was unfortunate, but didn't her husband say it was her house, too? And why couldn't she dig a hole into the wall of her house if she wanted to? She'd hoped it wouldn't come to sneaking out, but Zoran really left her no choice.

She wore the boots he'd given her and a pair of the more sturdy pants and a cotton shirt. Her outfit was all black, matching the mischievous ninja-like mood she was in. At her waist was her tyrant of a husband's throwing knives. Hey, she'd asked him. It wasn't her fault he was stubborn and forced her to resort to borrowing without permission.

Turning down the hall in the direction she'd seen Zoran walk in that morning, she looked around. Their apartment was adjoined to a long red hallway. As she made her way, she saw portraits, statues, and tapestries decorating with subtle beauty. She ignored them all, not really interested in fine art except as markers for direction.

Coming to the first turn, she frowned. The halls looked the same, only the decorations were different. Seeing a small panel on the wall with strange carvings, she looked at all four corners. Three were the similar in design, one was different. She tried the hall with the different symbol.

She got lucky. The hall led her down a straight path, past several closed doors and a shorter hallway. She kept going straight and hit upon the front gate. Sunlight streamed through the opening. The guard on duty looked her over, stopping to stare at her hair. He seemed to have heard of her, because he merely nodded his head and allowed her to pass without speaking.

Pia narrowed her eyes and made a face behind his back. These stupid Qurilixen and their hair fetish! She cursed them all with baldness.

Going into the soft haze of the triple suns, she took a deep
breath of air. She instantly felt better. She was in a
courtyard. Glancing up in surprise, she realized she lived in
the tall mountain she'd seen from the festival ground. From
the ground, because of the angle, you couldn't see the
windows or balconies that were adjoined to the homes.
They were carved just so, that even from a distance it
looked just like a mountain cliff. It was truly an
impenetrable fortress. Pia was impressed.

A path went down one side of the courtyard to the forest.
Another split off to a tiny village nestled in the valley. The
red earth streets were carved to perfection and the town
looked very tidy. Pia walked slowly away from the forest.
Past the village she could see the edge of the festival
grounds and the platform where she'd first met the King
and Queen. The tents were all gone and the field looked
barren.

The villager's homes were of rock and wood, so that even
the poorest of families looked to be prosperous. Pia could
see some of the villagers down below. They wore light
linen tunics and all had long hair. Pia touched her short
blonde locks, hating how she was suddenly self-conscious
about them. Taking a tie from her pocket, she pulled her
hair back into a small ponytail.

Suddenly, she heard the telltale strike of metal to metal.
She smiled mischievously. Today was her lucky day.
Lifting her shirt, she took out the knives hidden in her
waistband and bounced them lightly in her hand. It was
time to have some fun.

* * * *

Pia grinned at the surrounding men. It hadn't taken long
for her to draw a crowd. At first, everyone had stared at
her--especially her short hair--in wonderment. Then, when
she took her knives and began to throw, the men had begun
to gather around to watch her. They nodded their heads in
grudging respect of her skill and soon no one cared that her
hair was short or that she was a woman invading their
practice field.

Pia smiled to herself. It was the same everywhere she
went. Warriors were easily won over with a little show. She

tossed the last of Zoran's knives at the throwing post and turned to look at the small crowd.

"Any challengers?" she called to the men. The men smiled in return, looking around their ranks.

"I'll take that challenge, my lady," one of the soldiers said. He was a scruffy looking lad with long lips and an easy smile.

"And you are?" Pia questioned.

The man bowed gallantly before her, his nature effortless in its good humor. "Hume, my lady."

"Well, Sir Hume," she said loudly, an impish grin lining her features. "I hope you don't mind losing to a woman."

The surrounding men howled with laughter. Hume waved his hand gallantly at them, completely unconcerned.

"If I have to lose," he said most courteously. He took up her hand and bowed low over it. "Let it be my heart to one as lovely as you, my lady."

Pia smirked, not taking notice of the gallantry. She snatched her hand away and waved him back as she went to retrieve her blades. The crowd laughed louder at the man's bold banter and the lady's firm dismissal of it. All of them were taken by the beautiful woman who threw better than most men and smiled so straightforwardly that it made their single hearts melt.

Pia walked up, lifting the hilt to Hume in offering.

"No, my lady," he murmured graciously. His eyes sparkled. "By all means, you go first."

* * * *

Agro cleared his throat. "Excuse me, *Draea Anwealda.*"

Zoran turned up from the papers he was still trying to get through. He lifted a finger before concluding the last sentence with a slight sigh. He hadn't been able to get the documents read the night before. His mind kept thinking of Pia and the boring trade agreement couldn't compete. With a sigh, he reached over to a nearby table and grabbed a pen. He quickly signed his name before handing the documents over to a waiting soldier, saying, "Deliver these to the King immediately."

The man nodded and was off.

Zoran stepped out of the small one room building, which he loosely referred to as an office, onto the practice field. Smiling, he nodded at Agro. "What brings you out?"

"Ach, the wife is pregnant and she's kicked me out of the house again," the man said, waving a dismissing hand as if it were not big deal. "She says I make her crazy, but I tried to tell her she's always crazy at this time."

Zoran chuckled and began walking toward the far end of the field to the village. He'd seen the man's slender wife. She was the only person who could make this giant tremble with fear.

Agro was a beefy monster of a man with two green eyes that were currently blackened with matching bruises. He had an easy smile that was always full of mischief. He'd grown up around the four Princes, knew them well, and was well liked by them in return.

"She do that to your face while kicking you out?" Zoran asked, motioning to the black eyes and still chuckling.

"Ach, no! That was your brother, Ualan. He got a bit testy at the Breeding Festival and needed to vent," Agro said. "And I might have said a few things that aggravated him."

Zoran's smile faded slightly.

"So how's your new blushing bride?" Agro asked. Zoran wondered at the man's roguish grin. He was up to something. "Word is she hasn't been out since the wedding. You keeping her tied up somewhere?"

"Ah," Zoran waved the question away.

"I see it's true you disfigured her," Agro said with a smirk.

Since Agro was like a brother to him, he let the insolence pass.

"I don't know why you would've done it. She has a glorious color to her hair. When the sun hits it, its like spun gold," Agro said.

Zoran nodded, but then, taking in what the man said, he stopped and frowned. When had this man seen Pia outside? He hadn't been there when he'd introduced her to his parents at the festival.

Unhampered, Agro continued in his mischief, "Yeah, she's a beauty all right. Not like Yusef's little firebird who's all vigor and flames. No, your wife is all air and light. Why, those eyes of hers, what would you say are they brown? Green? I couldn't rightly tell. Ah, it doesn't matter--"

"What are you talking about?" Zoran asked when it became clear the man intended on rambling until he stopped him.

Agro grinned.

"Where is she?" Zoran demanded hotly, his face snarling. His stomach tightened into knots and he placed his hands on his hips.

"Ah, so you don't know that your wife's gone and joined the military?" questioned Agro needlessly.

"Joined the...?" Zoran began in confusion. In order to join, she'd have to get his permission. "What are you going on about?"

"She's practicing right now with the men," Agro said, motioning Zoran's attention to the growing group of soldiers around the knife post.

Zoran frowned, storming forward. He told himself it wasn't possible. Pia was locked safely away in their home. There was no way she could have gotten out.

Agro watched the Prince in curiosity. He knew Zoran well enough to know he wouldn't like his beautiful new bride around the rowdy soldiers without him. He also knew that an unruly wife was just what the Prince needed. Zoran was too serious. He ran his life like he ran his military. He needed a little conflict at home to loosen him up and add smile lines to his tense, sober face.

Zoran came around the group of men and froze. Hume was throwing his knives at the post. Pia, his wayward wife, was standing next to him, clapping good naturedly as the man hit his mark.

Zoran's limbs tightened in outrage and, for a moment, he couldn't move.

Pia laughed as Hume copied her throw and hit her marks. A bright smile came to her face as she glanced around. She missed the hard countenance of her husband at the edge of the crowd.

Hume, his wide lips grinning from car to ear, teased, "Would you like to try again, my lady? I'm trying to take it easy on you."

"Hume!"

Pia jolted in alarm at the gruff bark. All eyes turned around at the noise. She blinked in confusion to see her husband. She'd thought he would be off guarding something. She glanced over at Hume.

The soldier stepped forward and bowed to her husband, as he answered, "Yes, *Draea Anwealda*."

"Since you have so much energy, lead these men through a march of the east field course," Zoran commanded.

"Yes, *Draea Anwealda*," Hume said. He began calling out orders.

Pia trembled, seeing how all the men stood at attention, only to solute Zoran at the order to march. Her heart hammered in her chest as she turned to watch her husband. Instantly, she saw his authoritative pose. He wasn't a guard. He was the commander. How could she have missed it?

The men filed into an orderly line and jogged off without giving her a backwards glance. Zoran stared hard at his wife, trying to control his anger. Agro, who watched Pia's stubborn expression from behind him, slowly slipped away, grinning like a fool.

Pia swallowed. They were alone on the field. Unable to come up with a single thing to say, she smiled, shrugged and turned to go gather the knives from the post.

"Don't you move," Zoran said. His tone was soft but there was no doubt that it was a command.

Pia froze, despite her instinct to run away as fast as she could. She kept her back to him. A grimace purposefully formed on her features as she waited.

Zoran took a slow step to her. Pia tensed. He continued past, going to grab his knives from the post. Clenching them in his fist, he marched back to stand in front of her. His arm rose, motioning to a nearby guard, who was passing, to come to him. He handed the knives to the man and ordered that he put them in his office. The guard bowed and obeyed, leaving the couple once more alone on the field.

Pia gulped and looked Zoran directly in the eye while she waited for him to speak.

"Who let you out?" he demanded after a long, hot pause in which he glared at her.

Pia frowned at his hard tone, growing irritated with him. She'd been having fun until he showed up and ruined it.

Bitterly, she murmured, "Don't you mean to say, how did I escape my prison?"

"Pia," he said, his eyes narrowing.

"Warden," she said insolently in the same tone. She crossed her arms over her chest and mimicked his militant stance.

"Do you think this is a game?" Zoran asked, outraged that she would openly defy him on his field--the place he commanded. He'd never wanted to kiss anyone as bad in his life.

"It's your fault I'm out here," Pia said. Her brow rose on her face, daring him on into a fight.

Zoran realized that she wasn't scared of him. She seemed to thrive on his growing anger.

"My fault?" he growled in disbelief.

"I asked you nicely to let me out of the house during the day. I wouldn't have had to sneak out behind your back if you hadn't forbidden me to throw your knives," she fumed. "I tried to reason with you, tyrant."

"I told you no!"

"I'm not your lap dog," she said. "I'm not one of these men you can order about."

"You are my wife," he said, as if that one thing gave him the right to be angry.

"This is all I know how to do, Zoran," she proclaimed waving her hand about the field.

"I thought you could sew," he answered with a dark snarl.

"And I thought you were a royal guard, so I guess we're even. I only told you I could sew to try and get out of the house," she said honestly. She uncrossed her arms and put them on her hips. She took a menacing step forward. Poking him definitely in his rock-hard chest, she said, "I'm sick and tired of you, Zoran, and your macho, controlling attitude. Either you get your act together and resign yourself to the fact that you didn't marry a homemaker, or give me my divorce. The choice is up to you. But I'll not be kept a prisoner anymore."

As she screamed the word divorce at him, he glanced around. A few villagers were gathered below them, pointing and watching the royal couple in awe. He saw Agro, a frown on the man's lips, as he tried to usher the curious onlookers away.

Pia wasn't concerned with the villagers. She was too mad. Zoran's eyes flash with a golden fire, as he shot forward and grabbed her arm. Tugging her behind him, he began leading her away from the field.

Pia stumbled, tripping over her feet as she tried to dig her heels into the ground to stop him. When that didn't work, she jumped and landed on his back. Her arm wound around his neck as she squeezed.

Zoran stumbled in amazement that she actually tried to attack him in public, though he shouldn't have been surprised. Her long legs wound around his waist. Zoran jerked, throwing her over his body.

Pia flipped over his shoulder, through the air, and landed hard on the ground. She grunted as she fell forward, bruising her knees. Zoran descended upon her. Wrenching her arm behind her back, he hauled her to her feet.

Pia struggled against him, moaning slightly when he pulled her arm higher. She refused to scream. Her body tensed waiting for any opening to escape. Her lungs heaved for air.

"Behave," Zoran ordered, giving her a hard shake. He pulled her back into his chest. His fire-laden eyes shone with excitement. Pia tensed. His mouth came close to her throat and she felt his teeth on her neck, biting lightly.

"Let me go," she ordered with a growl.

"Do you concede the fight?" he asked against her flesh, goading her.

"Never," she said. "I'll never concede to you, you lying bastard!"

Zoran pulled back from her throat. With a swift jerk, he twirled her into the air. Pia screamed in surprise. He caught her easily over his shoulder and stormed into the castle.

"*Draea Anwealda*," the guard said at the front gate. His eyes were wide as he saw the struggling, screaming Princess over the Prince's shoulder. The Prince nodded at him as if nothing was amiss.

Pia glared at the soldier as she was carted away. Suddenly, she dug her nails into Zoran's back, clawing him.

Zoran flinched, arching as he loosened his hold. Pia kneed him in the chest and pushed up, falling over his back to the floor. Hitting the ground in a summersault, she rolled, hopped instantly to her feet, and ran for the castle entrance.

"Stop her," Zoran ordered the guard, striding after his wife.

The guard instantly moved in her way, blockading her. Pia smiled cruelly. This man was obviously underestimating his prey. She ran faster. His arms widened as if to catch her. Pia ducked at the last possible second, kicking his legs out from under him. The surprised soldier landed on his back but sprang forward to grab her ankle as she tried to rush past.

Pia fell to the ground, bumping her chin on the hard earth. Her teeth jarred in her head and she kicked at the soldier's head, barely missing.

Suddenly, Zoran's hand was on the back of her hair, hauling her up. Pia moaned loudly, more in outrage than in pain.

"On your feet," the Prince bellowed to the soldier, who instantly obeyed and stood back up.

This time Zoran wasn't so pleasant in his restraint. He hooked a large arm around her neck and dragged her before him. When Pia tried to bite at his arm, he flexed his muscles and cut off her air. She began struggling for breath, clawing at his arm to be free. Her head spun and her arms weakened. When her scratches lightened, Zoran loosened his hold. Pia gasped for air, clutching at his arm. He marched her down the long hall, dragging her when her feet stumbled at the awkward angle. He turned the corner to his home.

The door was still wide open and he frowned. He threw Pia inside, automatically taking in the hole in the wall and the tampered with panel.

"Shut," he hollered. The door slid closed.

Pia stumbled forward but didn't fall. Panting, she glared at Zoran. Bitter hatred shone in her gaze. She wiped her sore chin. There was blood when she drew her hand away.

They stood for a long time, staring at the other. Slowly, Zoran took a deep breath.

"What am I to do with you, Pia?" he asked softly. No one had ever dared to stand up to him like she had. She aggravated him, made him mad with lust, and taunted him to the point of explosion. She was bold, cunning, smart, strong.

The gentleness of his tone took her by surprise, but she blinked in quick recovery. Her jaw throbbed, as she said, "You tell me, *Draea Anwealda*. That's your title is it not, oh prison guard."

"It means Dragon Lord," Zoran answered, not liking the way the title came out of her snarling lips. It wasn't respect he heard in her voice. "I'm a guard. My official title is Captain of the Guard. I control all the Draig armies. It was you who assumed I was of lower ranking."

"You let me assume."

"You never asked."

Pia's mouth tightened.

Zoran relaxed. He took in her bloodied face and was sorry for it.

"How's your jaw?" he asked, his voice becoming tender once more.

Her answer was a stubborn scowl.

"Damn it, Pia," Zoran fumed in frustration. "I'm not trying to be a tyrant. I'm trying to protect you. It's not safe for you out at the training ground. Accidents happen all the time. I don't want to see you get hurt."

"Did you ever think that I don't want your protection," Pia said. "And if it's the men you're afraid of, don't be. I can handle them. It's not like they see me for anything more than one of the guys."

At that Zoran frowned. He'd seen the look on Hume's face as well as the others. They were all smitten. And why wouldn't they be? She was absolutely ravishing.

Zoran lowered his head, sighing. He could tell she really believed what she said. She truly didn't know the effect she had on his men. She had no clue as to her own feminine power. She had no idea what her bright, open smiles could lead men to believe. He'd been young once. He knew the hormones that raged within the younger soldiers. If they thought they had a chance with such a woman, married or not, they would take it without thinking.

Running his finger through is hair, he said in frustration, "What, then, do you want from me, Pia?"

Pia hesitated. As she looked at him, she didn't know how to answer. A myriad of emotions flooded her. She wanted his respect. She wanted his.... She took a deep, trembling breath. She wanted him to look at her with longing. She wanted him to think her beautiful--when she knew she was not. She wanted him to touch her, to kiss her.

"Freedom," she answered simply.

Mistaking her request, he turned his tortured gaze to her. "I can't give you a divorce. I told you that already."

"I meant freedom to leave this house, to be myself, and do what I want to do. If you want me as your wife, Zoran, then treat me as a wife, not one of your men. Respect me as your wife. Respect that I'm not some simple woman who is content to cook and clean and stay home all day. That's not who I am. I was raised on a military base. I was taught to fight and defend myself. That's who I am. It's what I do."

"You wish me to treat you as a wife," Zoran murmured. He braved a step forward, amazed when she didn't turn and run. He watched her carefully, ready for her to strike at him. She didn't move. He stopped before her, not touching her, as he said in a low tone that gave her whole body chills, "Yet, you do not act as a wife."

Pia swallowed, knowing he meant that she didn't go to him as a wife goes to a husband. She stiffened, too afraid to answer. What could she say?

"You do not kiss me when I ask for it," Zoran continued. His eyes bore into her, as intimate as a caress of his hand, though he didn't move to touch her. "You do not look at me with pleasure or desire. You don't ask me to touch you. You don't come to touch me."

With each sentence, his words got softer.

"There's more to marriage than..." Pia frowned, looking at the floor. She couldn't say it.

Zoran brooded in silence, waiting for her to speak.

"You ask that of me, yet there's no honesty between us. I didn't even know what you do all day until I snuck out and discovered if for myself. We're strangers, Zoran. Don't you see? How can I...? How can we...?"

"All right," Zoran said, lifting his finger to her shoulder. He trailed his touch lightly down her arm, not pressing forward with his whole hand. He had to touch her, needed to, even if it was the barest of caresses. "Here's the deal. You want something. I want something. You give me what I want. I'll let you have what you want. You'll be given full freedom to roam outside these walls, so long as you let me know where you are and so long as you listen to me and heed me. This is my world, Pia. I know the dangers in it."

Pia froze, instantly rejecting the deal in her head, but agreeing to it in her body.

"What do you want?" she asked, shaking.

"I want you," Zoran began seriously. Pia gasped at the bold statement. He drew his hand down her side to her quivering ribs. "I want you to answer two questions for me."

Pia's face fell. She wondered at the disappointment curling in her limbs.

"Is that your only stipulation?" she asked in hesitation.

Zoran edged closer, letting his hand fall full on her side. Taking his free hand, he brushed at her bloodied chin, wiping it partially clean. "Do you want there to be more?"

"No." Pia shook her head. It was a lie.

"You're sure?" he persisted. He worked his hand beneath her black shirt to her waist.

Pia tried not to tremble. Was it just her or did his mouth draw closer? She stared at it, wishing he'd force another kiss on her.

"Yes, I'm sure," Pia breathed.

"Do we have a deal then?" Zoran asked. "You'll answer two questions--fully and honestly?"

Pia thought of her freedom. Slowly, she nodded her head. Her voice was weak, as she answered, "Deal."

"Tell me how you got this scar."

Pia blinked. The question took her by surprise and she jerked away from his searching hand. She pressed her lips and said simply, "It was a knife. Next question?"

Zoran's arms fell to his sides, away from her. He tried to hide his disappointment. He wouldn't be put off. "Whose?"

"Is that your second question?"

"No, it's part of the first," he murmured, drawing closer to her.

Pia would've sworn his eyes changed to a golden hue. She couldn't think straight when he looked at her like that.

"The deal was for fully and honestly," Zoran said. "Whose knife?"

"My father's," Pia answered. Her jaw and her eyes hardened against him.

"Your father," he repeated, somewhat awed. "Why did you call it a gift?"

"It was the last thing he ever gave me," Pia said. Her short hair had come loose in their fight and she nervously pushed it back behind her ears.

"Why?" Zoran's hand reached to touch her again but she didn't seem to notice it. Her eyes drifted into deeper thoughts.

"I answered your question," Pia's voice wavered and her eyes cleared. "What is the second?"

"How did you come to owe so much money to Galaxy Brides?" Zoran expected her to say gambling or something insignificant.

Pia's lips tightened and her eyes watered. She looked at him for a long time. When her mouth finally opened to speak, she clipped, "I've changed my mind. Keep your freedom. I don't want it."

She tried to pull away. Zoran tightened his hold on her waist. "Why won't you trust me?"

"Could it be because you don't trust me?" Pia asked. "You keep me prisoner in this house all day. I honestly have no idea why you wanted to marry me. You won't tell me who you are or what I am--"

"You're a Princess. I'm a Prince. We live in a castle with the royal family," he stated bluntly.

Pia blinked, waiting for his face to break into a teasing grin. It never came.

"Are you serious?"

"Extremely," Zoran mused with a dry smile that held little pleasure. "You are a Princess of the House of Draig. The Queen is your mother, the King your father, your husband a Prince. This fortress we live in is a palace. I'm the second oldest which makes me the leader of the military and in charge of security and defense."

"Second?" she asked, listening very intently to everything he said. She could see the truth in his eyes. She was a Princess.

"You also have three new brothers," Zoran continued. His face gave nothing away. It had been his request for honesty and he would show her he could be true to his own word. "Ualan, the oldest will be King when my father dies. Yusef, beneath me, is the Captain of the Outlands. Olek, the youngest brother, is ambassador."

"That's why the Queen was so concerned with my hair," Pia said. "I didn't understand it earlier, but she was afraid I was going to embarrass the royal family. That's why you don't take me anywhere, isn't it? You're ashamed of me."

Zoran didn't answer as she rushed on.

"Prince Zoran," Pia said, shaking her head. "I should've known. That's why you don't want to divorce me. You're a Prince and it would disrupt your precious family honor and reputation. You'd much rather hide your hideous, ugly wife away from view."

"That's not true. I'm not ashamed of you. I just don't know if I can trust you. You don't seem to care about my family's honor or your own. You have no concern about how your actions will reflect on our reputations. You just do whatever you want, never listening to what I say."

"That's because you haven't said anything to me," Pia said. "You didn't tell me I was a Princess and that my action affected a kingdom."

"Would you have cared?" Zoran eyed her hair. "I asked you not to cut your hair, and you did anyway."

"No, you *ordered* me not to do it. Everything you've said to me has been an order not a request. There's a difference, Zoran. If you would've spoken to me reasonably, I might have listened to you. I might not have done it."

"I told you it would be considered a disfigurement," Zoran defended. "I told you it would shame both of us."

"Can we get over the hair already?" Pia asked in despair. "I know it's ugly. I'm ugly. I get it. There's nothing I can do about it. It will grow back. Now let it drop!"

Pia's body lost some of its fight. Her dejected expression tore at Zoran's chest and an unfamiliar anguish overcame him. She shook her head at him, turning to walk away.

"Just leave me alone, tyrant."

Zoran watched her go.

Chapter Ten

"Pia, wait," Zoran demanded.

Pia stiffened. For once his words sounded more like a request than a command and she couldn't deny him. She stopped, her head hanging down, and didn't look at him. She was too embarrassed.

"There's more I have to tell you." he said, ready to come clean.

"Oh, there's more?" Pia sighed, weary from their verbal battles. She would much rather use her fists. Sarcastically, she drawled, "What? Do you have another wife somewhere? Some children hiding out in the next room? Oh, don't tell me, there's some evil monster on the loose and I got voted as the sacrificial offering."

Zoran stalked to her, spinning her around into his arms. Her body stiffened in surprise, but he didn't back down. His eyes flashed with liquid fire.

"Quit saying things like that. I would never let harm befall you. You're my only wife. It's my duty to protect you," Zoran expressed earnestly, tenderly brushing back a strand of her hair.

"I don't need your protection, Zoran. I can take care of myself. I have always taken care of myself." Her words were soft.

"Then take something else from me," he urged gently. Zoran was emboldened when she didn't struggle to be free of his hold. He pulled her closer.

Pia shivered. Her eyes glazed as he claimed her mouth with his. His kiss was soft, taking its time as he moved his mouth over hers. Slowly, she tried to respond. Her mouth parted, offering to him.

Zoran growled, deepening the kiss. He found her hair, crushing her face to him. Pia moaned lightly into his mouth. She lifted her hands to nestle on his strong, protecting arms. Maybe being protected wouldn't be so bad.

To Pia's surprise, Zoran tore his lips away with a frustrated growl. Her body ached, begging him on. She lifted her hand to stop him but then pulled it back to her side.

"I'm sorry," she said. "I know you're trying."

He looked at her, confusion tapering through his gaze.

Pia pulled out of his arms, pushing at his forearms until he let her go. "You don't have to kiss me if you don't want to. It's fine. I understand and--"

Zoran grabbed her back up into his fierce embrace. Pia moaned in surprise of the suddenness of his attack. This time, when he kissed her, he was none too gentle, letting her feel his slashing teeth, his hungry mouth, the onslaught of his uncontrolled desire.

Zoran wanted her badly, always wanted her, but had tried to hold back from her. He told himself that she needed him to be gentle. But when she moaned against his mouth, it was like a siren's song calling him to his death. He knew he should stop, but he could little refuse the passionate link between them. His body was on fire, taking over his mind until he couldn't think to slow his assault on her body.

He readily found her breasts, tearing at her shirt to get to them. Her scent was in his head, drugging him until he was trapped in a web of mindless obsession. He pulled away, only long enough to see the couch. Sweeping her up into his arms, he carted her to it and roughly laid her down. Pia shuddered, as he immediately came over her.

His lips were on her neck, eagerly licking and biting at her tender flesh. He found her waistband, pulling back long enough to strip her pants from her body in one swift movement. Then, when she lay naked beneath him, he devoured her breasts--teasing the tips with this tongue and teeth.

Pia gasped, her hands weakly falling back in surprise at his onslaught. Zoran groaned, a truly animalistic sound, against her. She didn't hold back for long. Her fingers sought to fulfill an adventure of their own. Trailing over hard muscles and sinewy flesh covered in his thick tunic, she pulled him to her.

Zoran's hands found her scar. He followed it with his mouth. Licking it, he trailed down her side. Pia's stomach tightened and arched. Zoran's body tensed, wanting its release desperately. In his fervor he forgot that he should slow. He forgot that she needed him gentle. The way her hands pulled at him, it didn't appear as if she wanted him gentle.

"Argh," he growled passionately, painfully. He came over her once more. Onslaughting her throat with his kisses, he groaned, "I want you. I want inside of you. I've got to have you now."

Pia shivered at the hoarse admission. Suddenly, his hands were at his waist, freeing his all too potent arousal. His arm mindlessly pushed her leg over his shoulder to open her up fully to him. Now that she didn't fight him, he couldn't hold back. His body was desperate to end the pain of his suffering.

His mouth dipped to taste the wetness of her center fire, making sure she was ready for him. She was and Zoran growled at the sweet taste of her. Her hips bucked against his hot mouth and his warrior's body took it as an invitation to conquer. Everything about this woman drove him to madness. He lost all control with her.

"Pia," he moaned into her panting lips. "I can't hold back ... ah. I need to be inside you. I need to feel you."

Pia tensed. Excitement and fear flooded her blood, sped faster by her racing heart. She didn't understand him. He looked as if he was in agony.

Zoran lifted up, guiding himself to her moist opening. He tested her depths, feeling the tight muscles of her body working around the tip of his erection.

"Ah, you're so hot," he moaned in pleasure and approval. "You're so tight. Oh, Pia."

Pia gasped. He was a big man and though her body sought him, his size hurt.

"Zoran?" she asked, confused by the pain where need had so readily been. Her body tightened, making it worse.

Zoran groaned to feel her squeezing him. She was like nothing he'd ever felt before. The brazen whores who visited the planet had never felt so good, so tight, so hot, so achingly moist. He growled and pushed a little more, his hips beginning to work in shallow strokes as he drove persistently forward.

"Ugh," Pia quivered in pain. Suddenly, she pushed at him, her caresses becoming resistance, as she was frightened by his uncontrolled claiming. Her legs flailed by his head, trying to knock him out of her.

Zoran felt her body jerking and thought she urged him on. With a flex of his hips, he embedded himself deeply into her. And, though she didn't accept his full length, it was enough to cause a conquering yell of manly satisfaction to escape Zoran's lips.

Pia's eyes widened. Her body burned with liquid fire, a white hot pain that tore her apart. His body withdrew. Reacting on instinct more than reason, she swung viciously for his head. Zoran grunted in surprise, poised to thrust again. Pia smacked him another time, slamming his face with her fist so hard that he fell off the couch.

One of Zoran's hands reached for her in his confusion. He stopped as he witnessed the abused horror on her face.

Petrified with fear, she shook. Pia jerked into action. Taking off across the room, she ran naked into the bathroom, knowing the paper thin door wouldn't be able to stop him if he wanted to come through.

Zoran watched her run, his head beginning to clear of the pleasurable fog she'd worked around him. He could still feel the wetness of her on his body. But, he could also detect her fear of him and was mortified by it. The bathroom door shut and he heard her scurrying across the floor to get away from him. Looking down, he froze. What had he done? The wetness he felt was her blood.

"Pia," he groaned hoarsely. The evidence of his viciousness glared at him from his still risen member. What had he done? It wasn't lost on him that he who'd sworn to protect her, had been the one who'd hurt her. Never had any of the women he'd been with bled. Remembering how unusually tight she had been, the desire drained from his limbs. His body burned, aching to go after her, to protect and comfort her.

Pia cowered on the bathroom floor, panting in apprehension. Her stomach throbbed and twitched with each movement, but she ignored it. She'd been in worse pain. What scared her was the look on his face when he'd done it. He hadn't been the cool headed commander she was used to. His face had contorted in bittersweet agony. His eyes had glowed pure gold with an intent she didn't understand. He'd wanted to control her, to conquer her and claim her. Pia couldn't relinquish that kind of control. Staring at the door, she waited to see if he would come for her. He didn't.

As she relaxed, she realized her body didn't hurt as badly as before. There had been pleasure before the pain, a sweetness that stirred in her limbs anew. Looking down at her body, she saw blood on her thighs. She shivered, stumbling to the hot spring. Catching her reflection in the mirror, she saw her ugly face staring back at her. She saw the blood on her chin from the fight.

Princess Pia, she snorted to herself with a look of utter disgust. *You're no more a Princess than a toad is a Prince.*

How could he have looked at her like that? She could barely bring herself to look at her reflection.

With angry jerks, she cried--cursing herself for what she was. She pulled at her hair in anger, hating herself for cutting it, for disfiguring herself more in his eyes. How could he look at her? How could he need her? She didn't deserve it.

Pia threw herself into the bath, scrubbing angrily at her skin to wash the blood away. And when the blood was gone, she kept scrubbing, trying to wash the pain from her aching heart.

* * * *

Zoran stood outside the bathroom door for a long time, feeling the rush of her agony wash over him and believing it was his doing. He swallowed, wanting to run away from the torture of it. He didn't run. He stood, moving to a chair and opening himself up to the torment of it. He sat, making himself take in her suffering. Then, he heard her cry, a soft sob she tried to muffle to silence. He cursed himself for a monster, truly hating himself for the first time in his life.

* * * *

Pia awoke the next morning on the bathroom floor, curled in the vague warmth of Zoran's overlarge robe. Her body was so stiff from the hard stone that it took a moment before she could even move. Her eyes opened, automatically going to the bathroom door. She'd stayed up most of the night, watching to see if Zoran would come after her. He didn't and Pia wasn't sure what she felt was relief.

Taking a deep breath, she pushed to standing. Her stomach twinged slightly and she remembered all too vividly what had caused the ache. Going to the bathroom door, she lightly slid it open. Hesitantly, she poked her head outside.

"Pia?"

Pia jumped to hear her name. Glancing over, she saw Zoran was sitting on the couch. Her first reaction was to slam the door and continue hiding out like a coward. But Pia wasn't a coward. She stood tall, regally wrapping his robe around her trembling body as she looked boldly at him. Her confidence wavered as she saw his handsome face, and she had to look away.

Zoran looked as if had waited there all night for her. Taking a deep breath, she lifted her chin and stepped out of the bathroom.

Zoran watched his wife. He'd sent word to the field that he would be late. He wanted to wait for her to come out on her own. Leaning forward, he looked at his hands, not knowing what to say to her. He'd seen her fear, felt her rejection, and it hurt him deeply. He still wanted her so badly, and she could barely bring herself to look him in the eye.

There was an awkward silence. Pia's hand tapped along the outside of her upper thigh. When he didn't speak, she glanced up.

"Pia...?" he began, his voice full of question. There was a rift between them and neither one knew how to cross it.

Her mouth opened, but no words came out. She hesitantly walked toward him. Zoran didn't move.

Stopping several paces away, she said the only thing she could think of, "Shouldn't you be at work?"

To Zoran the words sounded bitter and hard. She didn't want him there. He couldn't blame her. Slowly, he stood and said, "All right, I'll go, Pia."

When he turned from her, Pia had the strangest urge to run to him. Her eyes devoured him now that he walked away. Zoran disappeared into the bedroom. When he came out, she hadn't moved. He'd changed his tunic, donning another black one.

He looked at her wan features from across their home. There was nothing he could say to appease her. How could he even begin to say he was sorry? "You're free to leave. I'll reprogram the door for you."

Pia nodded weakly. She wanted to run to him, but her fear of rejection and ridicule held her back.

Zoran said a few commands and then turned to her.

Pia repeated the words, "open" and "shut" at his signals. Her voice was hoarse and strained but the door obeyed her.

Before he left, he nodded his head once at her and said, "I'm sorry, Pia. I never meant to hurt you."

Pia's legs weakened as the door shut behind him. She sunk wearily to the floor. Her heart poured out of her and she cried anew.

* * * *

Zoran didn't come home that day. Pia went only as far as the outer halls, stopping to look for him, debating whether or not she should try and find him. She wanted to say she was sorry too. That she shouldn't have run away. That she could now remember the pleasure of his touch and wanted to be a wife to him, if he could still bring himself to have her. She turned around each time, too much of a coward to make it to the end of the hall.

Zoran also didn't come home that night. Pia waited up for him, falling asleep on the couch sometime during the early morning hours. When she awoke the next morning, she was still alone.

* * * *

Zoran took the soldiers through night drills, letting them rest in hour-long shifts. The war games were normally great fun, though Zoran's heart wasn't in it. He watched with a melancholy the men could easily see on their leader's stern face. As dawn approached, Agro, who was always one of the first to volunteer for the night games, drew near him.

"I'll finish up here," Agro said quietly. They'd all seen the way their leader was pushing himself. "Why don't you go to your wife?"

Zoran's expression said it all. Agro stepped back from the man, gulping to see the warrior's raw pain and self-loathing. Zoran shook his head in denial, continuing to yell out his orders.

* * * *

Pia lifted her hands in the air, slowly falling back to arch her stomach before her legs moved over into a leisurely back flip. The exercise was helping her sore insides to relax, though it did nothing for her downtrodden spirits. She watched the exercise room ceiling go past as she fluidly repeated the process. On the third try, she froze, stomach arched. Someone was at the door.

She flipped herself around to her feet. Brushing her hands, as she rushed through the living room to the front hall, she yelled, "Open."

Even though she should've known it wouldn't be Zoran, she was still disappointed. Soon, her disappointment turned to surprise.

"Nadja?" Pia asked, blinking to see the woman she'd known from the ship.

"Hello, Pia," Nadja said, her voice soft. Her light brown hair was pulled neatly back and her blue eyes shone pleasantly from her porcelain skin. She held a small bag in her nervously twisting hands. When Pia only looked at her, Nadja asked, "Do you mind if I come in?"

"Oh, yeah," Pia said. "I'm sorry. It's just I've been cooped up in here for so long, I feel as if I've forgotten my manners."

Nadja smiled, her nervous stance seeming to relax. Pia ordered the door shut behind her.

"Can I get you anything?" Pia asked, beginning to move toward the kitchen. "I think we have juice."

"No, I'm fine," Nadja said. She looked around the Japanese style home and smiled to herself, "I see you got the Princess suite, too."

Pia laughed, almost feeling relief to learn that someone as tolerable as Nadja was a Princess. She'd been worried she'd have to spend the rest of her life surrounded by women like the brassy Gena. "You too?"

Nadja nodded and an instant camaraderie was struck up between the women.

"It's just so nice to see one of the other women from the ship," Nadja said as Pia led her in. "This planet has entirely too many men, which wouldn't be so bad except they are all so mannish."

Pia laughed, instantly understanding. "So which Prince did you get?"

"Olek."

"Ah, the ambassador." Pia nodded wisely.

"What about you?" Nadja asked, though she'd already been told by her husband.

"Zoran."

Nadja noticed the woman's eyes clouded slightly as she said the name.

"What do you have there?" Pia asked, hoping to change the subject.

"Oh!" Nadja lifted the bag. "Before I show you, I have to apologize in advance."

Pia frowned.

"It was my husband's request," Nadja said. She reached into the bag and pulled out a hair extender. "He said your husband cut off your hair and asked if I could...."

Nadja hesitated, swallowing in embarrassment.

"Grow it back for me," Pia said with a wry grin when Nadja didn't finish. The woman nodded. "Zoran didn't cut my hair, I did."

"Oh," Nadja exclaimed. "I didn't mean to insult you. I like your hair short."

"It's all right," Pia laughed. Nadja had been quiet on the ship but she found she liked the agreeable woman. "I guess its called disfigurement. It means I shamed myself or something. You should see the looks the people gave me when I went outside. It was like an evil spirit came into their midst. I was waiting for mothers to rush their children away screaming."

Nadja giggled. "Well, it's a planet of men. Go figure they'd come up with a tradition to keep their woman looking soft."

"The Queen stopped by just to look at it," Pia continued with a look of vast amusement. "I thought she was going to throw up on me."

"Mede was probably mad at her son. She says they are a handful," Nadja admitted. "The Queen isn't so bad."

Pia looked at her in disbelief.

"So, do you want me to grow it for you?" Nadja asked, lifting the extender. "If anything, it should give us something to do today."

"Why not," Pia answered thoughtfully. She thought of Zoran. He really did seem to like her longer hair. Suddenly, the idea of pleasing him excited her. She glanced at Nadja, eyeing her in concentration. Nadja blushed at the bold look and seemed shaken.

"What?" Nadja questioned, looking down her front.

"Do you think you could help me with the other stuff too?" Pia asked, her voice dipping shyly.

"Other stuff?" Nadja questioned, blinking in surprise to hear the woman so modestly spoken. "What other stuff?"

Pia waved her hand at Nadja. "You know, beauty stuff--dresses, hairstyles, makeup.

Nadja chuckled softly, a smile coming to her face. "Sure, I'd love to. But, honestly, I don't think you need all that."

Pia looked down.

"I mean," Nadja said, detecting something amiss in the woman's response to the compliment. "You have a strong, natural way about you that the men around here seem to respond to. I wish I could be more like that."

"What?" Pia asked, furrowing her brow in amazement that anyone could be jealous of her. "You want me to teach you how to defend yourself?"

Nadja's face lit up with such a force of excitement. She hadn't been asking that, but the idea fascinated her. Her father never let her learn such things as self-defense.

"Oh, could you?" Nadja asked. "I mean, you'll probably hate teaching me. I don't even know ... I don't know anything."

"I'd love to," said Pia, finding she really would. Fighting was the one thing she could do well, and that she could give back to Nadja pleased her greatly.

Nadja bounced in giddy anticipation. Grinning like a fool, she said, "All right, let's get started."

* * * *

Pia felt like a changed woman. After disappearing for a few minutes, Nadja brought back with her a servant laden with makeup and hair accessories. Pia admitted that dresses were being made for her and Nadja sent the man to the village to see if they were finished.

Nadja extended her hair down past her shoulders. It wasn't as long as before but it was a nice compromise. Nadja also taught her a few easy tricks for pulling the hair into different styles and showed her how a little darkening of her eyes could really bring them out, though she continually claimed Pia didn't need the makeup.

Pia showed Nadja a couple self-defense moves, promising to teach her more at a later date when they were more properly dressed for it. Afterwards, Nadja had invited Pia to come over for dinner. Pia refused. Nadja nodded in understanding without even needing to hear the reason.

Pia waited, all dolled up, for Zoran to come home. The dresses weren't finished, but the seamstress had sent word that they would be delivered the next day. She waited in a comfortable outfit of cotton pants and a tight blue shirt. Zoran didn't show and it was getting late.

Pia, unable to stand waiting any longer, started for the door yelling at it to open. Stepping out into the hall, she paused. A soldier was coming at her.

"Sir Hume," Pia said in surprise.

Hume stopped, looking up at her hair and face. A slight smile of awe came to his feature as he bowed. His eyes stared at her, refusing to dip down to the floor. "My lady, Prince Zoran wished me to inform you that he has been called away on duty."

"Duty?" she asked in surprise. "What duty?"

"I'm sorry, my lady, I do not know," Hume said. "The King sent him away not but an hour ago."

"And when will he be back?" she asked, frowning. "Can you tell me that?"

"Two days, my lady, maybe more," Hume said. "He wished me to tell you that if you had a need for anything to call on this."

Pia took the hand communicator he gave her. Turning it over in her palm, she studied it and frowned.

"The Queen will be happy to assist you." Hume belatedly finished with a bow.

"Wait," Pia ordered to stop his retreat. Grimacing, she asked, "The Queen?"

"Yes," he said. "She possesses the other communicator. Just push the button if you have need of her."

"Great," Pia mumbled wryly. She tilted her jaw up at the man as he again bowed. Backing up, he stared at her, grinning like a fool. At his look, Pia frowned at him, wondering if Hume had suddenly gone mad. He backed up to the end of the hall and she said, "Uh, thanks."

Chapter Eleven

Zoran was exhausted. He hadn't slept for three days. Gripping the center horn of his mount, he swung up behind the beast's bare shoulders. The *ceffyl's* wide back shifted low at the weight of its warrior rider, used to the rough handling. His fanged mouth darted open with a hiss of its long tongue. It had the eyes of a reptile, the face and hooves of a beast of burden, and the body of a small elephant. It was wickedly fast for an animal of its size and equally as deadly.

He'd been all over the swamplands, tracking the Var scent to the outer edges of the kingdom. The thick moss-covered trees dripped with moisture from the recent rainfall and a hot steamy fog lifted over in dense patches. The ceffyl's hisses kept most of the large swamp life at bay. Its thick hide could withstand the bite of the poisonous *givre* that swam freely in this part of the kingdom.

Zoran lifted his feet to set before him as the animal trudged its way through deeper water. Its foot sunk slightly stirring up a nest of red and black tailed *givres*. The ceffyl howled in annoyance but kept moving to drier land.

Zoran frowned, letting his feet slide down over the sides of his mount, ignoring how the swamp water made his pants stick to the animal's sides. He longed for home and his bed. His mission had been fruitless. Whoever had tried to break into the royal offices was long gone.

He wondered if Pia would welcome him back and briefly considered sleeping in his small office on the practice field. Looking up at the sky, he knew he couldn't for the same reason he had to turn back home without completely tracking his prey. The coronation was tomorrow night and he needed to set things right with Pia before then.

Not knowing what he would say to her when he saw her, Zoran made the last leg of the journey home.

* * * *

Zoran left his mount in the stables. He ignored the soldiers as he passed them on the practice field. Coming to the knife post, he glanced briefly at the gathered crowd. For a moment, his heart stopped and he searched for Pia. She wasn't there. It was his brother, Ualan, and Agro who drew the crowd.

Seeing him, Ualan nodded in greeting. His brother looked wearied, and his frown only deepened as Agro spoke to him. Zoran nodded back. He was too tired to do much else.

"Hey," Zoran heard Agro taunt Ualan to the pleasure of the crowd. "What about eyes closed?"

Zoran couldn't help the slight smile when Ualan stopped him from leaving. His brother closed his eyes and spun, blindly throwing the blades as he turned. Four landed in the pattern of a cross on the post, the last landed in between Agro's feet. Agro jumped back slightly with a hearty laugh of amusement. Ualan quietly nod and continued down the path to the castle.

Agro smiled an impish grin and waved at Ualan's back. He'd been left in charge of the training. Before Zoran could speak to the men, Agro commanded them gruffly, "Ach now, you pups, back to work."

"I see you are working them hard," Zoran called, amused. He yawned, watching the men depart.

"Ach," Agro grumbled good-naturedly. He picked the blade out of the ground. "You've worked them hard enough to last a year. What's wrong with a little sport now and then? If you lightened up, maybe your face wouldn't look so damned ugly."

Zoran chuckled, lifting an arrogant brow in disbelief at the baited comment, "Me, ugly?"

"Aye, you," Agro nodded. He went to the post and pulled out the rest of the blades. "I think it's your temper as of late. Half the men are scared to cross your path for fear you'll work them into the ground."

Agro absently threw the blades at the post. They all hit in random order. Retrieving them, Agro gave the blades to Zoran. Zoran looked at them briefly before sighing. The Prince tossed them out of old habit and they landed in a straight line.

"Is it the wife?" Agro asked perceptively.

Zoran took a deep breath. Suddenly, everything rushed out of him in a frustrated confession.

"She's ... *argh* ... she's so aggravating at times and so damned ravishing the next. I can hardly keep my head straight. I'm trying, but I don't understand what she wants. One minute she looks at me like I should kiss her, the next like I'm insane for trying. Hot, cold, hot, cold, she makes my head spin in circles until I can hardly see straight," Zoran admitted with a frown. Agro chuckled knowingly, leaving the knives in the post. Zoran continued, "I'm a man, Agro, a warrior. I've outsmarted and outguessed some of the worthiest of adversaries. I've conquered entire armies against the worst odds, but I can't seem to conquer her. I can't figure her out."

"Hum," Agro mused. He walked to the post and pulled the knife blades.

"You're married," Zoran said, forlorn. "Are all married women like this?"

Agro chuckled as if at a private joke. A wealth of husbandly wisdom filtered in his eyes. When he came back, he threw the knives and said thoughtfully, "Maybe the problem is that a woman doesn't need to be conquered, *Draea Anwealda*."

Zoran's brow furrowed in thought.

Agro turned to give the last blade to his friend. "Maybe she needs to be won."

* * * *

Pia flinched, barely making a sound as the medic, Tal, sealed the gash in her side with his laser. She lay on her couch, arm raised above her head. Her hair was pulled back into a serviceable bun for exercising and her clothes were lightly drenched with sweat. Lifting up to watch the medic work, she gave a hard sigh.

"Are you sure you wouldn't like me to deaden the pain, my lady?" the medic asked when she jerked at a particularly deep section of the wound.

"No," Pia answered between her tightened lips. Sweat beaded her brow, but she answered, "It's fine. Just keep going."

Nadja stood behind him, worrying her hands. Her wide blue eyes filled with what looked like tears. "I'm so sorry, Pia. I didn't mean to kick you that hard."

Pia chuckled, sucking in a breath as she was again seared with the laser. Refusing to cry out at the pain, she said, "It's nothing, Nadja, quit fretting. I should've been ready for it. You've got some power in those legs of yours. Next time, we'll just make sure we're no where near the sword display."

Nadja relaxed some, though her face was still pulled tight.

Pia closed her eyes waiting for the man to finish. Hearing the door slide up, her eyes popped back open. Instantly, she moved to stand. The laser bumped and seared off course. She frowned slightly. The medic huffed and turned it off.

"You have to sit still," he ordered.

"Zoran," Pia breathed, ignoring the medic as she stared at her husband in the doorway. He looked tired and incredibly handsome. His eyes scanned over the room, glancing over Nadja and the medic.

Coming forward, he eyed Pia's side. His wet hair was brushed back from his face. He'd stopped by his father's to quickly bathe and change his clothes before coming home. His voice dark with worry and little sleep, he demanded, "What happened?"

"It ... it was an accident," Nadja said to the big warrior. She trembled before him as he looked at her. Slowly, she glanced at Pia, feeling sorry for the woman. Nadja's husband might be a big man, but Pia's husband was a giant. It was no wonder the woman didn't talk about him too much. "Pia, I'll see you later."

"Thanks, Nadja," Pia mumbled in distraction. She tried to give the woman a smile, but Nadja had already turned away. At the medic's insistence, she laid back down to let him finish. As an afterthought, she called to the woman, "Remember to practice!"

"Pia?" Zoran asked. His heart had stopped in his chest to see the medic. As he eyed the wound, assuring himself she was going to live, he tried to breathe. "What happened?"

She frowned, ready for a lecture. Zoran mistook her look as displeasure in seeing him. How could he blame her after what he did?

"It's no big deal," Pia grunted. "I was showing Olek's wife how to kick. She accidentally kicked me into your sword stand. It was a simple mistake."

Zoran glanced at the exercise room.

The medic finished and Pia sat up.

"Don't worry," she said with a stiff sigh. "Your precious weapons are unharmed. Nadja cleaned it up."

He didn't care about his weapons. Frowning, he glanced at Tal, not wanting to discuss any marital discontentment in front of the man.

"Try to take it easy for the next couple of day, my lady," the medic said, putting his things back into his bag. "I'll come back in a week to smooth out the scar. If you like I can get the other one, too."

Tal nodded at her ribs. Pia hastily pulled her shirt down over them.

"No, it's old," she shrugged as if it was no big deal. "Don't worry about it."

"*Draea Anwealda,*" Tal said, standing. He leaned over to grab his medic bag.

"Tal," Zoran acknowledged, tilting his head to walk him out. Pia watched the men, before turning to examine Tal's handiwork. The scar was thin. Compared to the burns, she hardly noticed it.

Speaking in the Qurilixen tongue, Zoran asked, "How is she?"

Tal answered in the same, "She'll heal fine, *Draea Anwealda*. The wound was deep and she should take it easy."

Tal frowned, glancing back toward Pia on the couch before turning to the Prince.

"What is it?" Zoran insisted.

"Nothing really," Tal began, with a frown. Cocking his head, he asked, "Has Lady Pia had any extensive surgeries?"

"Why?" Zoran questioned, he too glanced at Pia. She was poking at her ribs and grimacing after each jab.

"It's just her skin, my lord," the medic said, sighing. "It's normal but it appears to have been altered recently. The levels are healthy, like a newborn's, but when I took the laser to it, it didn't want to heal as if it had been worked over quite extensively within the last six months. We usually only see such occurrences with postoperative patients. I had to set the beam fairly high. The condition isn't noticeable except ... well, except when she has to have medical attention like this."

"She hasn't said anything to me. Did you ask her about it?"

"She said no, but that's what puzzles me," Tal said, shaking his head in medical awe. "Her tolerance for pain is incredibly high--too high, especially for what I have seen in the other non-Draig women. The laser level I used would've made grown Draig warriors black out from pain. She barely even flinched."

Zoran glanced at Pia again. She was stretching her arm up. Her eyes narrowed slightly as she lowered it down, testing the wound's limitations.

"I took a reading of her nerve endings to make sure there's no damage in them," Tal continued. "She's completely healthy--very healthy in fact."

"Thank you," Zoran said, puzzled by what the man said.

"Whatever she's been through," the medic continued as he turned to leave, "it had to have been something terrible."

"Thank you," Zoran repeated.

"What was that all about?" Pia asked when Zoran came back inside. Frowning absently as she lowered her shirt over her ribs, she inquired, "Is there something wrong with me?"

"No," Zoran answered, before lying, "he was updating me on the soldiers' medic reports. Some of them got in to a brawl the other night. They're fine."

"Oh," Pia said. Her eyes devoured him, starved for the sight of him. She looked down at her lap. "So, is that where you were? With the soldiers?"

Zoran tried to smile, but the three long days of no sleep were getting to him and he yawned instead. "No, I had to attend some official business for the King. Nothing exciting."

"Oh," Pia mumbled, wishing he'd tell her more, but confident by the look on his face he that he wouldn't. He yawned again. Black circles marred the skin beneath his light brown eyes.

"I asked Hume to tell you I would be gone," Zoran said softly. When he looked at her, he still wanted her. He wanted to hold her, kiss her, protect her. Right now, he wanted to curl his body around her and sleep next to her. With shame welling within his warrior chest, he knew that she probably only wished to be protected from him, not by him.

"Yes, he did," Pia said. "Thank you for the courtesy and for the communicator. I didn't use it. I left it on the dresser for you."

There was a silence. Pia bit her lips, wanting to say so much, wanting to apologize for overreacting the other night, wanting more than anything to give it another try. But the words stuck in her throat.

"Pia--" he began.

"No," she interrupted, moving to stand. He looked so worn. "Why don't you go get some sleep? We'll talk tomorrow morning."

Zoran, too exhausted to protest, nodded. He wasn't sure that anything he tried to say would come out right anyway. He slowly turned to the bedroom, glad that she hadn't tried to kick him out of his own home. The sight of her beautiful body, her beautiful face, stayed with him as he fell onto this bed, instantly asleep.

Pia sighed, watching him walk away. He could barely keep his eyes open, let alone think straight enough to talk to her. Hearing him fall on the bed, she waited. Then, going to peek in on him, she sighed. He was fast asleep.

Quietly, she snuck into the bedroom. Her eyes roamed over his body, making sure he was uninjured. She'd been so worried about him the last several days. Luckily Nadja had kept her so busy with training and beauty lessons that she hadn't been able to dwell on it too much.

Pia took the boots off his feet, dropping them on the floor. He sighed, but didn't wake up, hardly even moved. Then, covering him with a blanket, she hit the button for the curtain dome. Darkness fell over the bedroom as she softly shut the door.

* * * *

Zoran groaned, looking around in the darkness. His eyes shifted, piercing through the dark bedroom with ease. Throwing the covers off his body, he noticed he was still dressed but his boots were on the floor. Yawning, he scratched the back of his head, not taking time to wonder about it. Throwing his feet over the side of the bed, he stretched his arms.

Making quick work of his clothes, he changed to a more comfortable outfit before going quietly to the door. It was in the middle of the night, but he was starving. The front room was just as dark when he passed through. His eyes automatically went to the couch. Pia wasn't there.

His gaze narrowed in curiosity as he heard a soft curse coming from the exercise room. A dim light showed from within. Pia was inside, bent over in pain as she gripped her wounded ribs. As he watched, she forced herself to stand, took a fighting stance and kicked lightly into the air. Stiffening, she held the stance for several seconds before letting her leg come back down to the side.

Zoran's gut pulled into knots. She was so exquisite. Her hair was pulled back into a bun and he noticed that the locks looked thicker, longer. He couldn't help himself, couldn't stop his feet as he silently crossed over the floor. She jumped in the air and kicked harder, testing her injury's limits. With a gasp, she fell back, unable to land as gracefully as she'd hoped. Zoran swooped forward on instinct to catch her.

Pia jerked in surprise to land in his arms. He slowly righted her, letting her go so she could stand. She looked at him, her hazel eyes wide.

"You shouldn't be pushing yourself like this," Zoran murmured, his eyes filled with concern. He moved his hand as if he wanted to touch her, but he held back, remembering all too well the last time he'd held her. "You should be taking it easy."

"My father always said it's good to know your limits when you're wounded." Pia answered, absently rubbing her side. "Besides, I couldn't sleep."

"Nightmares?"

She sniffed wryly at that. "Uncomfortable couch."

Zoran chuckled. He wanted to tell her that she didn't have to sleep on the couch that she could sleep with him on the bed, but thought better of it. She would surely take the gesture the wrong way--even if a part of him meant it 'the wrong way.' After what had happened, he still couldn't help it, he wanted her. Only now he wasn't sure he deserved her.

"How about you?" she asked. "I was sure you'd sleep through tomorrow."

"Hungry," he grinned, pleased that they weren't fighting.

"Ah," she said, moving to walk past him. Shooting him a sidelong glance, she said, "Good plan."

Zoran watched her go by, before following her to the kitchen. As she began rummaging through the refrigerator, he hopped up on a counter to study her.

"What do you feel like?" she asked, peeking up from over the door.

Looking at her mouth, he murmured, "Something sweet."

Pia gulped. Her heart caught in surprise. Shaking her head, she smirked, "You didn't buy anything sweet. You bought health food."

Zoran laughed. Reaching over his head, he pushed the cabinet behind him open. Blindly searching, he arched his back and dug to the back of the top shelf. Pia shut the refrigerator door and came over to watch him. His shirt lifted as he moved, revealing a teasing peek of his muscular stomach. A roguishly victorious smile dawned on his face, as he drew out a bag.

"What's that?" Pia asked.

Zoran smiled, drawing out a cookie. Pia's eyes rounded. He wiggled it at her. "Just a little something I picked up at the local bakery."

"Oo, I want one," she insisted, holding out her hand.

He eyed her, a teasing light coming to his face. "No, this is my last one."

To prove his point he dropped the empty bag in the sink.

"Hey," Pia protested. "I can't believe you were hiding those all this time. Here I have been eating nothing but fruit and vegetable salads. By the way, I've been meaning to ask, you're not a vegetarian are you? Because I'm sorry, but, if I have to kill the cow myself, I'm going to get a steak."

"No," he said. "I just haven't been hunting in awhile so there's no meat."

Pia liked the idea of hunting. "Can we go?"

"Where?" he asked impishly, making a great show of looking at the cookie and smelling it. A big, contented smile crossed over his features to drive her crazy.

"Hunting," Pia insisted.

"We'd have to camp," Zoran said. "All the good meat is to the North this time of year."

Her expression said, *so?*

"Do you know how to track?" Zoran asked.

Does tracking men count? Pia thought. "Sure."

Zoran thought that camping in isolation with the beautiful vixen before him didn't sound so bad, though hunting for food had no place in his sudden fantasy.

"I'll see if I can arrange it," he answered.

Pia smiled brightly at him. "Now, hand over that cookie. If you only want to look at it, I'll draw you a picture."

"What? You want this cookie right here?" Zoran questioned, his handsome face turning with mischief. Pia nodded, bringing her hand expectantly closer. He took a bite and moaned dramatically, nodding his head in delight. Talking with his mouth full, he admitted, "Mm, this is really good."

"Oh, you really are incorrigible!" Pia said playfully, coming forward. Without stopping to think, her hand rested on his strong thigh and her body came between his legs. His brow rose and he lifted the cookie above his head. Pia jumped, using his leg for leverage as she tried to grab it.

Zoran laughed, dipping it down within her reach only to snatch it away when she got too close. Pia chuckled, feigning anger. Zoran tilted his head back to take another bite.

"Oh, that's it," she said. She pushed up on his legs and pressed her knee between his thighs. Kneeling over one of his large thighs, she tried to steal the treat away from him. Zoran crushed the whole thing in his mouth, his cheeks puffing up as he chewed enthusiastically.

"Oh!" she huffed, hitting his chest.

"Careful," came his muffled warning as she wobbled on her precarious setting. He automatically fitted his hands to her hips to hold her up.

"What else do you have hidden up here?" Pia stretched up, trying to see the top shelf.

Zoran swallowed. Her breasts were really close to his face. His grip tightened slightly on her hips. His body lurched. Unbidden, torturous thoughts entered his mind.

"Ah-hah!" Pia cried in victory, finding an unopened bag. Her body lowered and his thigh bumped between her legs. A jolt of awareness shot through her at the intimate contact. Zoran gave her a small, smoldering smile. Pia turned bright red and instantly slid down. Pretending there had been nothing in their shared look, she wiggled the fresh bag. "I think someone has a little sweet tooth."

"Hey," Zoran said in instant protest, as if seeing what she had for the first time. He hopped down off the counter to go after her. "Those are mine."

Pia's face rounded in mock horror and she took off running with her prize. Calling over her shoulder, she taunted, "Not anymore."

When Zoran caught up to her she had the bag opened and was beginning to stuff her mouth full. Pia lifted the bag high over her head, turning to keep an eye on him.

"Mees ar verre goomph," she mumbled her taunt, laughing and covering her mouth.

Zoran swept her into his arms, reaching and grabbing the bag from her. Pia protested, doing her best to chew and swallow over her fit of laughter.

"Ah, great," Zoran mourned before turning to her. He pressed her firmly to his chest with one arm as he examined the bag. In his most serious tone, he said, "You know the baker only makes these once a year and these were the very last of what he had."

Pia swallowed, still giggling, "You're a Prince. Can't you exploit your power and pass a law or something? Or threaten to throw him in the dungeon if he doesn't bake you cookies?"

Zoran grinned, pleased by the easy way his title passed by her lips. Taking the opportunity, he said, "Speaking of being a Prince, I need to tell you something."

Pia, realizing he held her closely, artfully pushed back from him. Her face fell slightly, "I already know about the coronation."

"Oh?" he questioned in surprise, disappointed by her withdrawal.

"Yeah, Nadja told me. I already know you have to ask me to go and need me to act happy for the sake of the kingdom or whatever." Pia shrugged. She quickly pulled the bun out of her hair to show him it was longer. "She also grew my hair out for me so I wouldn't embarrass you."

Zoran's eyes dipped over her face. He really wanted to kiss her. His mouth burned with need, as did his body.

"So when is it?"

"Tomorrow night," he answered. He lifted his hand to touch one of the golden locks. "You don't mind going, do you?"

"No," Pia yawned, "it's fine."

"It's late," Zoran murmured. He grew braver and touched her cheek. His voice didn't waver, as he boldly suggested, "Why don't we go to bed?"

Pia blinked, swallowing nervously as she glanced away.

Zoran saw her anxiety and was sorry for it.

"Pia," he began, softly. An ache started in his chest. He wanted to go to her, but held back. "The other night I didn't mean to hurt you. I...."

Zoran looked down her body and sighed, remembering the blood.

"Are you...?" he began, worried.

Pia flushed, more embarrassed than anything. She delicately waved the question away. "I'm ... it's fine. I've had worse pain. I probably overreacted a little. I wasn't sure what you ... was happening."

Zoran frowned.

Pia turned her back on him, embarrassed. "Can we not discuss this? Everything's fine. I just want to forget about it."

Zoran nodded, realizing she couldn't see him.

"Come on," Zoran urged. He drew his hand tenderly to her shoulder. He told himself to win her, not conquer her. Gently, he said, "It's late. Let's go to bed."

Pia tensed.

He quickly added, "I promise not to lay a hand on you unless you want me to."

Pia let him turn her around to face him. He tried to smile. Pia shivered, really wanting him to lay his hands on her. She would never ask for it. It was too embarrassing.

Pia allowed him to lead her to the bed. The bedroom was still dim when they crawled under the covers. Zoran's eyes shifted so he could study her face in the dark. She looked nervous, staring up at the ceiling. She gripped the coverlet tightly, working the smooth material. When he spoke, she nearly jumped out of her skin.

"Good night, Pia."

Pia shivered. Her body jumped with desire for him, but she didn't know how to ask for it. She looked over him, her eyes searching in the dark and not seeing him.

"Good night." Turning her back on him, she did her best to fall asleep.

Chapter Twelve

Zoran was gone for most of the day. Nadja came over in the afternoon to help Pia curl her hair and pick out an appropriate dress. To Nadja's relief, Pia was moving around as if nothing had happened and didn't seem to be holding a grudge about the accident. Nadja still felt really guilty, but Pia refused to listen to another apology, so she held quiet.

Blinking as Nadja darkened her eyelashes, Pia asked, "You said you father was a doctor, right?"

Nadja glanced down wearily from her task. "Uh-huh."

"Would it be possible for, say, a doctor to make your body more ... sensitive to...?" Pia frowned.

"Just be blunt," Nadja said. "I never knew you to skirt around an issue."

"I want to know if a doctor altered me to make me feel ... lust," Pia stated, her mouth twisting to hide her mortification.

Nadja giggled. She couldn't help it.

"I knew I shouldn't have said anything," Pia mumbled, turning away to look in the mirror. She eyed Nadja's handiwork indifferently.

"Are you feeling ... lust?" Nadja asked with a grin.

"I don't know," Pia said. "Forget I asked about it."

"I'm sorry," Nadja said. "No, it's not possible for a doctor to do something to you to make you feel lust. The only way I've ever heard of is through medicines. But you would have to take them on a regular basis and more than likely you would know if you were being dosed. Normally there would be telltale side effects."

"Oh." Pia looked dejected.

"Did something happen between you and Zoran?" Nadja asked, curling a strand of hair before pulling it up at the sides to create a cascaded of curls around Pia's face. Nadja felt sorry for her friend at the idea. Zoran was a beastly, humorless man as far as she was concerned.

"Nothing, well, we did ... and I hit him off," she admitted weakly. "There was blood."

"Oh?" Nadja began, then seeing Pia's meaning in her blushing face, she said, *"Oooh."*

"Is there something wrong with me?" Pia asked. She thought that perhaps the bleeding was her fault, like she wasn't built right or the surgeries had altered her insides.

"Oh, no," Nadja said softly. "No, there isn't anything wrong. It was your first time with a man?"

Pia nodded.

"Didn't your mom...?" began Nadja, trying to be delicate.

"She died," Pia stated flatly.

"What about your dad?"

"Dead."

"The blood is normal the first time," Nadja said delicately. Nadja didn't know firsthand and wasn't sure she was the best person to be giving this advice, but the relief on Pia's face was palpable. Nadja, remembering her mother's talk to her directly after the engagement announcement, repeated the woman's words, "Um, you're just being broken into sex. The second time shouldn't be bad and the third time better."

Pia nodded weakly, before turning to her hair. Eyeing the formal hairdo in the mirror, she asked, "This isn't going to be too much, is it?"

"It's a coronation," Nadja announced. "I think it will do perfectly!"

"All right," Pia said wearily. She'd never been to a formal function before. "Just as long as I'm not the only one wearing a dress tonight."

* * * *

"Pia," Zoran called. "Come on, we've got to go."

He frowned, knocking lightly on the bathroom door. Pia had been hiding from him ever since he got home. At first she said she was getting dressed and now she said she was too sick to come out.

"You'll just have to go without me," she called. "I'm too nauseous. I think I caught something."

"Pia--" he began.

"No, Zoran, I'm sorry. Just make my apologies to whomever. Go have fun," she called. "I'll see you when you get back."

"Pia, I need you there," he insisted. "It's your coronation. You need to be there for it. Can I at least come in?"

"No ... oh, fine," she ended with a growl, her tone growing stronger with irritation. "But you can't laugh at me."

A quizzical expression crossed over Zoran's features as the sick voice suddenly disappeared into a confident growl. He slid open the bathroom door with one finger.

Pia gulped, her pale face looking at him. Her hair cascaded down over her shoulders in curls. His gaze instantly roamed over her dark red gown. The satin was simplistic, hugging to her frame, parting at mid-thigh to bell out in a sweep of material around her legs. The sleeves were short, capped over the shoulder. The neck swung long, sweeping lightly over her breasts to give just enough teasing mystery to instantly drive him mad with desire.

Pia's breath caught, looking him over. He was handsome in tight black slacks and a red silk tunic of oriental influence. The upright collar was short and separated slightly at the neck. A row of small buttons worked their way down over his chest, stopping at the waist so that the material could part at the front continuing down to the knees. The dragon symbol was again on his chest in black.

Her eyes wide, she couldn't stop herself from saying, "You look so handsome."

Zoran grinned in manly delight at her breathless words. Her face flushed red and she shook herself to her senses.

"I can't go with you," Pia stated. Frowning, she looked down at her dress as if that could explain everything she was thinking. "I think Nadja overdid the hair and this dress ... it's all wrong."

Zoran stepped forward, his body lurching. Huskily, he said, "You look perfect."

"No, it's too much," Pia insisted. "I've got those black pants you bought me with the dragon emblem. I'll wear those."

Having decided, Pia strode past him. Zoran's arm shot out catching her about the waist. He curved his arm around her, making her back up so he could continue to look at her. He wasn't quite done with his examination.

"It's perfect," Zoran repeated, giving her a heated look over the satin. He flexed his hand on her waist. Unable to stop himself, he groaned. Leaning over, he cupped her face and kissed her gently. Pia jumped slightly in surprise. Her lips parted and he deepened the kiss. Instantly, her arms wound about his neck in encouragement.

Zoran felt her melting against him and had to pull back. He slid his hand over the satin covered curve of her lower back. If this continued, he wouldn't be making it much further than the bedroom for the rest of the night and his father would be livid.

"Um," he sighed, pulling her back. He licked his lips. "We can't do this. We're already late."

"I don't have a dragon," she said, her eyes wide as she looked up at him.

"What?" He blinked in confusion. He was still too busy staring at her shaded lips. He'd never seen her in makeup before. He thought her beautiful either way.

Pia touched the patch on his chest. "I don't have a dragon emblem. I think I'm supposed to."

Zoran chuckled. "Wait, I'll find you one."

Pia walked slowly behind him as he went to the bedroom. When he came back he was holding his armband from the Breeding Festival. Pushing at it, he bent it smaller to fit her arm.

"I wish I'd thought to get you some proper jewelry," Zoran admitted. "But this will have to do."

Pia let him slide it over her wrist, adjusting the dragon to wind around her upper arm. She smiled. She loved it. It was perfect.

"What's on your feet?" Zoran asked, seeing her black boots.

Pia grinned. "Can you believe the woman tried to make me wear dress slippers? I had her give me these instead."

She pulled her skirt to the side to show the knee high black boots over her bare tanned legs. Zoran's eyes instantly traveled higher to her exposed thigh. If she lifted just a bit higher, he would see the curve of her naked hip. This was going to be a very long night.

"They're perfect," he said, his voice a bit husky.

Already he could picture her in the boots and nothing else. Or even better, that dress pushed up over her hips as he took her from behind. His gaze traveled up her waist to her cleavage. How much trouble would he get in if they didn't show up? Maybe the King wouldn't notice. Maybe....

Clearing his head, Zoran grunted roughly, "We need to go."

* * * *

The main common hall of the Draig mountain palace had steep, arched ceilings with the center dome for light. The red stone floor was swept clean. A space was left clear for dancing. Banners of the family crest lined the walls, one for each color of the family lines--purple for the King and Queen, black for Yusef, green for Olek, red for Zoran, and blue-gray for Ualan. Each banner had the silver symbol of the dragon boldly woven into it.

Lines of tables reached across the floor for dining, filled with villagers and attended to by servants who carted out endless pitchers of various drinks and set them out on the tables. Their murmuring voices could be heard all around the hall, as they excitedly awaited the start of the festivities. All of them craned to get a good look at their new Princesses sitting at the head table.

Pia was seated between Queen Mede and her husband. Aside from the three Princesses, the royal family all wore crowns. The Queen tried to talk to her a few times and she answered as politely and distantly as possible. The woman made her uncomfortable. Next to the Queen was King Llyr. He spoke mostly to his wife.

Looking past the King, Pia tried to smile at Nadja, but her lips were stiff. She never dreamed that she would be set up on display before so many people. Honestly, she hadn't known what to expect this night. Looking around the hall, all the curious eyes on her, she shivered.

Prince Olek was next to Nadja. He had a laughing smile and seemed very easy natured compared to his somber brothers. Pia could instantly see the man's complete infatuation with his wife. When Nadja wasn't looking at him, his eyes were all over her. She was happy for her friend. Although, she wasn't sure Nadja realized it herself.

Next in line was Prince Ualan. She couldn't tell much from the man's blank expression and he didn't pay her any attention. That was fine with Pia. Morrigan, his wife, was next to him. She nodded in Pia's direction. Pia didn't know Morrigan well, but returned her acknowledgement with a slight smile.

Morrigan and Ualan had been the last to arrive, just now being seated. From what she gathered, Morrigan had made herself a slave to purge her honor and had come tonight to ask royal pardon. She wondered what the woman had done to shame herself.

Smiling wryly down at her drink, she thought, *Maybe she cut her hair, too.*

Next to Zoran was his brother, Prince Yusef. He was an ungodly dark specimen, contrasting completely to his lighter toned brothers. He didn't say much when he was introduced to her and she had merely nodded in return. The man seemed preoccupied, as if his thoughts had nothing to do with the evening at hand and he was just there filling a space at the royal table. His wife was at home, sick.

"It's glad I am that all my sons have found brides. We're a house blessed." Pia looked over at the King as he spoke. He lifted his goblet proudly to the crowd before continuing, "Preosts, crown the Princesses."

Pia shivered as she was given a crown to match Zoran's, though it was smaller and much more delicate. The Preost fit it on her head and she was almost too scared to move under the unfamiliar weight.

After the Preosts were finished muttering whatever ceremonial blessing they spoke, servants began coming around with plates of food, serving the head table first. Pia looked absently at the meal. It was delicate and proper and made her long even more for a juicy, rare steak. Sighing, she dutifully picked up her fork.

Musicians began playing softly in the background to fill the hall with music. Pia looked them over, before turning to study the crowd. A group of blond warriors in the back caught her attention. The silent group was ignored by most of the hall. Only one servant approached them, seeming to hesitate as he filled their goblets. The men held still, not looking at the servant as he made his way around.

Pia dropped her fork, leaning to grab her drink only to flinch when she realized it was wine and set it back down untouched. Zoran saw the gesture and smiled. He waved his hand to a servant and asked him quietly to bring something other than wine for his wife.

Pia leaned over, not taking her eyes off the men. It was obvious they didn't belong in the hall. Seeing the largest warrior at their table shift his eyes around the room in displeasure, Pia narrowed her gaze.

Zoran looked down to feel her delicate hand working against his arm. Glancing at Pia's face, he followed her eyes to the table of Var warriors. The largest at their table, King Attor, turned his stare to the royal table.

"That man plans something," Pia said quietly, absently. "I'm going to make my way over there."

Zoran tensed. He squeezed his hand over her fingers. Pia blinked, coming out of her concentration. Zoran's eyes lowered in warning, "You are doing no such thing. That's King Attor of the Var. He rules the kingdom to the south. He's our guest tonight, and he's being watched very carefully."

Pia, realizing what she'd said, paled. She blinked out of her concentration. Seeing his serious eyes, she said, "Sorry, old habit."

Pia could see instantly that Zoran didn't like the man's presence in his family's home. His eyes were suspicious as he turned to look back down over the hall.

Zoran saw the Var King snarl slightly in anger, though the man reigned in his emotion well. He wondered at his wife's 'old habit.' This was no place to ask her.

"Why is he here?" Pia asked, her instincts quickening with the familiar rush of intrigue and danger. It was a sensation she hadn't felt for a long, long time and she clung to its familiar pull. "He does not look like a friend."

"He's not," Zoran allowed. It was a show of power to their people to prove the Princes were happily married and thus would produce many royal heirs to secure their lineage. It also showed they had no fear of the Var. "But his presence serves a necessity."

"Ah," Pia said, nodding in instant understanding. "It proves that we're unafraid of him to invite him openly to our home. Smart."

Zoran wondered at her cunning perception. He was about to ask when the servant came back and switched Pia's wine with juice. Pia blinked her surprise.

Zoran leaned to whisper in her ear. "I'll make a standing order in the kitchen not to serve you wine."

Pia shivered as his breath hit her throat. All thoughts of Var intrigue left her as she breathlessly turned her face to Zoran's. His lips were really close. Her eyes dipped, unwittingly inviting him to kiss her.

Zoran's heart lurched. Glancing up, he noticed his father's eyes on him. The king urged him with a nod to kiss his bride. Zoran smiled wryly, turned his gaze back to his wife.

"Thanks," Pia said, leaning back when he didn't move closer. She swallowed nervously, again becoming aware of the crowd, though her eyes couldn't focus on them and her ears couldn't hear them. Her heart was beating erratically in her chest. She inched to reach under the table to touch Zoran's leg.

"You're welcome," Zoran murmured, pulling back from her. He had the insane urge to haul her onto his lap and start kissing and groping her incessantly. Shutting his eyes, he took a calming breath. He needed a freezing cold shower. Hell, he needed to dip his overheated body into a river of ice.

A shout of laughter resounded over the hall in front of Pia. Pia blinked, turning her dazed attention to the sound that dared to break into her turbulent thoughts. Leaning forward, she saw a young boy limping to his feet from the floor. A group of Draig warriors were laughing at him. One foot turned in slightly and started to drag. Pia's face fell in horror. Without stopping to think, she jumped up from the table and rushed down to the floor to help him.

Zoran tensed as Pia flew past his back. Instantly, his eyes turned to the table of Var warriors, thinking she meant to go there. He stood, intent on chasing after her. Then, to his surprise, she turned and went down to where Hienrich was trying to prove his worth to the soldiers in an effort to be admitted into their ranks.

Several large Draig warriors chuckled as they watched the slender, sickly boy from the nearby table. Zoran knew that the boy wanted more than anything to be a soldier. He'd even dared to hound him at the practice field on many occasions. But, being that the orphan was born with a deformed foot that turned in when he walked, he wasn't the most likely candidate.

The boy, who was climbing back to his feet to do whatever trick the drunken Draig warriors had good-naturedly bid him to try, blinked as Pia sidled next to him. Hienrich paled to see the Princess watching him and tried to bow. The boy's position was precarious and he stumbled before righting himself.

Zoran saw the protective looks on his men's faces as she approached the boy, though they kept them guarded. Sure, the warriors gave the orphaned boy a hard time, but they were trying to make him strong of character. If he was going to fight with his deformity, he would have to have nerves of steel.

"Leave him be!" an angry Pia demanded to the table of stunned warriors. Zoran frowned at her forceful words. But, even as he watched her, he couldn't help thinking how beautifully defiant she was. Besides, it was nice to see her turning her fire onto someone else for a change--even if that someone was some of the highest ranking men under his command.

"What do you want with Hienrich, my lady?" Stot asked, a burly soldier with a beard. The soldier's face was hard, but he didn't raise his voice as he tried to protect Hienrich. Zoran knew the man often cared for the boy, letting him sleep over with his sons and taking him camping with his family to teach him how to be a proper man. Orphans were the responsibility of the entire community. And, whereas they didn't have a stable, permanent home, they were never left wanting. "Does he offend you? I'll have him removed."

Zoran watched, enthralled, as Pia's body shook in irritation. Standing up to some of the most fearsome men under his command, she declared, "He does not offend me! You, however...."

"I don't think your wife understands that Hienrich is being put through the paces to prove his worth as a soldier. Perhaps you should stop her and explain before she makes a scene," Yusef broke in at his side.

A grin threatened the side of Zoran's mouth, though he hid it well. Turning to Yusef, he said, "Perhaps you're right brother."

"My lady," the confused Stot defended, not understanding what he'd done wrong. "He knows we mean no harm. Don't you, lad?"

Hienrich dutifully nodded his head. He understood perfectly well. He too was confused as he looked at the Princess.

"See," Stot said.

"Yeah," another added, drunker soldier with a pock marked face. "He thinks to become a warrior, don't you, boy?"

The men laughed good-naturedly. Zoran stood, stepping leisurely around the table to fetch his loud wife. He was too aware that the hall was studying him for a reaction.

"Well, I'm a Princess," Pia announced, "and he'll by my personal warrior."

The hall was stunned. Hienrich's mouth almost fell to the floor at her declaration. Yusef took a drink, trying not to laugh at the mischief Pia caused. Zoran came up behind her, crossing his arms over his chest and said nothing.

Stot glanced at Prince Zoran in confusion of the declaration.

"If my lady wishes for a warrior," the bearded man said when he could finally talk. "Let us battle for the position. Do not insult us by naming a boy."

"Let us have a tournament," one of the Draig warriors called. A shout of agreement came for the men eager to do battle for the Princess' notice.

"Do you dare to question a Princess?" Zoran called with authority over the hall.

The onlookers fell instantly silent in respect. The warriors growled and looked darkly at the boy whose chest was puffing up with his new authority over them. Zoran sighed. He was going to be in for a headache of complaints after this incident. The men wouldn't take kindly to his wife publicly slighting their ability in favor of an untrained boy.

Pia turned in surprise to see Zoran behind her. As he saw her face, he didn't care how many grumpy men he had to deal with. Her open look of pleasure and gratification made it all worth it. She looked as if he'd just handed her a pile of stars.

"He's my warrior too!"

Zoran turned around to see Nadja standing next to Olek, looking very defiant.

"And mine as well!"

Zoran glanced to Ualan, who looked amused. It was his wife, Morrigan, who spoke.

Zoran glanced at his father and shrugged. The King merely gestured his fingers lightly, urging him to put an end to it. They could well deal with the ramifications of the wayward Princesses later.

"There you have it," Zoran announced to the hall. "You cannot deny the wish of three Princesses. Hienrich is now under royal protection and will be treated accordingly to his new station."

The three Princesses glanced at each other, a silent camaraderie building between them. Pia nodded her thanks for their support. The stunned hall picked up its celebration once more.

Zoran lifted his hand and motioned the musicians to start playing. Pia told Hienrich to come to the high table to join them. The boy nodded his head, his chest lifting with pride as he saw some of the nearby boys looking at him in respect and awe.

Pia looked expectantly at Yusef and then to the empty seat beside him. The boy beamed. Yusef glanced at Zoran, shrugged, and moved over so the boy could sit beside Zoran's seat. Pia waved a servant to bring the boy a plate.

As soon as the servant left, Yusef stood and went to join the musicians. They handed him an instrument and he began playing, paying more attention to the livening crowd than to his task.

Zoran saw Pia looking at him from the corner of his eye. She shifted slightly closer to him. He hid his smile, taking a long drink.

Chapter Thirteen

The feast was cleared and after dinner drinks were poured aplenty. The Draig were much freer with their affection than most humanoid cultures. They openly kissed and caressed their lovers as if it were no big occurrence.

After the commotion died down, Zoran glanced fully at his wife. She was staring at him. Her hazel eyes were wide in what he could only guess was an emotion akin to respect or adoration.

Pia bit her lip and leaned forward. Zoran tensed, feeling her hand hesitantly creep onto his thigh, her long fingers curling lightly around to the inside. Leaning her head down, she whispered to him, "Thank you for saving the boy. I couldn't stand to see them treat him so poorly just because he's different."

Zoran wanted to chuckle, but held back. Hienrich had been treated exceptionally well, being as he was even given attention by the burly men. He had a feeling that, after his wife's intervention, the boy wouldn't be so well received by the bitter warriors who were insulted by Princess Pia's actions. Undoubtedly, he'd have to front the money for a tournament and have a real warrior picked amongst them. He wondered if he would get permission from his father to compete.

However, as he felt her willingly touching him and saw the very tender, almost vulnerable way she was looking at him, he didn't care. Let her have her delusion. He would gladly suffer any number of her public misconceptions and faux pas in order to keep that soft look on her beautiful face.

The musicians kept playing. The quiet Yusef strummed with them on a guitar looking instrument and proved himself quite up to the task. Someone sang in the Qurilixen language. It was a beautiful sounding ballad.

Zoran glanced down to where the couples were beginning to dance. He reached over, lightly touching her cheek. Instead of answering, he said, "Dance with me."

Pia tensed. She shook her head in denial. "I can't dance."

"It's all just movement," he urged, taking the crown from his head and setting it on the table. He took hers off as well. His eyes dipped over her red dress and his tone lowered. "I've seen you move. You'll do fine."

Before she could again protest, his hand met hers on his leg. Standing, he pulled her up and led her around the table to the dance floor. The villagers turned to watch the royal couple with pleasure before turning back to their conversations.

Zoran turned, bowing slightly to his wife. Her head didn't move, but her eyes looked nervously around to see if any stared. Still holding her hand, Zoran lifted it to the side, cupping her fingers around his, and drew forward to wrap his hand about her waist. Pia shivered beneath his warm fingers.

"Put your hand on my arm," he whispered, his slight grin hiding what he was saying from the crowd.

Pia obeyed. She wrapped her fingers around his large bicep and she was pulled slightly closer to his chest so she felt the press of him brushing up against her breasts in whispering caresses. Her lips parted with a quick intake of air.

"Now just move lightly. Follow my lead, as if you were trying to sneak across the floor unheard." Zoran's eyes dipped to her mouth, tempted but restrained.

Pia nodded. That sounded easy enough.

Zoran began to slowly move. He was a wonderful instructor, leading Pia easily in the steps. Pia stared into his eyes, becoming oblivious to anything around them. She was amazed that a man his size could move with such grace and perfection. Her heart beat wildly. She was completely captivated by this giant of a man who held her.

Zoran grinned, dipping her back. He was pleased when she didn't tense, trusting him to hold onto her. Pia relaxed completely into his arms. Zoran pulled their extended arms in close and slowed his steps by a small degree, though still keeping time to the music. Pia felt weak. Zoran's arm ran up her back, urging her head to fall forward to his shoulder as he held her closer. To them, there was no one else in the room.

King Llyr looked meaningfully at his Queen, nodding to Zoran and his wife with pleasure. The Queen smiled to see them.

"They'll be the first to give us grandsons," the King said knowingly to her.

Zoran suddenly caught Yusef's look from the corner of his eyes. Following his brother's stare, he turned Pia around to look at the head table. King Attor was there with his Var warriors addressing his father. He danced closer, trying to hear what was said. Pia snuggled into his arms, sighing contentedly, completely unaware.

"Many blessings on your unions," King Attor was saying. "May your reign be long."

"As may yours, King Attor," his father said. King Llyr stood to show a respect Zoran knew his father didn't feel.

Zoran turned his wife again. Pia looked up in surprise at the sudden shift of movement. Zoran winked at her and dipped her across his arm. When she came back up she was smiling at him.

Pia's smile fell to see the serious look on his face. Zoran was looking after the departing Vars. She glanced over his shoulder, seeing the blond warriors walking out the side door.

Yusef ended his part of the song early and passed his instrument back to its owner, who took up immediately where the Prince had left off. No one noticed the change as the dancing continued. Yusef followed the warriors out of the common hall.

"You can go if you want," Pia said softly, watching Zoran's face.

Zoran turned back to look at her. A wide grin came to his lips as he swept her into a spin and brought her crashing lightly back into his arms. Leaning over without missing a step, he kissed her throat beneath her ear causing her to shiver. Murmuring against her hair, he admitted, "What I want to do is to dance with my beautiful wife."

Pia stiffened slightly in his arms at the compliment. Zoran drew back only to see her gaze had once more guarded itself against him. The song ended. Pia stepped back from him.

"Maybe we should go sit down," she said quietly.

Zoran was unwilling to let her leave the dance floor. There was nothing he could do about it. Though, he did guide his hand to her lower back to lead her to her seat.

As Pia sat, she saw the Queen smiling at her. She nodded stiffly and turned her eyes down to her plate. She rested her hands in her lap. For a moment, in Zoran's arms, she had almost felt like she was beautiful.

Over her head, the King nodded at Zoran in approval. Zoran automatically placed his crown back on his head, leaning to do the same for Pia before moving close to her. He wrapped his arm about her waist to draw her to him.

"Pia," he began in question, wondering what was wrong.

Pia glanced up at him, but she didn't have time to answer.

Zoran glanced down as Agro came to the head table, stepping up to speak quietly to the King. Zoran stood, coming around to hear what he said. Pia watched the beefy warrior's face. She couldn't understand what was said, but could tell something was wrong. They stiffened, their eyes narrowing. The men nodded and Zoran came back to his wife.

"What's happened?" Pia asked. To her surprise, Zoran smiled at her. Though, she could see the hard look in his eyes, his face was pure, deceiving pleasure.

"There has been trouble with the Var. Yusef's been hurt. I have to go," Zoran said seriously. "I'll ask one of the men to take you back to the house."

"I want to go with you," Pia said. She naturally gravitated closer to him. "I can help."

Zoran smiled. He raised a hand to touch her cheek. To those who watched on, they looked like a loving couple.

"No," Zoran said. His hard eyes bore into her. She could see he was concerned.

"But," she began, her face turning down in worry.

"Lean into me, Pia," Zoran commanded softly. His eyes dipped naturally to her lips. His hand fell to her arm. "We can't let anyone see that we're worried."

Pia obeyed and he was glad for it. Her face came close to his. She felt his breath stirring over her lips as he spoke. Her eyes naturally closed, waiting for his kiss, and not really caring that they were being watched.

"I need you to promise me you will go back to the house and wait for me," Zoran said. "I don't want to have to worry about something happening to you."

"Nothing will happen," she tried. She naturally slid her hand onto his thigh to rest. The smell of him was luring her forward, making want to nuzzle into his shoulder. His hand slid to her waist and worked over to possessively lie on her hip.

"Pia," Zoran growled low. His lips whispered closer and she shivered. "Promise me."

Her eyes opened and she looked into his. Slowly, she nodded. Zoran visibly relaxed.

The King and Queen had stood and were walking behind them. Zoran felt his mother's hand on his arm, urging him up. He glanced at her then back to his wife. She was nervously licking her lips.

"Hienrich can take me back," she said. Zoran moved to stand and her hand tightened on his leg. "Try to hurry."

Zoran's eyes softened and he nodded. He took up his mother's arm, pausing only long enough to give Hienrich a gruff order. Hienrich's young face turned very serious and he nodded solemnly. As soon as Zoran was out of the hall, the boy stood and turned to Princess Pia.

"My lady." Hienrich bowed. "I'm to escort you back to your home."

Pia watched him, hiding her smile. She nodded seriously at him. Standing, she let him lead her from the hall, completely unaware of the irritated stares of some of the drunken warriors.

* * * *

As soon as they were clear of the hall, Zoran and his parents ran for the medical ward. Agro hadn't been able to tell them much, only that Yusef had been attacked from behind while seeing King Attor out of the keep and off Draig land. The man seemed fairly confident that it wasn't the King and his ambassadors who had dealt the blows, but the Var were not dismissed as suspects in the tragedy.

Hearing Yusef howl in pain, Zoran's stomach knotted in outrage. None of them had thought the Var King would dare to be so bold. It had been hard not to run out of the common hall when Agro told them of it, but it would do no good to alarm the castle until they knew what was happening.

As they stepped into the medical ward, Ualan and Olek were right behind them. Agro had Yusef pinned to a bed as the doctor's worked. Ualan and Olek stepped in to relieve the man of his position. Agro backed away, his face strained. Yusef fought like a bear, but he'd lost so much blood that he was weakening quickly.

"They stabbed him in the back. He didn't have time to shift," Agro said.

The King nodded to the loyal man. Speaking low, he commanded, "Agro, gather the trackers and see if they can't pick up a scent."

"I'll lead them myself," the warrior declared hotly. Shifting into his fearsome Draig form, he took off down the hall with lightening speed.

"My wife," Yusef groaned from the bed, nearly incoherent.

Zoran waved over one of the guard's who'd carried his brother. Lowering his voice, he said, "Get to the Outpost and gather my brother's wife. Be discreet and tell no one what happened here tonight. Don't shift unless there's trouble and do not tell her what is happening. Leave her to us. We will deal with her."

The guard nodded in complete understanding.

Hearing Olek, Zoran turned his attention to his brothers. Olek was bidding someone to go after Yusef's wife.

"I've taken care of it," Zoran broke in. He waved the guard away to do his bidding. Moving forward to watch the doctors, he frowned. Under his breath, he stated, "They go to get her right now."

* * * *

Pia followed the silent Hienrich down the red passageway. If anything happened, she was sure she would end up protecting the young boy instead of vise versa. Feeling her side, she lifted her arm and tried to stretch out the sore muscle. She just hoped it didn't come to that.

"Here you are, my lady," Hienrich dutifully announced. He turned to stand guard outside the door.

Pia ordered the door to open. Then, looking at the young boy ready to fight to the death for her, she eyed him gravely.

"Maybe you should come inside and wait with me," she suggested.

"A soldier does not run from danger, my lady," Hienrich said, his jaw lifting proudly.

Pia nodded, though inside she thought it adorable that he was taking his new position so seriously. "Would you come inside, for me?"

Hienrich looked at her, his stubborn jaw setting.

Before he could deny her, she rushed, "Please, Hienrich. Prince Zoran is gone and I'm sure to be scared in this big house by myself. You would be doing me a great service if you would come inside and keep me company."

Hienrich debated.

Pia lowered her tone and wrung her hands lightly. "This door will surely hold anyone off who tries to get in. And, if they do get past, well then, I have you inside to protect me. So, please, come in. I would feel so much better with a man in the house."

Hienrich nodded, unable to fight the female logic. He knew well men were supposed to protect women and this woman was a Princess. His duty was twice as important. He walked in ahead of her.

"Maybe you could have a look around and make sure it's safe," she leaned over and whispered.

She smiled when Hienrich nodded to her, saying, "Stay here, my lady."

She waited patiently by the door as Hienrich made a great show of inspecting the entire house, disappearing into the different rooms. Pia eyed the oak door, knowing no one was getting through it. Seeing the hole she'd dug in the wall, she frowned. She really should get that fixed.

"All's clear, my lady," Hienrich said.

Pia let loose a long sigh of relief for his benefit. "Thank you, so much."

She began walking to the kitchen. Taking the awkward crown off her head, she set it on the counter. Smiling, she called, "You wouldn't happen to like cookies, would you?"

She poked her head out of the kitchen. Hienrich's answering smile of excitement was all the answer she needed.

"Why don't you have a seat at the table and I'll get some?" Moving her dress aside, Pia hopped onto the countertop and grabbed Zoran's hidden bag. Climbing back down with much less grace, she got a plate and poured some out for the boy.

When she came out of the kitchen, he was sitting eagerly at the low table. Pia gave him the plate and smiled at him.

Hienrich ate in enthusiastic silence, before looking up at the Princess. Almost shyly, he asked, "Why did you pick me to be your warrior?"

"Don't you want to be my warrior?" she inquired.

"Well, yes, of course, my lady," Hienrich said. "But usually the position is fought for in tournament. The others will be a little upset because of it. They are better suited and deserve the chance."

Pia shrugged. "I've found that someone is always upset no matter what you do. So what if their feelings are hurt. They'll get over it."

Hienrich nodded. "I haven't trained yet. I think I should before taking this position."

Pia nodded thoughtfully, amazed at the boy's logic.

"If you don't want me to leave your service, I understand," he said. "But I think the soldiers were getting ready to let me try out for them. They were giving me a test of strength tonight to prove I was worthy."

"Is that what they were doing?" Pia saw the earnest look on the boy's face and instantly understood that the men hadn't been picking on him. They were performing some barbaric rite of passage to see if the boy was ready to try out to join them.

"You speak very wisely, Hienrich," Pia said. "Well, stand up then. Let me see what you can do. If you impress me, I'll speak to Prince Zoran about you. I'll request that you begin training immediately. But, mind you, you must work hard. If you are to honor my family's name, I expect the best out of you."

"Yes, my lady," Hienrich said. He was instantly on his feet, standing at attention.

"Stay here," Pia said. "I wish to see you with a sword."

"Yes, my lady," he obeyed, standing at full attention.

Pia went to the exercise room, hiding her smile. Retrieving a small sword, she came back and eyed Hienrich. "Do you know how to use this?"

"Yes."

"Before I give it to you," she began with authority. "I'll teach you the very first lesson about being a fighter. It doesn't matter how big or small you are. If you are confident in your ability and can strike fear into your opponent. That's half the battle."

Hienrich nodded.

"Now, let me see your scariest face," Pia said, a smirk starting to curl her lips.

Hienrich did. Pia was stunned.

The boy's features shifted. His young skin turned dark beneath his clothes, hardening with a natural armor. His eyes turned yellow as a line grew out of his forehead. It pushed forward to make a hard plate of impermeable tissue over his nose and brow. Sharp talons grew from his fingers and short fangs poked out of his mouth.

Pia trembled, not suspecting the literal change. Automatically holding up the sword, she stumbled away from the snarling boy. He growled. A scream worked its way from her startled throat. All traces of the young boy were gone, disappeared into the visage of a monster.

Hienrich, thinking it was a test, roared louder, coming at her. He gave her his most menacing look.

"Back, Hienrich!" Pia yelled loudly. She gripped the sword, backing away. She had no wish to hurt the child, but she couldn't physically fight off his fangs and claws if he tried to attack. If he lunged for her, she wouldn't have a choice. She would have to defend herself.

Chapter Fourteen

Zoran sighed, striding through the halls to get home to Pia. Yusef was unconscious and in pretty bad condition. The doctor told them that he hadn't been given time to shift into Draig and the knife wounds had penetrated deeply beneath the surface of his skin. They were sure that he would pull through, though he was still in danger.

Hearing a scream, his heart gripped in his chest. Frantically, he ran the rest of the way down the hall to his home, yelling for the door to open. He would know his wife's voice anywhere. As he came through the front door, he saw she was shouting at Hienrich to back away. The unruly Draig roar of a child followed the sound of her rising voice.

Zoran blinked, seeing Pia cornered against the wall with one of his small swords lifted up. She was pointing it at Hienrich who had shifted and was growling at her.

"What is going on?" the Prince bellowed loudly to the boy in their native language.

Pia turned her eyes to Zoran. The wide hazel depths were shaken. Her mouth opened to explain but no words came out.

Hienrich instantly shifted back to human form. He bowed, answering in kind, "My lady wished me to show her my scariest face so that I may prove I'm worthy of training under you, my lord."

Zoran took in Pia's trembling lips and her death grip on the sword. She kept her gaze steadily on Hienrich.

"I think you were too scary," Zoran said to the boy. "Report to the field for training tomorrow morning. You will start as an apprentice warrior to the men. Now go."

Hienrich nodded and jogged out the door.

"And from now on," Zoran barked to the boy's retreating back, "be more delicate around the ladies. They are not used to such fierceness."

Pia watched the boy run off. Her limbs trembled. Zoran ordered the door to close and strode over to her. Pia dropped the sword from her shaking fingers. It clattered loudly to the floor, but she didn't care. She rushed forward into Zoran's arms, too shaken to do much else.

"He's not human," she breathed into Zoran's chest. He folded her into his embrace. "He's like a ... dragon. I didn't know."

"Sh," Zoran whispered, holding her close. He stroked the back of her hair. His body was stiff, witnessing her rejection of the Draig form. Inside, he tightened into knots. He had to tell her the truth.

Pia pulled back, looking up at his rigid face. Suddenly, she shook herself. "Some warrior I've turned out to be. It's not like I haven't seen shifters before, but I really thought he was going to attack and I didn't relish fighting off a young boy. I was so scared I was going to have to defend myself against him."

Zoran smiled, though it was tight.

Pia pulled out of his arms and he let her go. A thought occurred to her and she rushed, "How's your brother?"

"Not well," Zoran answered.

"What happened?" she questioned, trying to see past his blank expression. He was searching her, but she couldn't tell what he sought.

"He was stabbed in the back," he said, his voice cautious.

"Any witnesses?"

"No."

"Any idea who?"

"No."

"Do you think it was the Var?" Pia asked, growing exasperated with his short answers.

"Possibly," Zoran answered in frustration. Before she could ask another question, he said, "Listen, Pia, I need to tell you something."

"What?" she asked. Her face was confused. "Are we in danger?"

"I am Draig," he said bluntly, before losing his nerve.

Pia's eyes narrowed, not following. A quizzical smile came to her mouth. "Yes, I assumed you were of the House of Draig, as apparently we all are. We're the royal family--"

"No, Pia," Zoran broke in, his gaze tortured. His allowed his eyes to shift fully to a golden yellow. The skin on his face hardened and turned to brown armor. Pia jerked in surprise, stumbling backwards into the couch as she watched his handsome face contort. His hair remained the same, but his forehead jutted low as his brow protruded. Fangs grew between his parted lips and talon-like claws formed on his fingers. When his lips parted to speak, his voice was hoarse and came out in a fierce demon-like growl. "I am Draig."

Pia gasped loudly. She suddenly knew all the times she'd seen his eyes change in color, she hadn't been imagining it. He was a shifter. Her heart momentarily stopped beating in her chest. Her legs weakened and she fell back to sit on the arm of the chair. She should've guessed when she saw Hienrich. This meant all the men on the planet were shifters. They'd never let on.

She eyed him carefully. In a way he looked to be the same powerful man as before. She'd been all over the galaxy, had seen many creatures so the transformation itself wasn't shocking. But, to see the only man she'd ever been attracted to transform himself into something not quite human, unnerved her greatly. If she'd been scared about intimacy before, she was now petrified. Seeing him in Draig left her feeling vulnerable to him and Pia didn't like feeling vulnerable.

"Just give me a minute," Pia said, eyeing him. He wasn't growling and snarling like the boy had been. She knew this man. It was the same man who'd danced with her earlier.

Zoran relaxed at her softly spoken words. She was still staring warily at him, but at least she wasn't running away in fear. Zoran shifted back to his human form and took a step forward. She stood and moved slightly away from him to sit on the couch.

"Pia, I wanted to tell you earlier," he began.

"It's probably a good thing you didn't, considering the way I handled seeing Hienrich for the first time," Pia said, laughing lightly. Her eyes met his for a brief instant before turning away. "It's not like I've never ... albeit not one like you."

Pia glanced at him again. He still wore the long red tunic. It made him all the more commanding and handsome. Shivers racked her body, as she thought, *Never as breathtaking as you.*

Zoran took a hesitant step forward, moving to sit on the opposite end of the couch, not touching her. She was handling it well, considering.

"I," she hesitated, "ah, does it hurt?"

Zoran chuckled lightly. Draig was most comfortable. The tougher skin protected them from the elements. The eyes allowed them to see more clearly and to greater distances. In many ways, it was the human form that was handicapped. Although, it was the human form that could really feel. Its softer flesh could tremble at a woman's touch, could mold to a woman's gentle body, could claim her and make love to her. "No, it doesn't hurt."

"Can you control it?"

"For the most part," he answered honestly. "If I'm in danger, I shift as a reflex."

"Oh," she mumbled.

"I'd never hurt you, Pia, if that's what you're asking me," he said. He moved as if to touch her.

"No," she gasped. Pia's wide eyes met his and she jerked back. "I mean, not yet. I need to get used to it first. It's still a little bit of a shock. I didn't suspect...."

Zoran nodded. He was about to speak when a knock sounded on his door.

"Open," he called, standing to meet whoever came. He half expected it to be the soldier with Yusef's bride. It wasn't. It was one of the doctor's wives.

"Draea Anwealda!" rushed the woman. Her panicked voice switched to a thick English as she saw Pia. "Come quickly, you and the Princess!"

"What's happened?" Pia asked. She joined Zoran's side, but didn't touch him.

"You are needed in the medical wing," the woman said, her Qurilixen accent coming out fast to garble her words. "It's the Princess Morrigan. She has been poisoned!"

Zoran watched as she gave him a meaningful look and then glanced at Pia. Zoran studied his wife. She did look a little pale, but that could have been from what he'd just shown her and not poison. He wasn't willing to take chances.

"Come on, Pia," he urged. He didn't reach out to touch her, as he said, "We've got to go."

Pia followed him out to the hall, lifting her red skirt as she moved. Seeing a tapestry when she turned a corner, she noticed it had a depiction of the Qurilixen men in Draig form. Pia wondered how her usually observant nature didn't notice it before. The dragon obsession made perfect sense.

Zoran's family was already gathered in the medical ward when they arrived. Ualan looked tortured. He stared blindly at the operating room door. Yusef was on the bed in bad shape. His skin was pale and he was bandaged over his entire upper body.

Pia stepped next to Zoran looking for Morrigan. She couldn't see her. She did see Queen Mede. The woman was shaking her head, speaking frantically to Olek as she motioned at Nadja and Pia.

"Go with the doctor, Pia," Zoran said gently, looking at her. He motioned his head, careful not to touch her. The doctor was covered completely with protective gear, down to his goggles. It didn't look good. "He just wants to check you to make sure you're fine."

"I'll go with them," the Queen announced in support of her daughters. Pia frowned. She was secretly glad when the doctor turned and indicated that Mede should stay out of the room. The Queen blinked in confusion but obeyed the man.

"But," Pia began in protest of Zoran's insistent shove when she didn't move fast enough to suit him. "I feel fine. I haven't been poisoned."

Nadja's eyes widened in horror at the statement and she spun around to stare at Olek. Pia frowned, realizing the woman didn't know what was happening. Mede pushed Nadja forward.

"Go, dear," Mede said to Nadja. "Hurry."

Pia was led into the room followed by Nadja. The doctor turned to the women, taking out two handheld medic units. Without comment, he grabbed their arms and took a sample of their blood. Neither woman spoke as they watched the man go to a counter to test them.

Outside the room, the men were quiet, their faces drawn in worry. Morrigan had fallen to poison and possibly lay dying in the other room. Yusef was still unconscious. Suddenly, Ualan spoke, stating what they were all thinking.

"If any in our family die," Ualan swore. His voice deepened into a growl as his face hardened with a shift. Resembling a mere shadow of the beast he could become, he roared, "There will be blood."

"There will be blood either way," Zoran declared, his eyes dark. His heart hardened in his chest. He couldn't lose Pia. Regardless of what was between them, she was his whole world, his future.

Minutes later Pia and Nadja came from the back room. The doctor announced that their blood tested fine. Pia went to stand by Zoran, her face hard. They sat quietly together in the medical wing by the motionless Yusef, waiting for news of Morrigan.

Morrigan was very ill and didn't stop throwing up, even in her sleep. Her body fought with a bravery and in the end she won the battle for her life--albeit barely. Ualan sighed heavily with the news and was instantly ushered to his wife's side where he stayed.

The King ordered all the food and wine tested, starting with Morrigan's. The poison was instantly found in a goblet. The servant responsible for serving her the drink had been dealt with. It was soon learned he wasn't at fault. One of King Attor's men had distracted him as he was preparing to serve the royal drink.

The drink had been meant for the King and Queen. But when King Attor went up to speak, the servant had placed the goblet before Morrigan instead, as not to get in their way. He never realized Princess Morrigan wouldn't recognize the King's seal and would indeed take the drink for herself. It was a grim blessing that Morrigan drank it. If Mede or Llyr had taken a sip, they would've died instantly. The poison worked slower on humans.

The family relaxed to discover Morrigan was going to live. Pia didn't really know the woman, but seeing how close the family was reminded her of her parents and she felt their pain. She had no wish to see Morrigan harmed.

Their relief didn't last long, as the soldier Zoran sent to gather Yusef's wife came back alone. He looked worried, standing in the doorway, eyeing the royal family.

"Where is she?" Zoran barked, as soon as he saw the man.

Pia jumped slightly by his side at the harsh sound of her husband's ire. Her wide eyes turned to Zoran in confusion.

"My lady is gone," the soldier announced. "There looks to have been a struggle. We smelled Var blood, but no human. She should still be alive."

The King growled.

"We picked up their scent in the forest. I ordered the others to follow it," the soldier said to Zoran. He spoke in English and Pia was glad she could hear what was going on.

"You should call the soldiers back and get one of your best trackers on it," Olek stated quietly. "Let them think they have escaped into the shadowed marshes. Once we find their location, we'll go after them alone and reclaim her for Yusef."

"Olek's right," Zoran stated, switching his language in deference to the listening women. He didn't want to alarm them. "If they wanted her dead, they would've killed her right then. They take her for a reason. If they hear the men coming after them, they could be forced to get rid of her to escape."

The men looked at each other, nodding in agreement and knowing that the revenge was going to be theirs alone.

When it was determined that nothing else could be done, the royal family departed for their homes. Only Ualan stayed to sit vigil over his wife and brother, promising to send news if there were any changes.

Chapter Fifteen

As the door opened to their home and Pia stepped inside, she studied Zoran. It was late, but she wasn't anywhere near tired. Her body was too on edge by the night's events. They'd walked home in silence, but now that they were alone, Pia wanted some answers.

"Yusef's bride was kidnapped by the Var tonight wasn't she?"

Zoran didn't answer.

"You're planning on getting her back, aren't you? Or do you think they've killed her already?" Pia continued.

Still no answer.

"What did you say to your brothers?" she asked pointedly. "What are you planning to do?"

"Don't concern yourself with it, Pia," Zoran answered. "We will handle it."

"Why aren't you telling me anything?" Pia frowned. "Aren't I part of this? You twice acted tonight as though my life might be in danger--first in the hall when Yusef was attacked, then with the poison. Yet, when I ask to be told what is going on, it's like you don't trust me with the family secrets."

Zoran didn't say anything.

"You don't, do you?" Pia questioned, hurt. "Yet, you expect me to follow your word blindly when you tell me to do something. Pia, don't go to the practice field. Pia, go home. Pia, listen to me for I know what's best for you. What am I to you? Another one of your men to be ordered about? You are not my commander, Zoran."

Zoran's look darkened. He didn't trust himself to speak. She pulled completely away from him, shaking her head.

"I give up, Zoran." Turning her back, she walked away. "I don't understand you at all."

Zoran watched her go. He didn't know how to answer her questions. The truth was he was preoccupied. He didn't know what he was going to do to rescue Yusef's wife--only that it was up to him to come up with a plan. His brother lay dying and he didn't want to let the man down. Frowning in growing irritation, he stormed after his frustrating wife, following her into the bedroom. She was going to lecture him about trust when she refused to tell him anything about her past?

Pia glanced up, blinking in surprise to see him. She was sitting on the edge of the bed about to unzip her boot. Zoran strode directly for her, grabbing her about the shoulders and pulling her up to face him.

"Why should I trust you with my family secrets when you don't trust me with yours?" Zoran's nerves were shot and he was boiling for a fight of any kind. Seeing Pia's face, he picked the easiest stirred battle he knew.

"What?" Pia demanded, incredulously. She tried to shake loose, but he didn't let he go. His eyes boiled like hot lava. "What are you talking about? I have no secrets about your family."

"Why are you here, Pia?" Zoran demanded hotly. His eyes glowed with all the torment and passion inside of him. Too much was happening that wasn't in his control--Yusef, the Var, the kidnapping, his achingly gorgeous wife whose heart of ice he couldn't seem to touch.

"Where?" Pia asked confused. "Why am I in the bedroom?"

"Why did you marry me?"

"W-what?" Pia trembled. The word was no more than a whisper. Her eyes turned down and she tried to pull away.

"Why do you tremble and pull away whenever I try to touch you?" Zoran questioned, his voice lowering, though it was still murderously hard. He gripped her tighter and refused to let her go.

"I told you," she hesitated. "I have to get used to your--"

"Don't give me that," Zoran said. His eyes flashed again. He could sense that she wasn't scared of the Draig. She was hiding something from him. "You've been scared of me since that first night in my tent. I say you're beautiful--"

"Don't," Pia pleaded, trying to break free.

"I say it," Zoran persisted darkly, as if the words only brought him pain, "and you push me away. I touch you and you nearly jump out of your skin. I try ... I try to make love to you and you won't have me. Why, Pia?"

"It's not..." she tried. Her lips tightened and she didn't finish.

"Who was your father to you? Why did he give you that scar? Why do you owe Galaxy Brides all that money? What are you running from? Why are you here, Pia? Why?" Zoran shouted. He was tired of trying to figure her out. Tortured, he ground out, "Why did you marry me?"

"That's not fair," Pia whispered. "You made me marry you. I tried to end it, but you wouldn't let me."

"I don't believe that!" Zoran said. His breathing became labored as he tried to control himself. He didn't want to hurt her. He didn't want to say anything he might regret. "I can tell you want me. I can smell your desire for me even now. So don't tell me you--"

"You won't tell me what I deserve to know," Pia interrupted, not wanting to hear him finish. "But in return would have me bare my soul? It's not like we're in love, Zoran. Yes, I'm your wife and I'll be loyal, but don't act like we weren't an arranged marriage. You bought me from a corporation! I'm paid for, that's all you need to know."

"If you want to know my feelings, all you have to do is ask me and I'll tell you," said Zoran. The thought didn't seem to bring him pleasure and Pia wasn't sure she wanted to hear what he had to say. "I'll be honest with you about them."

"Let go of me," Pia demanded instead of asking. She gazed steadily to him, staring him down. She ripped out of his arms. "How dare you yell at me? I don't owe you an explanation for any of it. It's none of your business what I did or who I was before I got here. I don't ask you about your past. All I ask is that you trust me now. That you tell me what is going on. Why are we in danger? Why was the royal family attacked? Why do we need to fear the Var? Who are they to us? Nothing I ask has anything to do with your past. It's a threat to us now."

"You want my complete trust?" Zoran questioned. His gaze bore into her.

"Yes, by all means," Pia answered wryly. "I have done nothing not to deserve it."

His brow rose, thinking of several instances that he could used to dispute that fact. Instead, he asked, "And you will give yours in return? I have your promise?"

"What do you mean?" Pia questioned wearily, sensing a trap.

"I mean you'll tell me everything and I'll tell you everything. Both of our questions will be answered honestly--no refusals this time."

"Why does it matter?" Pia asked, touching her face, feeling the smooth texture as she remembered her scars. She thought of the dead Rayvikian. She thought of her parents. She thought of the life she'd led. She didn't think he would understand it. He came from such an honorable people. She didn't think he would see her life as honorable.

"It matters, Pia, because you are my wife."

Pia gulped. She wondered how long he would want her for a wife after she told him the truth. But, as she looked at him, she was tired of lying and hiding.

"Shift," she requested softly. Tears came to her eyes.

Zoran's brow narrowed in confusion.

"Just shift," she insisted, grimacing in light annoyance that he didn't automatically obey her.

Zoran slowly shifted to take on the Draig. His golden eyes looked at her swirling like molten lava. Pia looked at him carefully. Now changed, his chest heaved with deeper breaths. Pia went to him, lifting her hand to his face. She felt the roughened texture of his dark skin.

Zoran's gaze bore steadily into her. He felt her heart slowing. He felt her loneliness and her aching. To his surprise, she almost relaxed as she felt him in Draig form. He was careful to keep his hands back from her.

Closing her eyes, Pia continued to touch him, feeling his neck, as she said, "My parents were stationed on an Earthbase on Dagar Twelve. It's one of the moons in what's known as the Dead Man's quadrant. It's called the Dead Man's because everyone on the base didn't exist on record--anywhere. According to the Earth government, the base didn't exist. It's where I grew up."

Zoran held very still. Her eyes opened to look at him and she drew slowly back, letting her hand fall as she sat on the bed. Zoran didn't dare shift back. She actually seemed more comfortable talking to him like this and he wasn't about to do anything to make her close herself off again.

Pia took a steady breath. Zoran was still strong and strangely attractive. But, without the handsome human features or the tormenting look of his brown eyes, she could relax enough to speak to him.

"My parents were spies and assassins," Pia continued. "My father raised me. My mother was killed on assignment when I was about one. Ever since I could walk I was trained to be in the family business, as were the other children on the base. Then, when I was fifteen, the Earth government changed power and thus their politics. The Dagar base was forgotten for about a year, written off as a testing lab for mutated diseases. But, when it was discovered what we really were, the government decided they needed to cover us up. They sent a cleanup crew to kill everyone on the base--including children, babies, even the animals. We never saw it coming. Everything was destroyed."

"But you escaped," Zoran's rough dragon voice probed.

Pia stood and touched her side. Running her finger over the length of her scar beneath her red dress, she said, "All children on the base were outfitted with locators. If anything happened, if we became injured when we were out on the training courses or in some simulated assignment, the locators would go off and a personal medic droid would come retrieve us. They'd drag us to a safe hideout underground and doctor us up. Let me tell you, those droids came in handy and were well used. That's how we started the game of guessing each other's wounds. We had nothing better to do in the recovery unit."

She smiled wryly and shrugged as if it were a normal upbringing.

"My father was good man, Zoran. He was gone a lot on assignment, but he believed in what he was doing. During the attack, he became trapped beneath some rubble. I tried to pull him out, but I wasn't strong enough. He must have known something was wrong because he told me he loved me, grabbed his knife, and gave me this." She pressed her hand to her scar. "I saw him and the rest of my home blow up as the medic droid was dragging me away to safety."

Her eyes turned sad and she sat back down. Pia lightly traced her cheek with a delicate finger. Zoran moved silently to sit beside her. She blinked in surprise to see him shift back to human form.

"I think I like you better the other way," Pia admitted. "It's not so intimidating."

Zoran would've laughed if she wasn't so serious.

"Anyway, ah, after I got out of recovery, I learned most of my friends were dead. Everyone I had ever known was murdered, save for a remaining handful of people. Since we didn't exist, we had nothing, no one, no planet. The assistant director of the base took us under his wing. He had a lot of contacts and he got us out of there. We each gave ourselves a new name, complete with galactic IDs and fake birth certificates. I became Pia Korbin and, before we knew it, we were up and running again as a rogue agency for hire. I was sixteen."

Pia stopped talking. Her eyes were wet but she didn't cry. She lay back on the bed. Lifting up one leg, she unzipped a boot and then the other.

"Why Pia Korbin?" Zoran asked, watching the long line of her legs stretch into the air.

"My mother was Pia. My father was Korbin," she answered simply. "Pia Korbin."

Leaning back on his elbow, Zoran questioned, "What was your name before that?"

Zoran listened to her story in fascination. He wasn't really sure what to think. All he knew was that he really wanted to kiss her, pull her into his arms, and never stop.

Pia chuckled, kicking off her boots. "Seven. As in, seventh child born on the base, born on the seventh of the seventh Earth month."

"You became an assassin?"

Pia sat up. She suddenly realized how much she'd revealed to him. "I think I've told you enough. You should be satisfied with that. I more than answered your questions. You know how I got the scar."

"Pia," Zoran began. She was so beautiful in her red satin dress. It accented her tanned skin, hugged dangerously seductive to her curves. He wanted to touch her.

"It's late," she said. "I'm tired."

"No, you're not," he stated. When her brow rose, he added, "In Draig I can detect such things."

Zoran didn't want to tell her that he felt bits and pieces inside of her--that when she broke his crystal, they were forever joined. He didn't want her knowing she felt inside of him, if she would just open herself up. Until he had her trust and she his, he didn't want her having the power to use his emotions against him. He wasn't sure what she would do with such a power.

"I'm tired of talking about this," Pia corrected wearily. There was no use in denying it since he seemed so sure. She wondered what else he could detect in her. Could he feel the treacherous longing in her body? Could he sense her desperate need to be held by him? "Where did you learn to dance?"

The question took him by surprise and he stared at her.

"I never danced before tonight," she said. "It was fun. Thank you."

Zoran came edged closer to her. "You are a natural."

Pia flushed. "I had a good teacher."

He moved closer. "There are other things I would teach you if you'd let me."

Pia couldn't look away. "Do you really want me to kiss you? Or are you just being nice?"

That brought him up short. Her face was deadly serious, but her words had been soft. Carefully, Zoran asked, "How can you not know the answer to that?"

"I guess I do," Pia said, a deep sadness welling up within her. She stood from the bed and began moving to the closet to change. "I can't say I blame you. I understand perfectly. I mean I never was very pretty, even before the accident."

Pia froze mid-stride. Her arms dropped and she closed her eyes, biting wearily at her lips to keep them shut.

"Accident?" he probed, standing behind her.

"Your Draig must be off tonight," she mumbled. "I have to be tired. I'm rambling and not making any sense."

Zoran forced her to turn around and look at him. Pia's chin lowered to face the floor, not wanting to watch him force himself to touch her. He slid his hand down her arm to her waist to run his thumb over her wound.

"You think because of a little scar, you're not pretty?" he asked, awed.

"I think I'm not pretty because I'm not," Pia answered matter-of-factly. "I have no grand illusions. It's not like they taught a course on self-delusion in between tracking and hand-to-hand combat."

Zoran's hand continued to caress over the red satin, wanting nothing more than to peel it back from her flesh.

"I know you want sons and are duty bound to," Pia hesitated, "do this. I know you're honorable, Zoran, and will always do your duty. I only hope I didn't tarnish your honor by what I told you. I won't repeat it to anyone. And, really, none of the old crew knows I'm here. It's not like they're coming anytime soon for a visit."

"Pia, the medic told me that you," Zoran hesitated. Pia pulled away from him. Her face grew hard. Voicing a suspicion that had been forming in the pit of his stomach, he continued, "He said that you appeared to have had some kind of surgery recently. Is that why you owed Galaxy Brides? Is that why you had to agree to come here? To repay a debt?"

The expression on her pale features was enough of an answer. His heart dropped into his stomach.

"I want to understand," Zoran persisted. "Did something happen on one of your assignments?"

Again, her face answered yes without speaking. She held deathly still.

"You had to change your face, your appearance in order to disappear?" he questioned. "That's what the surgery was, wasn't it? You had to hide your identity?"

Pia nodded. Aside from the small gesture she didn't move.

"Is that why you don't want to be married to me? You were forced to come here and thought to get rejected so you could get out of your debt, but I chose you and ruined your plans?" Zoran felt as if his heart was ripped out of his chest. He wanted her so badly, but for her he was the losing side of a gamble she took to save her own life.

"You're very perceptive," Pia said, her tone cold. "Although, you got one fact wrong. If you didn't choose me, I would still have my debt. Whether it was you and this planet or some other guy somewhere else, in the end I would be married. That was the deal with Galaxy Brides."

Zoran closed his eyes and turned away. She'd been forced. He couldn't bear to look at her. It hurt too much.

Pia, misunderstanding his withdrawal, said, "I'm sorry you're the one who had to get stuck with me, Zoran, I truly am."

Zoran didn't move. Pia crossed over to the lights and dimmed them. He tensed, wondering what she was doing. His eyes shifted to see clearly in the dark. She found him easily, running her hands over his shoulder. She brought her fingers around to feel the front side of his tunic over his chest. Feeling her way down his unmoving body, she unbuttoned his tunic front and pushed it down his arm, baring his chest. His breath deepened. He watched her face carefully, knowing she was blindly feeling him in the dark.

"You said you wanted me to touch you," she whispered. Pia's fingers ran over his chest, willingly touching him. She glided her hands over his stomach. She found the waist of his pants and slowly worked them down over his hips, bending at the knee to take them to the floor.

Zoran wanted her to come to him willingly, but not like this. Not because she was the unlucky participant in a contract, not because she had a debt to fulfill. He wanted her to want him. It was a bittersweet ache she stirred. Though he smelled her desire and knew she did want him with her body, it wasn't enough for him. He wanted her to want him with her mind and her heart. She trembled slightly and he saw her bite her lip. He didn't move.

Pia took her hands and ran them over his calves and knees. She caressed her fingers delicately over his heated flesh, feeling the hair-roughened texture of his legs, moving up to intimately touch the sides of his hips.

"Is this how you wanted me to touch you?" Pia closed her eyes and swallowed. She couldn't see his expression, only felt his breathing deepen and stir against her.

Zoran saw her vulnerable face clearly in the dark. When he didn't answer, too enthralled by her to speak, she ran her fingers up his sides to feel his broad shoulders and neck.

"Do you still want me to kiss you?" she asked.

Pia hoped the darkness would help him forget who she was and what she looked like. Maybe then he wouldn't have to take her so fast in an effort to get it over with, like last time. She leaned in to cautiously kiss his chest.

"Like this?" Pia whispered. She kissed him again. Zoran's breath caught, but he didn't stop her. She lifted her hands to her dress and slowly drew the satin from her shoulders. It whispered over her body as it pooled on the ground, leaving her gloriously naked.

Zoran's body tensed, already hard with desire.

"Did you still want to touch me?" Pia whispered weakly. She stood vulnerable and naked before him, not moving. "Zoran?"

Zoran's hand tightened and lifted. He didn't want her like this, standing before him like a human sacrifice. He didn't want her as a whore he paid for. For, surely, that's how she felt. Why else would she be offering herself to him all of a sudden?

"You don't have to do this, Pia," Zoran murmured. His arms ached to hold her. His body burned with desire. Turning away from her was the hardest thing he'd ever done. He went to the dresser and began looking for a pair of light cotton pants. Finding them easily in the dark, he turned to find her clutching the red satin desperately to her chest. He imagined she felt relief. "I'm sorry if I made you feel you had to repay your debt to me in such a way. I never wanted to force you to do something you don't want to do."

Pia trembled. Her heart squeezed until she thought it would burst. She'd thrown herself at him, offered him everything he'd asked for--touching and kissing him willingly, allowing him to touch her if he wanted. He'd refused and the ache of his rejection was so painful, she could barely hear his words. Not even in the dark was she desirable to him. How could she blame him? Had she told him too much of her past? Was he ashamed to be married to a hired gun?

Pia knew that Zoran had tried to be a husband to her. He tried to do his duty, but it would seem tonight he didn't have the energy to pretend. Her body coursed with precarious emotions and she let the pain overtake her.

Zoran couldn't let himself look at her. If he did, his hard fought for resolve would crumble and he would go to her. Weakly, he said, "You can have the bed, Pia. I'll sleep on the couch tonight."

With a whispering slide of the door, he was gone.

Pia collapsed on the floor, naked and trembling. Her mouth moved to scream her agony, but only a gasp came out. Rocking in the dark, tears began falling soundlessly out of her eyes. She wanted to die.

* * * *

Zoran crossed naked to the bathroom, clutching his cotton pants. Tonight, a cold shower wouldn't be enough to drain the throbbing need from his loins or the torment from his body. She'd pushed him past the point of no return.

If he couldn't release himself inside her, then he would do the only thing he could. He would end the physical need with the fantasy of her in his head. And the other, more tortuous suffering, he would bury in his chest and pray that the pain didn't kill him.

Chapter Sixteen

Zoran left with the dawn, thoroughly exhausted. He'd ducked into the room only long enough to grab a tunic. His eyes had strayed to Pia on the mattress. She slept, sprawled out on the bed. Her arms and legs stretched in every direction.

His duty weighed heavily upon him. If he had to choose between going to fight the Var to retrieve Yusef's bride and facing the feelings he harbored in his heart for his uncaring wife, he gladly picked the first. At least against the Var, he knew it was a battle he could win.

About an hour after arriving on the practice field, Zoran saw the two trackers he'd sent after Yusef's wife. They said it had been hard, but they found her and her Var captors camping in the shadowed marshes. Zoran knew the area. He'd scouted through it before. It was an awful place. The rotting smell of molding plant life and animal carcasses masked even the barest traces of scent from most of their kind--from all but the elite bunch of Draig trackers who were chosen for their highly developed sense of smell.

He sent word to Ualan, Olek, and his father that they were to ride out immediately. Yusef still hadn't awakened and the doctor didn't sound as hopeful as the night before. The fallen Prince was worsening.

Zoran strode across the practice field with only his sword and knife for weaponry. He went to join his brothers, who were swinging up onto their *ceffyls*. Ualan's face was red. Zoran knew from his father that Morrigan had recovered enough to open her eyes early that morning. Whatever she'd said to Ualan had driven him from her side like he was being chased by a pack of demons. The rage would serve him well on this mission.

Ualan snarled darkly.

"There will be enough blood for all of us," Zoran growled in return, seeing his brother's mounting fury, though not exactly disapproving of it. Gripping the center horn of his mount, he swung up behind the beast's bare shoulders. The *ceffyl's* fanged mouth darted open with a hiss of his long tongue.

"Your wife will recover," Olek said to Ualan, joining them. "Her mind is well."

"Not if I strangle her into the grave," Ualan roared fiercely. His face shifted briefly in his rage.

The King rode up beside them. Olek and Zoran exchanged looks. Zoran could well understand his brother's frustration. He too felt it every time he thought of Pia. How he got the strength to refuse her when she offered herself to him, he would never know. Even now he wanted to hold her. His lips ached to feel her mouth. He snarled them into a hard line to keep them from feeling anything.

Ualan growled darkly, swearing under his breath as he kicked his steed into action. Murder flashed in his golden eyes as his *ceffyl* took off. The King looked at his sons. Zoran merely shrugged in return. He had no words to offer his father. He had no words to offer himself. Kicking their mounts, the three men were quickly behind Ualan.

* * * *

Pia was livid to discover Zoran had left to retrieve Yusef's bride without telling her. She had to learn about it from the Queen. Her anger was only made worse by the severe rejection she felt. She'd fallen asleep only after crying her heart out for hours. Her eyes were still puffy and her nose red, but she didn't care.

Queen Mede offered to stay and keep her company. Pia refused, stating she was going to work out and take a shower. The Queen almost appeared disappointed, but Pia didn't care.

The workout had done little to expend her frustrations. The cool shower did nothing to ease the tension in her body. Late in the afternoon word came around that Zoran and the men were back, carting one very alive Princess Olena.

Pia smiled, remembering the redhead who had sat next to her at the Breeding Festival. She liked Olena and was glad she was unharmed. Besides, any woman who could aggravate her husband by not telling him her name was all right by her. Right now, anyone who could aggravate their husband period was all right by her.

* * * *

Zoran didn't go home until late that evening. After taking Olena to her unconscious husband, he had visited with the doctors. To his relief, Yusef's condition seemed to have turned around. His brother still hadn't opened his eyes, but his coloring was better. They didn't know what caused the change, but Zoran wasn't about to question the good fortune.

Looking at his front door slide over his head, he thought, *I need all the good fortune I can get.*

Pia came into the room from the kitchen at the sound of the door. Her eyes hardened as she saw his blood-soaked clothes.

"So much for mutual honesty," Pia ground out.

"Thanks, wife," Zoran said bitterly. "It's good to be home. Your sweet concern for my life and my health overwhelm."

"Oh," Pia sighed in mock gratitude, "and thanks so much for telling me about going off to get Olena from the Var. I'm so glad we had that talk last night about honesty and answering questions. Your forthcoming nature has overwhelmed me. For awhile there I thought I was the only one honoring the bargain."

Zoran's eyes darkened. He was in no mood for this.

Pia really didn't care, as she stated sarcastically, "Oh, wait, that's right! I was the only one being honest last night!"

"Honest?" Zoran snarled, barking the word at her like a wild dog. "You want honest, wife?"

Pia trembled as he stalked across the room to her. His bloodied hands gripped her light cotton shirt and he nearly lifted her off the ground in his irritation. His power thrilled her. Her angry, defiant face excited him.

"Then tell me honestly to my face that you don't want me," he said.

Pia's chest heaved, drawing his eyes down.

"Tell me the truth! Tell me that you only offered yourself to me last night to pay off a debt. Tell me you truly didn't want to marry me and you are only toying with me!" Zoran demanded. He wanted the torment to end. He wished she'd just reach in and grab out his heart. He wanted her to stomp it beneath her boot--anything to kill its painful beating.

"Oh, yeah," Pia thundered back. "Then you admit that all I am to you is a bought and paid for whore that you are duty bound to sleep with for the sake of producing your sons!"

"Fine whore you are," Zoran said. Taking her hand, he roughly pulled it to his erect shaft. "A whore will usually slake a man's desires, not boil them to erupting and never follow through. If you are a whore, you're a lousy one, wife."

Pia snatched her hand away. "Don't you blame your condition on me! I offered to be a wife to you last night. You rejected me, not the other way around. I can't help it if you aren't attracted to me. I turned off the lights. I tried to make it easy on you! Any suffering you have is now your own doing. I wash my hands of it."

"Reject you?" Zoran fumed, his face coming closer. By all that was sacred, she was a beautiful temptress! "You were acting like a sacrifice. There's no passion in you for me. Do you think I relish the idea of forcing you to my bed?"

"I know you don't relish the idea of taking me to it!"

"By all the Gods, woman!" Zoran roared in disbelief. "Are you truly so stupid?"

Pia backed up, hurt. He was calling her stupid? It was like a slap across the face. Her injured hazel eyes stared silently back at him.

Zoran stalked her, not letting her get away. "I have done nothing but try to get you into my bed since the first moment I met you."

Pia gulped. She read the truth of it in his troubled expression. Zoran motioned to the couch.

"Hell, to my everlasting shame, I even practically forced you into it," he said, thinking of her blood on him. When she was backed against a wall, he stopped before her. "It's you who wants none of me."

Pia trembled. He was dirty from the heat of battle but she didn't care. His nostrils flared.

Softly, he reached a hand to her cheek and continued in an agonizing whisper, "You pushed me out of you, Pia, when I wouldn't leave your silken depths. You ran from me screaming. Is that how you would have me take you? Would you have me ravish you? Take you unwillingly? Force you to my bed until you tremble in fear at the very thought of my presence?"

Pia did tremble, but it wasn't with fear. Her whole body shook with the torrent of emotions flooding between them. It was as if she felt every fiber of his body calling to her.

"Is that what you want from me?" Zoran insisted. "Because even now I could do it. My body is on fire all the time for you. You're distracting me. All I think about is touching you. I can't even work anymore without seeing your beautiful face taunting me."

Pia's mouth opened to protest.

"Argh, no!" he yelled, shaking his head. "Do not yell at me for calling you beautiful. I don't know what happened to you to make you so damned unaware of your power over men, and may the Gods help me, I don't really care. All I know is that you are exquisite and I would have you."

Pia's mouth closed.

"I know I cannot conquer your unfeeling heart toward me, Pia," he whispered, tormented by his obsession for her. Closing his eyes, he begged, "But, please, tell me how to win you. What do I have to do to make you want me as I want you?"

Pia hands hesitated, lifting to touch his chest. A ragged breath left her. His words swam in her head. She wanted to believe him, but it was hard. "Zoran, please, I ... I never meant to hurt you."

"Then you don't want me?"

"No," she sighed. He tensed about to walk away. "Wait."

He stopped, turning to bore his eyes into her, searching. His face was hard.

"Let me finish," Pia sighed. "No, it's not that I don't want you. It's ... I never meant to act like a sacrifice. I never meant to torture you."

His heart skipped with a thin trail of hope.

"Before I met you, no man but one even approached me," she whispered. Tears came to her and she pushed past him, needing the distance. Weakly, she admitted, "Oh, I don't want to tell you. I should've just stayed away from this whole mess. I never should've allowed you to marry me. You don't deserve this."

Zoran turned.

"Urgh," Pia began, taking a steadying breath to keep from crying. Sighing, she said, "Fine. I don't know were to begin."

"Why did you come here?" Zoran didn't move, listening carefully for her words. They were soft and she didn't turn to him.

"I told you that I was an assassin and a spy. I had unique qualifications that, ah, allowed me to get into some very seedy places. It's not like we targeted good people. We targeted slave traders, mass murders, cannibals, torture artists--some of them so horrific it makes my head swim to remember what they were capable of." She turned to him, her eyes pleading. "I know it may not matter to you, seeing how I've taken many lives, but I never killed an innocent person. It's important you understand that."

Zoran nodded. His arms crossed commandingly over his chest.

"My last assignment ended about two months before I arrived here. I was sent to Rayvik. It's in the Ice Galaxy. My target ended up being a rival to the Mayor of one of the biggest industrial cities. He'd hired us to wipe out the competition. But, when I saw what sort of man the Mayor was, I retreated and didn't finish my mission. I reported back and was waiting for my orders when...."

Pia's eye narrowed.

"What?" Zoran urged.

"I got drunk. The Mayor's son thought it would be fun to drag me out into the alley and rape me. I killed him and ran away. The Rayvikian Mayor owns a torture club and there's a hefty price on my head to get me there alive. I contacted Galaxy Brides and here I am." Pia's voice was cold as she quickly finished the story. "He was the only other man to ever ... try to ... be...."

Pia waved her hand, dismissing the statement. Zoran already knew the man hadn't been successful in completing his task.

"What unique qualifications did you have?" he asked quietly.

"Last night I didn't tell you everything. When my father ... during that explosion, I was hit too." Pia turned to study his reaction. "I was burnt over sixty percent of my body.

Since the Rayvikians were looking for a scarred woman and the surgeries to correct it would be exceptionally expensive, I had no choice but to become a bride. It took the Galaxy Bride doctors two weeks of constant surgery just to smooth the scarring out."

"So it was either me or terrible death," he concluded.

"I'm sorry, Zoran," Pia whispered. "I know it wasn't what you wanted to hear, but now you know everything. I understand if you want to send me away."

"Where would you go?" he asked, coming toward her.

"I don't know. I have some contacts. I could feel around for a job. As long as the doctors didn't take my picture, I'll manage to disappear."

"Is that what you want?" he asked, carefully studying her.

"No," she whispered, honest.

"What do you want?" Zoran asked, taking another step forward.

"I don't know," she lied. Oh, but Pia did know. She wanted him to kiss her. She wanted to stay here and have him tell her she was beautiful for the rest of her life. She wanted him to love her as she undeniably loved him.

Zoran easily sensed that she was lying.

"Take off your clothes," he ordered her.

Pia blinked, meeting his bold gaze. When she didn't act, he went to her.

"Take them off," Zoran stated more firmly.

"Why--?"

"Do not question me," he broke in darkly. "Just do it."

Pia stiffened but obeyed. Slowly lifting her cotton shirt over her shoulders, she then pushed off her pants. She kicked them aside.

"Don't move," he demanded in a whisper. "I want to examine you."

Pia stood tall. Zoran didn't touch her as he inspected her with the exactness of a commander to his very lovely female soldier. He took steps around her, his eyes devouring every curve. When Pia tried to turn to see what he was doing behind her, he snapped, "Eyes straight."

Pia's breathing deepened. Zoran took a hand to her backside, cupping it in his palm. She tensed.

"Very nice," he murmured in a low, possessive tone. Giving the fleshy mound a squeeze, he said, "Firm."

Pia jumped, trying to move. Suddenly, teeth were on her neck, biting lightly. Zoran let his fangs grow slightly to press in warning to her soft skin.

"I ordered you not to move," he whispered. "If you give me reason to, I can rip the throat from your neck."

Pia held still. Leisurely, he lips took the place of his teeth and kissed her before pulling away.

"What are you--?" Pia tried to ask, her voice weak.

"Silence," Zoran demanded, his tone harsh. He'd heard enough of her words. It was his turn. If it killed him, he was going to make her realize that she desired him as badly as he did her--even if that meant ordering her about to do it.

"Zora--?"

"Silence!" Leaning close to her ear, he whispered, "For someone who was raised on a military base, you certainly lack discipline. Speak again without permission and I'll have to reprimand you."

"Zoran, what are y--?"

Zoran growled, smacking her hard on her backside with the flat of his palm. Pia jumped in surprise even as she almost moaned in pleasure. She bit her tongue. Her knees tried to buckle, but she didn't let them.

"That's better," he urged after time had passed and she didn't move or speak again. He knelt behind her and lightly kissed where his hand imprinted red on her flesh. Coming back up to her ear, he stated, "I don't want to have to punish you, but I will. Do you understand?"

"Yes," she gasped.

Zoran smacked her firmly on her other cheek. This time his hand stayed boldly planted on her heated flesh.

"Yes, what?" he challenged.

"Yes, sir." Pia sucked in a fast breath. Her eyes closed as she nearly swooned.

Zoran firmly hit her again, feeling her tremble beneath his hand. He smelled desire pooling between her thighs to tempt him. He smiled so she couldn't see. Maybe Agro had been wrong. Maybe Pia didn't need to be conquered, but commanded. He was just the commander to do it. Perhaps if he took her will away from her and told her what to do, her brain would stop getting in the way and she would give them what they both wanted.

"Yes, sir, I understand," she answered.

"Good," Zoran murmured, rubbing his hand teasingly over her hip. He growled into her shoulder, "Very nice."

Zoran came around. Pia's eyes were closed and her lips were firmly pressed together. He took his time watching her with his sultry gaze, waiting until she looked at him before he moved.

When Pia finally peeked at him through her lashes, the look on his face was devilishly handsome. His mouth curled at the corner as he purposefully made a show of looking at every naked inch of her. When his gaze stopped at the hair between her thighs, he licked his lips in anticipation.

He lifted his hand, just as high as her breasts. Turning his palm to her, he ordered, "Step forward."

She did.

"Put your breast in my hand. Let me feel it," he ordered.

Pia looked up at him. Her backside still stung with the pleasure-pain of his touch and she didn't think to disobey the command. She stepped up to him and pressed her chest forward, not moving her arms.

"Rub it," Zoran ordered softly. His blank eyes were hiding a wealth of powerful emotions. But he wouldn't frighten her away with them yet. "Make your nipple pucker into my palm."

Pia closed her eyes and obeyed. Raising her chest with ever increasing pants for air, she caressed herself with him.

"Now, the other," he commanded when the nipple became almost instantly erect.

Pia moved. She let her other breast get the same torturous treatment.

"You like that, don't you," he growled. "Tell me you like it."

"I like it," she breathed.

Zoran reached around and spanked her hard. Pia's hips bucked.

"I like it, sir," she corrected instantly.

"Oh," he murmured in a low tone. "You like it when I spank you?"

He spanked her again. Her breast pressed harder into his unmoving palm.

"Yes, sir," she cried. She was rewarded with another slap.

"You're a disobedient woman, aren't you, Pia?" he whispered, though there was no disapproval in his tone.

"Yes, sir."

"You need to be taught to obey me, don't you?" he probed.

"Yes, sir." Pia groaned. Her body ached with need. The very significant places within her throbbed for him.

Zoran pulled his hand away. Pia blinked in surprise.

"Undress me," he ordered.

Pia instantly went to him, no hesitation. She grabbed his battle-stained tunic and pulled it over his head. Then, with the same urgency, she pulled the pants from his hips. She gasped at his hard erection. He lifted his feet to help her with his boots. When she finished, she moved to touch him.

"I didn't give you permission," he said quietly, though he was pleased with her willingness.

Pia drew back.

"I'm sore from fighting," he said, bringing to mind one of his most predominant fantasies of her wet body in the shower. "You will wash me and massage me. Come."

Without giving her time to respond, Zoran turned and marched straight for the shower, turned it on, and stepped in. Sitting on the seat, he placed his arms to the side. It would be sweet torture, but he would let her get used to his body. He watched as she dutifully followed him in. Her nipples, still straining, were instantly moistened with droplets from the shower.

His motioned his fingers to the soap, and said simply, "Wash."

Water sprayed all around her body, wetting her hair. She pushed the locks away from her face and reached for soap. Eyeing him, she didn't know where to begin. Seeing her dilemma, he lifted a foot. Pia dropped to her knees and began gliding her fingers over his flesh.

Zoran's gaze narrowed as he watched her. His body strained painfully, but he didn't hide his arousal from her. He wanted her to see it. He wanted her to feel and explore him. She gripped firmly, massaging his calf muscles with her strong fingers.

Pia felt him tense as she worked her way up to his thighs. He was so strong--pure muscle. She rose on her knees, massaging his legs. Her eyes stayed focused on his arousal and the two soft globes beneath it as she worked her way over his large thighs. It quivered as she neared it.

Pia didn't dare touch his erection as she worked over his hips to his stomach and chest. She rubbed and cleaned all the battle sweat from his glorious skin. Zoran watched her with eyes of liquid fire. She explored his arms and neck. She slid her fingers between his stronger ones as she lifted and washed his hands.

"Stand," she whispered, unable to get his back.

Zoran's brow rose on his manly face.

"Please, sir," she whispered.

He nodded and stood for her, turning around.

Pia rubbed his shoulders more thoroughly from behind. His head dropped and she heard him sigh as she eased the tension from them. She gave the same careful treatment to his back that she had the rest of him, only hesitating as she reached his taut backside.

He turned to eye her and she quickly touched him, massaging and cupping him in her palms as she finished.

Pia drew her hands away. Zoran turned, towering over her. The shower washed off all the soap she'd put on his body. He looked down pointedly at his arousal and said, his voice hoarse, "You missed a spot."

Pia looked down and didn't move.

Zoran took her hand in his, squirted more soap into it, and brought it forward to his member. Moving her hand, he had her cup the base, rubbing the soft globes before moving her fingers around his shaft, lathering himself with her hand. His eyes stayed steadily on hers as he forced her to stroke him several times. It was almost more than his body could take.

Pia felt the unyielding power of him beneath her palm as he made her learn his body. It tortured her and, although she remembered how hard of a fit he was inside her, she suddenly wanted to try it again. Didn't Nadja say the second time wasn't so bad?

Zoran almost lost himself as she tightened her fingers. She took over, stroking him more insistently in her own desire. He groaned and forced her hand from him.

"I think I'm clean enough," Zoran stated, his voice husky. He looked her wet body over. He wanted nothing more than to touch it. If he did, he would never be able to draw this out like he planned. "Wash yourself, wife, and then come into the bedroom."

Pia gulped. Her mouth was dry.

Zoran looked her over with a dominating consideration. "Don't bother to get dressed."

Pia shivered. Zoran strode out of the shower. He grabbed a towel and didn't look back. Collecting herself, she did as he commanded, washing as quickly as she could with shaking fingers.

Chapter Seventeen

Pia couldn't quite get herself to walk across the house naked. She tried. But, in the end, she grabbed a thick terry cloth robe off the wall by the sauna and wrapped it around her shivering body.

Zoran had been exquisite to explore. The feel of him amazed her, the hot texture of his flesh, the deep folds of his muscles, the size of his.... Just thinking about it made her blush furiously in embarrassment and she couldn't finish the thought.

When he looked at her in his commanding way, she really wanted to obey him. She wanted to please him and she wanted to be pleased by him. Her body ached for his touch, knowing that a set of explosives would go off at the lightest of his caresses.

Pia poked her head out of the bathroom door, looking out into the front room. It was empty. Slowly, she inched out, padding barefoot across the wooden floor. She paused to see that the bedroom door was closed.

Pia's heart hammered in her chest. She panicked. Spinning on her heels, she made a move for the front door. Her lips parted ready to call out a command for it to open. She was too late, Zoran had heard her.

"Lose the robe and come here."

Pia shivered. When she looked, he wasn't there but the door was open. A soft flickering came from the bedroom and Pia saw the dancing flames of numerous candles haphazardly trailing along the dresser and floor like twinkling stars.

She clutched the robe to her chest, slowly going to him. Curiosity overcame her fear and she stopped at the bedroom door. Zoran was lounging on the bed naked, waiting for her. Her eyes widened, instantly turning down and away.

When she merely stood, clutching the robe in a deathlike grip that turned her knuckles white, Zoran frowned. He felt her heart beating as if it were his own. He'd detected her hurried footsteps as she came to him only to stop. And, as he heard her heading toward the door, knew she contemplated running away. It would seem he still had some taming to do. Zoran idly smiled, up to the challenge.

Moving stealthily from the bed, he was soon before her. Pia tensed. Zoran grabbed her belt and jerked it from around her waist.

"Take off the robe," he said quietly. Her lips tightened and he lowered his mouth to them. Whispering against her, he let his mouth brush hers, as he urged, "Please, take it off. I'm aching to touch you."

Zoran's hands lifted to her shoulders, delving beneath the material to brush across her skin. He forced the robe from her shoulders and it pooled onto the floor.

"Better," he murmured, as if to himself.

Pia shivered.

"Do not try to hide from me again," Zoran instructed. "From this moment on, I'll look at you and touch you whenever and however I wish. And you will touch me. This is what we both want. You are my wife. You will stay as my wife. None of the other things matter."

It wasn't a question.

"Get on the bed," he told her.

Pia moved in silence and laid down on the low bed, watching as Zoran came over her. She eyed him trustingly, noting how his fiery gaze filled with pleasure when he saw her body beneath his.

"Give me your wrists," he commanded softly. His thighs straddled her. His erection moved close to her skin.

Pia was past the point of conscious reasoning. His words demanded, but his eyes and face begged her not to refuse him. Trustingly, she lifted her hands up to him.

Zoran crossed her arms at the wrists. Taking the soft belt from the robe, he watched her eyes as he bound her wrists together. She wiggled slightly, but didn't fight. Lifting her arms over her head, he made quick work of tying her to the top of the bed. He pulled her hands to make sure she couldn't free herself.

"Do you want me to touch you?" he asked.

Pia nodded, at a loss for words.

"Where?" His lids narrowed over his eyes.

Pia's lips parted, but she couldn't have made a sound if she tried. Her breath came out in ragged pants.

"How about here?" he questioned. Zoran took a finger to her hands, running over her arm to her throat, over her speeding pulse, down her collarbone to sweep across the tops of her breasts. "Do you want me here?"

Pia nodded. She closed her eyes as his fingers narrowed in on her nipples, twirling lightly around them so they budded. Her body stirred with an intense longing.

Zoran thoroughly caressed and explored her upper body, before moving to touch her stomach, rubbing over her legs, whispering past her feet. Pia had never felt anything like it before. Her heart ached. She wanted to cry, but the feelings were so good that instead she moaned. By the time he made the journey back toward her hips, she was squirming against her bindings.

"Where else do you want me to touch you?" Zoran asked.

Pia's stomach tightened and as he drew a finger closer to her heated center, she arched slightly in mindless offering. But Zoran had other plans. Pulling his hands away, he met her open mouth with his, taking in her ragged breaths. Her legs worked beneath him, stirring helplessly against the coverlet.

"Ask me to kiss you," he whispered against her lips.

Pia didn't ask. She arched up, taking his lips with hers. Zoran groaned as her mouth opened and her tongue sought automatically to taste him. He gave back to her with all his expert skill, setting her ablaze with the full tide of his restrained passion. Her knee lifted to rub against his hip. Using all her strength, she tried to pull him closer. Her hands fought to be free so that she could force him to her searching body. She wanted to touch him, explore him, as he had her.

Zoran's mouth broke free. His lips moved down across her body in the same path his hands had taken moments before. He trailed his tongue along her old scar, kissing her hip. His mouth breathed hotly to her center. He nipped at her inner thigh, kissed her from her knee down to her toes before traveling back up the other side. By the time he finished, he'd staked claim to every inch of her, worshipping and conquering at the same time. His lips found one ripe breast, biting and teasing it mercilessly, licking it roughly with his tongue.

"Oh!" Pia screamed.

Zoran growled, giving the other side the same attention. He bit lightly and her hips thrashed up. He bit harder and again she spasmed.

A slow smile came to his lips. Having an idea, he leaned over the bed and took a tapered candle. Holding it high so that the wax would cool some before it dripped on her skin, he let a drop fall across her chest.

Pia gasped loudly, her back arching beautifully for him. Every nerve in her body tingled with pleasure. Her skin was alive, awakened completely for the first time.

He dotted a red trail of wax down the valley of her breasts, over her stomach, to the side of her navel only to stop before hitting her delicate center.

"Zoran." Her breath caught delicately. Oh, but it was the most wonderful torture. "Please."

Those sweet words were what he'd been waiting for. Her eyes sought his, pleading. He licked his fingers and put out the flame before dropping the candle onto the floor.

"Please," Pia gasped, not sure what she was begging for. Sweat beaded on her trembling flesh.

Zoran smiled at her. His large body taut with his desire. He came up over her to kiss her. Her limbs were restless and weak.

"Please?" he repeated softly against her lips. "Do you want me to end your torment?"

"Yes, please, Zoran."

He kissed her again, liking the soft way his name fell from her lips. He moved his hand to her stomach, reaching to test her depths. Gently he rubbed his fingers against her moist center. Shockwaves of pleasure flowed over her and she cried out.

"Open yourself to me," he urged. Pia trembled, a little nervous as he brought his legs between hers. But his fingers felt so good rubbing against her that soon she was mindless to anything but the feelings he put inside her body.

Zoran guided his hips to fit next to hers. Poising himself above her, he kissed her again, stealing her breath from her chest.

Suddenly, the big warrior hesitated. "I don't want to hurt you."

"Zoran," she sighed against his mouth. "You're not hurting me. Please, don't stop now."

"But, before," he began.

"Shhh." She kissed him straining against her bonds. Her body was pulsating with the pleasure he'd given her. "Please, don't stop."

Zoran groaned. Tenderly, he entered her, testing her warm depths. Pia moaned, reaching up to him with her body. This time, he was slow, giving her body time to adapt to his size.

"Oh, Pia," he moaned and he filled her completely. He pushed his hips until he was flush against her. "I've wanted you so badly. Tell me you want me, too."

"Yes," she trembled. "I want you, Zoran."

It was all the encouragement he needed. Words were beyond him as he moved inside her. Pia tensed, never having felt anything as sweet as Zoran's possession. He made love to her slowly, savoring every emotion. His hips thrust in an even rhythm, working into her as he lifted his body above hers.

Then, when they couldn't draw it out any longer, he brought her to meet his climax. Zoran tensed, yelling loudly his conquering possession as he released himself into her. Pia whimpered at the onslaught of pleasure, beyond everything but the man above her. Her whole being shook as tremors racked her body. Everything inside her exploded into one glorious moment.

Out of breath Zoran collapsed next to her. Pia was too scared to open her eyes, scared that she'd wake up from the dream. Zoran released her wrists, drawing them down to kiss the reddened flesh.

"Look at me," he urged. Pia opened her eyes. Rising up on his arm, he sighed. "You look so beautiful right now."

Pia looked down. Zoran followed her eyes and chuckled. Flicking his finger over her skin, he gently pried the wax from her body.

"Was...?" She peeked up at him from between her lashes.

Zoran smiled, seeing the vulnerable look on her face. Lightly, he kissed her. "You were perfect."

Pia gulped, but didn't protest.

Zoran groaned, forcing himself to sit up. Walking naked and unashamed through the bedroom, he blew out the candles. Pia watched him, loving the look of him. He eased the coverlet out from under her. Pulling her into his arms, he held her close.

Pia closed her eyes. She was overwhelmed with her feelings. She didn't want to face them or give them a name. But even if she didn't say it, she knew she loved him. She loved him like she'd never loved anything. It terrified her.

Zoran had forced her to face the depths of her passion, knowing she needed him to control her. When she discovered those depths, he'd released her. His was a gift more precious than any she had ever received. She didn't want it to end, but knew, like everything, that it must end. A gift, such as he, was too precious to hold onto forever. The gleam he had for her would soon tarnish and disappear. And she would be trapped with the distant memory of it.

* * * *

Zoran's hunger for his wife was insatiable. He'd thought that finally realizing his passion for her would get her out of his head. It was no use. She could walk across the room and he would want to make love to her. Each and every time he went to her, she would blink in surprise that he could want her again.

But he did want her and he took her. After stiffening, followed by a moment of weak incoherent protest, Pia melted easily into his arms each time. When Zoran left for work in the morning, she was almost relieved, ready for the break. However, when he came back in the evening, she was eager to discover what new delights her husband had to teach her.

He was gentle each time and Pia wondered at the restraint. She saw the eagerness in him tempered back. That first time on the couch had been wild and rough. He'd been almost crazed. She wanted to try that. She was too embarrassed to ask.

He made love to her on the couch, in front of the fire, with the flames turning their skin a golden hue. He caught her in the exercise room, swept her sweat-laden body into his arms and claimed her in the hot spring, teaching her to ride him astride, controlling her hips with his large, strong hands. Mostly, he took her to his bed. He didn't bind her again, didn't drip wax, keeping his love play tender and sweet. He treated her like a delicate flower.

It was wonderful, but Pia was no delicate flower.

During the day, Pia spent time with the other Princesses, excluding Olena, who spent every moment caring for Yusef. Pia even started to like Queen Mede some, though she was still hesitant around the woman. She took her meals in the common hall along with the rest of the family. A high alert had been set on the kitchen and staff after Morrigan's poisoning, so it was a little more tense than usual when they gathered together. The men didn't join them often, taking their meals wherever they practiced and strategized.

When Nadja mentioned how Pia was training her to fight, Morrigan had been only too happy to join in the lessons. So, when they weren't roaming about the village with the Queen--during which time, Pia noticed they were always followed at a distance by a Draig guard--they were self-defense training in Pia's home.

Pia frowned, eyeing the punching bag in anger. Her muscles were sore, but it felt good. Morrigan hadn't showed up for her knife throwing lesson, but Pia was secretly glad for it. She was in no mood to be pleasant. She wanted blood.

Pia had been kicking the punching bag, pretending it was her husband's face. She'd told Zoran everything about her, but he still didn't confide what was going on. They were lying in bed, their bodies sated, when she'd asked him, "Have you found the men who attacked Yusef?"

"No," had been his answer. "But we will."

"Do you suspect a threat?" she asked, snuggling trustingly into his warmth. She traced patterns over his chest with her fingers. "Do they plan something?"

"No, they merely took an opportunity to strike," he murmured into her hair, giving her temple a light kiss. "We have nothing to fear from the Var."

And she had believed him! She should've detected his lie, if not for her being distracted by his warm kisses on her neck and the erotically bold hand on her hip.

"No threat, huh?" she asked, kicking the bag in quick succession until her leg hurt so badly she had to stop before falling over.

Pia had tried to go out to the forest for a jog by herself, only to be stopped by the same Draig guard who had been following them for the last several days. When she tried to skirt past him, demanding he step out of her way, he'd told her that the forest was off limits and he wasn't to allow her to enter it. When she asked why, he told her that the Var enemy had been sensed within the colossal forest and it wasn't safe.

The Princesses, it seemed, were not to go anywhere alone. The castle security was on the highest alert and it was suspected another attack would undoubtedly befall the royal family. Her life, along with the other Princesses, was in danger.

When she'd tried to go anyway, the Draig warrior had called out an order and she was surrounded by an entire battalion of soldiers--they just popped out of the trees like they'd been watching her all along. She hadn't even suspected they were there. Then she was informed that she would be subdued by any means necessary if she persisted in trying to defy the ... oh, and this was the best part ... the *Captain of the Guard's* order.

"Nothing to worry about," she growled, kicking with her other leg. "I'll show that overbearing, lying barbarian Zoran nothing to worry about! When I'm through with him he'll wish the Var had attacked!"

She continued to mutter under her breath. She couldn't believe she'd trusted him and he was treating her like delicate little housewife! How dare he patronize her! She'd faced worse threats than a barbaric Var King bent on taking over a kingdom. And even if she hadn't, there was no reason why he shouldn't trust her enough to tell her what was happening.

Honesty and trust, she thought bitterly. That's what he'd said he wanted between them. Obviously, what he'd meant was her honesty and her trust, oh, and her complete and utter submission to him!

Pia wailed on the bag, denting it with her fists and feet. This time she didn't stop until her body collapsed on the floor, her heart thundered so hard it nearly exploded from her chest, and her lungs burned with the need for air that couldn't be gasped fast enough.

* * * *

"My lord, your presence is requested in communications."

Zoran turned around from where he watched a hand-to-hand combat training on the practice field. The young soldier who spoke was looking at his brother, Ualan.

At the soldier's words, Ualan looked up from were he held his knife to a young warrior's throat. Sighing, he tapped the man's neck, indicating the kill shot. Standing, he nodded at Zoran before tossing the blade to him. Zoran caught it with one hand, barely blinking as he turned back around to watch a practice fight.

Ualan had been in a bitter, dark mood since before they'd left to reclaim Princess Olena. The soldiers normally tried to avoid the future King as if he carried the blue plague.

Zoran, whose body sung with pleasure each time he thought of his beautiful, passionate wife--which was about every three minutes--couldn't have been more opposite in temperament. He even commanded the men with a small smile on his face, which surely the whole military had noticed. He still was hard, pushing the men to be the best, but there was a gaiety to him that the men had never seen before.

Zoran wanted to make love to his wife almost every waking moment. Even after he'd claimed her and his body was well spent, a small part of him wanted to do it again. He couldn't get enough of her. He wanted to feel her beneath him, wanted to taste her lips with his. He was addicted. He wanted more of her, wanting to explore the wild untamed depths of her passion.

In the past, he'd never restrained himself when it came to seeking physical pleasures. But the whores he'd been with had been experienced and understood what he wanted. Pia was still innocent. He'd seen the way she reacted that first time, running away crying into the bathroom. Now that he had her trusting him, he didn't want to risk sending her off just because he had the urge to bend her over the dining room table and take her wildly from behind. Or because he wanted her to tie him up blindfolded and dominate his flesh into a pleasure-pain frenzy.

No, he had to be gentle. Not that gentle was bad--he just knew the other, rougher stuff could hold amazing climatic rewards. However, faced with the prospect of some or nothing, he would gladly take the some and not complain one bit.

Glancing over his shoulder, Zoran watched as Ualan walked off. Nodding to the out of breath soldier his brother had just knocked down, he motioned to him to rise and join the others in hand-to-hand combat.

Zoran looked to the sky, detecting the blue sun's position. He'd have to wait about another hour before he could knock off early for the day and give the men a break. Thinking of Pia, he smiled, suddenly having the strangest urge to run home.

Chapter Eighteen

Zoran rushed home. The last hour of practice had been torment as his body jolted with the excitement and promise of his desire. The training period was nearing its end and Zoran would be given a long break, which he planned on spending with his wife, so long as there was no war to be fought. He was happy to report to his father that nearly a quarter of the men were ready for their final testing. It was an impressive group that would be moving on, joining the official ranks of the army.

The training session had lasted three years. Those who didn't move went on for another three years--though that wasn't unusual. It was normal for the Draig legions to spend twelve or more years mastering their basic skills before moving to a more specialized field.

Instantly, his Draig senses detected Pia in the exercise room. Envisioning her body glistening with sweat, his body surged. Dropping his sword on the table, he went for her.

Pia was punching at the punching bag and didn't hear him. He heard her mumbling to herself, but he couldn't make out the words. A big smile on his masculine face, he watched her back side flex with a kick. She'd been working out a lot lately and he could definitely see a difference from when she'd first arrived.

"Hello, Pia," he said softly, his voice automatically dipping into the low, come-hither tone that usually sent chills along her spine.

Pia stiffened. Her arms dropped and she didn't turn to him. Looking down, she slowly unwound the protective bandages from her hands.

Zoran's smile deepened and he took a step forward.

"Dare to touch me again, dragon," she said in a low tone, before turning to glare at him, "and I promise to send your nose into the back of your skull."

Zoran's smiled faltered in puzzlement, surprised by the evilness of her dark tone and by the way her eyes were looking emotionlessly at him.

Pia's gaze dared him to try and touch her. He didn't move as she came toward him, thinking maybe she was playing a game. But, then, to his surprise, she continued past. Without a backwards glance she went into the bathroom, shut the door on him, and turned on the shower.

Zoran moved to follow her. Sliding open the door, he stepped into the bathroom. Her clothes were stripped from her body, piled on the floor, and she was scrubbing her skin with an incensed fury.

"Pia?" he questioned, worried.

"Get away from me, Zoran," she said, turning to work on her hair. She lathered it with the same incensed passion she'd given her skin before quickly rinsing it. "If you take a step closer, one of us won't be leaving this bathroom alive."

"Pia," Zoran said darkly. She put conditioner in her hair and quickly rinsed it. Demanding, he asked, "What goes on here?"

Pia threw open the door, glorious in her wet nakedness. She grabbed a towel and wrapped it around her body.

"Out of my way, Zoran." Her sinister expression spoke volumes.

"Not until you tell me what's going on," he countered, crossing his hands over his chest. He stared at her menacingly.

Pia was still too angry to take heed. Blinking deceptively, she dropped the towel and strode toward him. Zoran's eyes automatically dipped down her body to watch it. His mouth became dry. She stepped up to him and stopped.

"According to you," she stated with false sweetness. "Nothing goes on here at the palace. Everything is fine."

Pia's lips curled into an instant snarl and she gave him a mighty shove. Zoran, who had been staring at her heaving breasts, thinking how much he wanted to push her up against the counter and rough ride her, was taken off guard. He lost his balance. His arms flailed as he tumbled backwards into the hot spring.

Pia didn't turn back as she heard him splash. His dark curses followed. A slight smile of shallow victory came to her face as she went to the bedroom and shut the door. Taking the dresser, she pushed it in front of the screen to block him from entering. Then, she dressed slowly into some comfortable cotton drawstring pants and a loose shirt, and went to bed early.

* * * *

"None of the men will fight us," Zoran said irritably to his brothers. He glanced from Ualan to Olek and then back again. He'd just spent one very long and uncomfortable night on the couch. Pia had locked him out of his own room. When he ordered her to let him in, she'd just laughed and told him to get lost. Then, that morning when he said he needed to get a change of clothes, she'd stuffed his tunic through a shallow opening between the sliding door and the top of the dresser. Snarling to his brother, he growled in irritation. "They say our mood is too black. They are frightened we will kill them."

Zoran looked over at the men who had carefully edged across the exercise field to get away from the angry Princes. He couldn't say he blamed them. But it didn't mean he had to like it. Their frowns deepened. With the only outlet for their rage quickly retreating, they were stuck.

"What the hell are we supposed to do now?" Olek growled, voicing their sentiments as he stormed away to the palace. Zoran and Ualan were quick behind him.

* * * *

Olek and Nadja's home was filled with lush plant life and giant fish tanks that took up two entire walls. In the center of the front hall was a natural water fountain, relaxing and calm in its resplendent beauty. It did nothing to soothe the sour temperaments of the four Princesses.

Looking around at the other high-backed chairs, Pia noticed the other women looked as dismal as she felt, especially Morrigan whose unusually pale face and red eyes screamed that she was hungover. Stretching her arms over her head, Morrigan yawned. It was the most movement she'd made in awhile.

"Hienrich is now training as a soldier. I released him from his duty to us," Pia said in answer to a question about the boy.

Olena didn't understand, but the others nodded in understanding.

"So, have any of your husbands lied to you about who they were?" the dejected Princess Olena asked. She was the newest member to their miserable ranks. Her red hair was pulled back into a bun and her green eyes flashed with continuous mischief, even when she wasn't up to something. She looked none the worse for wear after her ordeal with the kidnappers, but she also wasn't speaking of it.

"I thought mine was a prison guard," Pia chuckled darkly to herself. *Just another one of Zoran's lies.*

"I used to call mine a gardener," Morrigan mused, tucking her hand beneath her head on the high-backed chair. Mumbling softly, she said so as not to disturb her delicate head, "And a caveman."

The women chuckled. Nadja just blushed shyly, and admitted, "I call mine a dragon."

"They're all dragons, if you ask me." Morrigan winked at Nadja.

Nadja halfheartedly laughed as she rose to answer a summons from the door. Blinking in surprise to see the Queen, she allowed her in.

Mede stepped into the intimate circle of women and nodded. "I heard you all were hiding out here."

Pia turned her eyes down, not wanting the woman to try and cheer them from their mutual sulk. Misery loves company and the Princesses were beyond miserable.

"How's Yusef?" Olena asked, suddenly blushing at the outburst. She refused to glance around at her comrades.

"Still awake," the Queen answered. "And still with his brothers. They speak of fighting and fighting always makes warriors happy, for it's something they know how to do."

Olena nodded, leaning back in her chair and trying to pretend like she didn't care either way. No one was fooled.

Mede glanced at the hungover Morrigan and raised her delicate brow slightly. Morrigan had to turn away. To her credit, the Queen said nothing.

Nadja suddenly asked if anyone wanted something to drink. Morrigan balked and instantly declined, turning a shade paler. They all laughed, despite their mood.

"No, dear, we're fine," the Queen answered. Silence followed. Mede was disappointed that the women weren't going to continue to talk freely. She'd heard their soft laughter and had been anxious to be a part of it. She knew the women were troubled in their own ways. She couldn't blame them. Her sons were great men, but were sometimes too stubborn for their own good. Announcing, she said, "Daughters."

The Princesses looked at her expectantly. Pia's eyes narrowed as she studied the Queen. Mede came forward and took a seat amongst them, looking them over in turn.

"Enough of this. This planet is in desperate need of more women and I intend to see that each one of you explores the power you possess," the Queen said.

Pia sat forward in curiosity to hear the woman out.

"Your husbands are warriors," Mede stated. "I expect each of you has a clear idea now of what that means. But just because they made the rules, doesn't mean you can't use them. You have more power than you think. So, tell me your problems with my sons and I'll give you the Qurilixen solution. I think it's time that the royal woman had the upper hand for once."

Pia lowered her eyes, thinking about that. If she gave the Queen a chance it was possible she could have a very powerful ally. It was time she got the upper hand against Zoran. No more of this sulking! She was going to beat the warrior at his own game!

Slowly, one by one, the women smiled, growing more and more trusting of the earnest Queen. The Queen nodded, happy. Yes, this was how it was supposed to be with daughters. She'd waited too many years to let her sons ruin her plans for a giant family.

"Pia," the Queen began, looking pointedly at the woman. In that moment, Pia was well aware the Queen knew her hesitance for her, but was being patient. "Why don't you go first?"

Pia sat up, looking around at her new family. Something struck inside of her. This was exactly what she wanted. It's what her life had been missing ever since her world exploded that night all those years ago. She wanted a home. She wanted a place to belong and to fight for. And--to coin one of Zoran's phrases--*by all that was sacred*, she was going to have it, whether her commander of a husband liked it or not.

* * * *

Zoran hurried home, his heart hammering in his chest. He'd been visiting with Olek and Yusef in the medical wing, waiting for Yusef to get the final results from his most resent blood test so that he could leave the medical ward, when his mother's servant came to retrieve him.

Leading him into the hall, the servant had given him a missive from his mother. It said the Queen had been to his house and there was an emergency at home. She didn't write what, but that it had something to do with Pia and a sword.

Thinking she'd hurt herself again, he ran to be with her. The door slid open and he rushed in, his heart thudding in fear, his whole body tense. His eyes flew to the couch, remembering how he'd come home to find her with the medic.

Urgently, his hoarse voice called out, "Pia!"

"In here," came the soft answer from his bedroom. He looked, seeing that the door was no longer blocked. Rushing forward, his eyes were desperate to see for themselves that she was well. Once in the bedroom, his eyes darted around. Nothing.

Suddenly, a sword poked into his back. Pia's voice washed over him, as she commanded, "Move and I'll skewer you."

Zoran tensed, ready to do battle. Her next words stopped him from disarming her.

"Prince Zoran, Captain of the Guard, you are now my prisoner," Pia stated. Behind him, she grinned. She wore one of his dark tunics with a red dragon surrounded by a shield on the chest and nothing else. Her bare legs poked out from beneath the folds. Her eyes unabashedly roamed over his firm backside.

The Queen had been most helpful in her advice to the Princesses and now that Pia had a plan of action, she felt three-hundred percent better. Mede told her that with a man like Zoran, she needed to be bold. She had to command the commander, conquer the conqueror in order for him to respect her completely.

Zoran was used to being in charge, doing what he wanted, having every order followed. Her husband answered only to one man, the King. So, in order to earn his trust and his respect, she had to be the one in charge--bold and unflinching, in absolute control. She had to make him realize that he had to answer to someone much more important than a King. He had to answer to a wife.

Zoran waited to see what she would do with him. Excitement and fierce desire flooded him at the dangerous game she played.

"Pia," he began in warning.

"On your knees, prisoner," Pia said. When he didn't readily obey, she kicked him in the back of the knee, forcing him to drop to the floor. "You will speak only when asked a direct question. Do you understand?"

Zoran said nothing, his jaw lifted.

Pia chuckled, letting him hear that she was unconcerned with his defiance. "I have ways of making you talk, prisoner."

The blade again poked his back. His groin filled--hardening and becoming eagerly erect.

"Take off your shirt," she said huskily. Her voice was quiet. "Let me see that you have no weapons."

Zoran grinned. He couldn't help it. With one swift movement, he obeyed. Tossing his shirt to the side, he knew she would find the knife behind his back.

The tip of her sword slowly edged over his shoulder by his neck. He watched the blade as it barely missed the tender flesh of his throat. She took the knife from his waist and he heard it being tossed aside.

Pia studied the hard lines of his back. Not a measure of fat marred his flawless body, as muscles sculpted his taunt flesh in a symphony of masculine perfection.

"Put your hands above you head before I cut it off," she demanded quietly.

Zoran stubbornly refused. The blade dipped by his flesh, brushing it slightly as she lifted his chin up with the blade. He lifted his hands and placed them on the back of his head.

Pia went forward, lashing his wrists tightly together with leather straps. He could have fought her, struck her down while her hands were busy tying him, but he waited, letting her little plan unravel. His nostrils flared, detecting the awakening perfume of her feminine pleasure as she dominated him.

Pia was busy looking over his back and strong arms, liking the way his muscles bulged beneath his flesh, erotically pleased by the look of the dark leather restraints to his wrists.

"Now what?" Zoran chuckled, mockingly.

Pia shook herself back into action. With the back of her hand, she knocked him over the head. "Quiet!"

Zoran instantly obeyed. His breathing deepened.

Throwing a long strip of leather rope over a high beam on the ceiling, she tied one end to Zoran's hands and pulled. Zoran was forced to stand, his hands brought high. Pia tied the other end to his wrists as well, trapping him up.

She smiled, very pleased with herself. As she came around to face him, she rested the sword over her shoulder. Zoran's brown gaze dipped with a scorching fire over her attire. She looked damned sexy in his war council tunic. His eyes glinted with golden purpose, causing her to frown.

"Shift and I'll be forced to run you through," she said, her face very serious. As if to prove her point, she took the sword to his waist and held it to his stomach. Zoran tensed, his eyes piercing daringly into her, challenging her to lose her composure.

Pia was enjoying herself immensely and didn't even flinch at his fiery look. She moved to set the sword on the floor beside her.

"You'll never get away with this," Zoran said, like a good defiant prisoner. His jaw hardened.

"I already have," Pia mocked.

"What do you want?"

"In due time," she said, "but first...."

Pia made a great show of studying him. Her eyes moved over his nipples, already budded with the excitement of his straining body. His long hair fell over his shoulders, a lock caught between his determined eyes to slash across his bold nose. Every defined ridge of his stomach flexed with his deep breath. Taking a finger to the center of his chest, she pressed her nail, scratching down to his navel to the little treasure trail of hair she found there.

"Let's just make sure you don't have anymore weapons hidden, shall we?" she mused. It wasn't lost on her, as she unlaced his pants, that his entire body was a hot, hard weapon. With a jerk, she tugged the material from his hips, baring him to her completely. His pants hung about his ankles. Pia eyed the full length of him, already at full arousal. She almost gasped seeing it, but quickly caught herself.

"Why don't you disarm that weapon?" he suggested. His voice was a guttural plea. "It looks as if it could be dangerous."

Zoran's body tensed when it looked as if her hand was going to touch him, but at the last minute her course changed and she leaned over to take a knife from his boot. Bouncing it on her hand, she turned and threw it across the room, embedding it into the wall. Zoran body leaped in excitement of her skill.

"I think I can handle it," she answered, turning back. "Besides, only good prisoners are rewarded in such ways."

Zoran's eyes lit. He instantly understood the rules of her game.

"Kick off your boots."

Zoran instantly obeyed, kicking off his pants in the process to stand before her naked.

"Ah," she nodded in approval. "Glad to see you understand who is in charge here."

"Where's my reward?" he asked, his body straining for her.

"What do you want?" she asked, pursing her lips together and looking him over.

"Your clothes," he answered, eyeing her with a hunger. "Take them off."

"What?" Pia asked, smiling prettily. She took up the edge of the tunic and lifted it over her thighs. Giving him only the barest peek of her nether hair, she dropped it back down. Zoran groaned in protest. "Sorry, you are in no position to command me."

"Untie me, Pia," he ordered. His body lurched to take her.

"No, I have a few questions for you first."

"What?" His eyes darkened suspiciously. Suddenly, he pulled with renewed force to be free. The binds were too tight.

"Tell me about the threat of the Var."

"There's no threat--" he began.

Pia slapped him across the face, leaving the imprint of her hand. She demanded again, louder, "What is the Var threat?"

"They have been sensed outside the forest. It's believed that they plan to overthrow us and take the Draig throne. It's possible they seek to harm anyone of the royal family, though they more than likely will go after the King and Queen first," Zoran answered. As he said the words, he could tell she already knew as much.

Pia stepped up to him. He tried to pull away, but she pressed her body into him and lifted on her toes. To his surprise, she dragged her tongue slowly over his cheek where she'd struck him only to lightly suck the tip of his ear between her teeth and bite.

Pia felt his heartbeat quicken. She soothed the bite with her lips, before whispering, "Much better, prisoner."

When she pulled back, his eyes were swirling golden fire. Pia dragged her hand into the sensitive bend off his throat before trailing down.

"Why did you not tell me this before?"

Zoran didn't answer. Pia frowned up at him and flicked his nipple with her nail. His body jerked.

"Why?" she insisted. Again she flicked him. Zoran closed his eyes, moaning in pleasure.

"I wanted to protect you from it," Zoran answered, mindless to what he said. He only knew he didn't want her to stop her wonderful torture.

Pia rewarded him with soft licks to his erect nipples. He rewarded her with a groan of longing so intense it shook her to the core.

"What do we know for sure?" she demanded.

When he didn't readily answer, she lifted her tunic slightly for him to see her upper thighs. His head turned, eagerly waiting her unveiling. She stopped right before she reached her naked sex.

"We know the Var have been..." He gulped. She lifted the tunic higher. "They've been overbold as of late. We..." He saw her hips clearly, her legs parted slightly in her dominating stance. "...know they plan something, we just can't seem to discover what."

When his words stopped her movement stopped. Zoran tilted his head as far to the side as it would go. He could almost see the bottom curve of her breasts.

"We believe they have broken into the royal offices to study blueprints of the palace," he offered hopefully.

Pia tossed the tunic over her head and stood before him naked. Zoran's mouth fell open, ready to devour her.

"Pia," Zoran moaned, the words were a plea. His eyes dipped over her skin. Her smell was driving his enhanced senses mad. The beast within him stirred with lust until he could only think of taking her. In his most commanding tone, he ordered her, "Untie me now."

"One more thing," she said instead. "What are we doing about this problem?"

"The war council has been called to meet tomorrow," he rushed. "It's our law that the Var be given a chance to defend themselves before we declare war. The noble households have been alerted and those who wish to will come. Now, untie me."

Pia eyed him one last time, taking the opportunity to go to him. Taking her hand to his erect member, she boldly stroked it. His face tightened as she played with him.

"Good prisoner," she murmured in the most seductive tone he'd ever heard.

"Climb on me," Zoran urged, thrusting his hips into her fingers as he dipped his face forward in an effort to catch her lips. He missed. "And I'll show you how good I really am."

Pia backed away from him. Her body was heady with power in the face of his need. She'd learned what she needed to for now. Turning around, she didn't think as she bent over to pick up the sword.

Zoran saw her backside as she leaned over and howled. He lurched against his ties. They wouldn't give. It didn't stop him from trying. Pia smiled. Slowly rising, she stopped with her backside still pushed out to him as she glanced over her shoulder. He was fighting his restraints with a force she had never seen in him. His eyes were powerful in their liquid glory.

"Oh," she teased. "Do you like it when I do that?"

He nodded, reduced to nothing more than grunts and moans. His nostrils flared, smelling her. She detected a slight shifting above his eyes as his brows lowered.

Pia turned with the sword. She blinked with innocence. "I would let you go, but I'm scared you might try to punish me for my insolence. I might just have to leave you there."

Zoran growled, his expression saying he had every intention of punishing her in the most pleasurable way possible.

Pia was surprised when he didn't speak. It was as if he was reduced to the most basic of primal instincts. He was a dragon and by the look in his eyes, he was going to mate.

Thrilled, she swung the sword over his head, breaking through the leather that held him to the ceiling. His bound wrists dropped, still tied. He stalked toward her. Pia dropped her sword in her haste to back up. Zoran lunged. His wrists hooked over her head, capturing her to him.

He breathed in ragged pants for a moment, as he reveled in his capture of her. Then, he ordered, "Get on your hands and knees."

Pia gasped at the force in him as he threw her toward the bed. She landed on her stomach. Zoran was instantly behind her with his supernatural speed, kneeling as he forced her legs apart. He hooked his wrists around her neck and pulled her to kneel before him. She groaned in excitement of his rough passion.

Zoran aimed, too far gone to stop himself as his animalistic aspect took over. Striking with a calculated accuracy, he pulled back on her neck to embed her completely on his shaft. He shouted in ruthless gratification. Pia gasped. His thighs pushed her legs apart, opening her helplessly to him.

Controlling her with his bound wrists Zoran thrust, driving hard and fast as he rode her in frenzied passion. He forced her to match his need, howling and grunting his enthusiasm behind her.

Pia thrilled in the uncontrolled fury of his claiming. Soon her body was pushed beyond where it had ever been.

Zoran pumped his muscular hips, slamming her back onto his thick erection. It was the most magnificent feeling of indulgence and power. Even as he controlled the movement, he knew that Pia had all the power over him.

She'd conquered his heart with her bold ways. She commanded him completely.

Pia screamed, moaned, gasped, breathlessly begged for him to continue. His name left her lips with a desperate plea for more. She couldn't take it, she felt the end coming for her, and she felt him riding her higher, higher--*ahhh!* Pia tensed, trembling uncontrollably as she quaked in climax.

Building wonderful friction with each thrust, Zoran didn't slow, plunging faster, faster, deeper, claiming. Feeling her moist heat--so luxurious and hot--quivering around him, he was lost. With a yell, he tensed. His stomach tightening painfully as he spilled his seed within her.

Jerking her back onto him a few last times, marking her as his, Zoran rode the tremors out, frozen behind her like a statuesque god. Pia groaned as he unhooked her neck and allowed her to fall to the mattress.

Zoran shivered as she slid off his lowering arousal. Sanity gradually returned. He looked down, guilt trying to invade him as he realized what he had done. Pia didn't move. He climbed back. To his surprise, she rolled over. A soft purr came from her throat as she looked at him. Her neck was red from where he'd controlled her, but she didn't seem to notice.

Her body singing with delight, Pia licked her lips. The feelings inside her were too good not to experience again and again. She pulled forward to stand before him. Grabbing onto his bound wrists and giving them a firm jerk of control, she eyed his lowering member and said, "Where do you think you are going, prisoner? Your prison sentence isn't over yet."

Zoran's surprise increased tenfold. She'd enjoyed his rough passion as much as he.

Pia jerked his arms again and moved her fingers to his spent manhood. Taking him firmly in hand, she decreed, "I'll give you time to recover. But mark my words captive, you will be showing me more of that."

Zoran grinned, his eyes narrowing. Oh, he had a lot more to show her. To his amazement, his loins twitched in her hand. He wouldn't have thought it possible, but his member tried to rise to the occasion.

"So how many times can you go?" she challenged. Pia licked her lips as she smiled mischievously. Looking his naked body over, her brow rose and she asked, "And exactly how many different ways does this thing work?"

Chapter Nineteen

Zoran was exhausted, having no desire to get out of bed and leave the warmth of his wife's body. Pia snuggled into his side, her head lying on his arm. Seeing her parted lips, he could not stop himself from kissing her.

Pia moaned sleepily in protest against his mouth, although she didn't draw away. Weakly, she mumbled, "No, Zoran, no more."

He chuckled, teasing softly against her temple, "But you said one more time."

Pia lifted one very lazy lid to eye him. She had indeed said one more time, but that was last night and they'd done it one more time, and one more, and one more.... Her body was too sore to even contemplate another bout so soon.

"Tyrant," she said before laughing softly.

"I take it you no longer want to shove my nose into my skull," he whispered. His kisses lightly found her temple as his nose nudged her.

Pia finally managed to open both eyes to look at him. Looking him over seriously, she said, "You shouldn't have lied to me."

Zoran's smile faded. "I didn't mean to lie. I meant to protect you."

"I don't need you to protect me. I can take care of myself."

"Pia," Zoran began only to sigh. It was getting late and he needed to meet with the war council. Already his brothers were probably waiting for him. "It's my duty to protect you and every other person under Draig rule. I know you can handle yourself, but don't ask me not to do my duty."

Well, if he puts it that way, she thought, secretly liking the fact she was under his protection. She was too tired to pick a fight. So instead, she teased, "Well, you might lead the Draig armies, prisoner, but I command you."

"Is that so?" Zoran laughed at her audacity. But as he looked at her lovely face, surrounded by her tousled blonde hair, he knew it was true. She did command him. He would never dare to tell her as much.

"Mm," Pia agreed. A mischievous smile came to her lips, as she said, "Hey, I guess that means I really control the Draig armies."

"If you had a need of them, I would gladly send them to conquer the world," he said gallantly.

Pia chuckled. Nodding her chin down his body, she admitted, "I saw that it leaked, but I had no idea it leaked out your brains."

Instantly, Pia's face turned red at the admission.

Zoran's hearty laughter filled the bedroom, amazed that she could still be embarrassed after the night they had. Knowing he had to get dressed, he finally pulled away from her. Thinking on her words, he ran hand onto her stomach and whispered, "No, not my brains, but, perhaps my son."

Pia froze, never having stopped to consider that their actions would have such a consequence. Sitting up, she pulled the covers with her. His hand fell off her stomach, as he too moved to get up.

Zoran saw her reaction and was sorry for it. It didn't seem she had changed her mind in that regard. She didn't want his sons. It might already be too late for her to decide against pregnancy. They'd come together often and it was possible that even now his child grew within her. Would she resent him for it? Would she do the unthinkable and try to end it? Deciding it was better not to mention that little fact, he let the subject drop.

Pia trembled to think herself a mother. She knew nothing about motherhood or pregnancy. Seeing the expression on his face and afraid he was going to press the issue further, she hastened, "Don't you have to be there in order for the war council to convene?"

Zoran smiled, remembering how she broke him under torture. She'd gotten that piece of information out of him when he taught her that kissing and sucking weren't only for mouths and tongues. As a hardened warrior, he might have shamed himself by caving so easily to her soft lips, but it had definitely been worth it.

"Yes," Zoran groaned. Seeing his war council tunic crumpled on the floor, he shook it out.

"Are you sure I can't go with you?" she asked. They'd been over it the night before and Pia knew he wouldn't be changing his mind. She was right.

"Princesses aren't allowed, only occasionally the Queen," he answered. "Besides, they are terribly dull. We basically grunt and stare at each other for hours and refuse to answer each other's questions."

"Grunting and staring," Pia giggled softly, giving his body a meaningful look. "I don't see anything boring about that."

* * * *

King Attor denied all charges with a smirky grin. He knew as long as he was under the protection of the convened council, he wouldn't be touched. Nothing was accomplished during the seven hours of talks. But, then again, nothing had been accomplished in the centuries of fighting that had occurred between the two kingdoms. Death attempts on both sides were nothing new, though none had occurred for over a hundred years.

Zoran was in charge of military matters, representing the Draig with a Var warrior of equal ranking opposite him. Olek presided over the whole affair, doing his best as ambassador to keep the peace, though all brothers knew he would like nothing more than to spill King Attor's blood for his insults to the royal Draig family.

After the meeting, it took another four and a half hours to insure that Attor and his men were gone. A thorough search of the castle revealed nothing and the high alert was taken off the village so that the villagers could again leave their homes using caution.

Zoran was exhausted from his night with Pia. It was hard not to grin during negotiations every time he thought about it. His vixen wife had drained him dry. However, strangely, his body was eager to go back to her. He wondered if he could give her another night of passion. His body was willing to try.

He stripped from his clothing and climbed into bed beside his sleeping wife. He knew that soon they might be facing another war with the House of Var. Feeling Zoran's arms around her waist, Pia yawned, turning around to look at him.

"What happened?" she asked, dying to know. She'd tried to wait up for him, but had fallen asleep. She'd spent most of the day poking at her stomach, trying to see if anything was different within her. Not sure what signs to look for, she just sighed. She didn't look fatter. Aside from the numbing sensation created by a night of loving, she didn't ache.

"Nothing was achieved," he admitted.

Pia sighed, sensing the truth in his words.

Reaching behind him, he pulled out a box and set in on her chest. "I wanted to give you something."

Pia blinked, looking down. The wooden box was old, looking very much worn. "What is it?"

"A gift," he admitted.

To her surprise, she noticed he almost seemed embarrassed. That piqued her curiosity. "What for?"

"I was going to give it to you the night of your coronation, after we got home, but ... well," he lightly shrugged. "So much happened that I never had a chance."

"What is it?" she asked again, almost too scared to touch it.

"Just open it," he urged.

Pia did, unhooking the delicate latch. Inside were five very beautiful knives. They were used, but in good shape. Touching the delicately engraved silver hilt encrusted with black onyx, she breathed, "They're beautiful."

"I know they're old," Zoran admitted. "But they were the first set given to me by my parents the day I became a man. I don't know, maybe I should've gotten you jewelry instead."

"Are you kidding?" Pia laughed, excited. "You can't maim a man with a set of earrings. These are perfect."

Zoran chuckled, nuzzling her neck with a soft trail of kisses. "Ah, my bloodthirsty wench."

"Can I try them out tomorrow?" she asked hopefully. "I've been promising to teach the other girls how to knife throw. It would be perfect!"

"Who do you want me to get as your target? I believe Hume is still fairly taken with you," Zoran mused.

Pia punched him. "I meant the knife post out at the field."

"I don't see why not," Zoran said. "We can go tomorrow morning if you like."

Pia was lifting each knife in turn as she spoke. When Zoran tried to move the box away, she growled and made as if to bite his hand.

"You can't sleep with them," he chuckled. He buried his face into his pillow and yawned.

"But--" she began.

"No, I'm setting my foot down."

Pia giggled but let him take the box and set it on the floor. He came back to wrap his arm around her warm body, trying to dig his fingers beneath her cotton shirt to the flesh at her waist.

She stroked back the hair from his face, saying, "Good night."

Zoran kissed the tip of her nose. Pia turned in his arms and pretended to go asleep. It wouldn't do to keep tempting fate until she learned a little bit more about this pregnancy thing. She'd have asked Nadja, but the castle had been on high alert and she hadn't been allowed to leave her home.

"Goodnight, Pia," Zoran sighed, nuzzling her neck. Holding her in his arms, he fell asleep.

* * * *

The warriors cheered good-naturedly as the four Princesses, wearing dark breeches and tunic shirts, aimed knives at the practice post. Olena was the first to throw. She did fairly well, as each knife made it into the center. The gathered soldiers clapped and stomped. She glanced at Yusef, trying to act like she didn't seek his approval. A white bandage slashed across his arm but he looked well.

Nadja was hopeless, missing the target completely on all five tries. She glanced at Olek in embarrassment. The men applauded anyway. Morrigan managed to hit the post on her turn, though they weren't centered. She curtsied as she received her cheers. Ualan wasn't there to watch her victory. She had told the Princesses that she had left him in bed asleep.

"Maybe you ladies should let a man show you how it's done," a voice from the crowd called.

"Ach," Agro cried. "You're hardly a man, Hume!"

Pia flashed a grin at Hume, who immediately crushed his hand over his heart. She took her new set of knives Zoran had given her, weighing them carefully in her hand as she tested them. Getting to the third one, she lifted it and studied the blade. Frowning, she went to her husband and handed it to him. Zoran uncrossed his arms and took it from her, letting his finger slyly glide over the pulse at her wrist. His mouth twitched but gave nothing away as Pia shivered.

Pia looked him directly in the eye, moving her hands to his waist, she lifted his tunic aside and let her nail scrape lightly over his skin as she retrieved a replacement blade from the back side of his waist. His stomach tensed, but his face gave nothing away as she withdrew a blade and began testing it as she had the others. His eyes, however, glinted with just enough liquid fire to leave her body very excited.

When he glanced curiously at the replacement blade, she announced loudly for all the men to hear, "You need to check the balance on that one. It will pull a fraction to the right."

With hardly moving a muscle, Zoran threw the blade over her shoulder. It stuck just to the right of the target. The men laughed heartily in approval.

Not turning around, Pia said, "Told you."

Zoran's lip curled up at the side, excited by her confidence. He stood, waiting for his wife to take her first turn, his stomach tight as he waited to judge her skill for himself.

Going before the target, Pia took a deep breath. She'd seen the challenge in Zoran's gaze. She would make him proud.

Flinging one of the blades at the post, she didn't wait for it to land before rapidly dropping to the ground to throw two more in roll. Then, coming to kneel, she threw the last two. The fourth blade struck against Zoran's to knock it free, before sticking in its place. On the fifth throw, she turned her arm and it missed the post completely. The warriors watched in stunned silence, their eyes following the path of her last throw. It was a foot before Hume, sticking hilt up and tipped forward to the man.

"You missed," Hume said, to break the silence. The men went wild cheering. Pia took a graceful bow. The women jumped in excitement, basking in Pia's victory.

Morrigan turned amongst the commotion to see her husband storming onto the field. The women, hearing her gasp, followed her gaze. Pia and Olena exchanged looks of amusement.

"Careful," Olena teased Morrigan, pulling close to the woman. "Or else we might think you actually like the barbarian."

Morrigan blushed, turning her eyes away. Pia handed Olena the blades for her next turn.

"My wife is missing," Ualan whispered furiously into Zoran's ear. "Have you seen her?"

Zoran frowned at Ualan's words. Without uncrossing his arms, he nodded his jaw to where Morrigan stood with the other Princesses.

Olena glanced at Yusef, he nodded his head. Pia, seeing the woman's look, whispered, "It would seem Rigan isn't the only one enamored by her warrior husband."

Olena let a mischievous smile light her eyes. "We've got a bet going. All I have to do is hit this post with these five blades and I win."

"Come," they heard Prince Ualan say.

Pia and Olena turned around to watch Ualan leading Morrigan off to the forest. They shared a look.

"Zoran tried to lead me around like that," Pia said, shaking her head in disapproval. "He had to carry me off kicking and screaming. I nearly got away, too. I did get a few good punches in."

Olena laughed, "I hid in the forest for a night, but broke my arm. Yusef had to come rescue me."

"We're waiting!" came a cry from the crowd.

Pia glared good-humoredly at Hume. Wryly, she called, "Don't make me aim higher, Sir Hume."

Pia meant his chest, but the rowdy warriors were only too ready to guess something much bawdier.

Zoran gulped. Pia looked in confusion at the men's snickering. Olena laughed, understanding the men all too well.

Pia crossed over to Zoran as Olena threw. Standing beside him and affecting a similar, cross-armed stance, she said from the side of her mouth, "What did I just say?"

"You indicated you were going to rid him of his manhood," Zoran said, cracking a smile at her innocence.

"Oh," came her reply. Pia bit her lips, but gave nothing away. "Want to wager on my next throw?"

Zoran turned to look at her. "What did you have in mind?"

"If I hit the post five times, I win," she stated under her breath.

"Too easy," he dismissed, shaking his head.

"Blindfolded?" she suggested.

"No consideration for distractions," he added. "You miss, you lose."

"Fine," Pia said. They barely looked at each other. To everyone else it seemed they discussed Olena's technique. Olena threw her last blade. It hit, but went too far to the side and instantly fell back out with the weight of the hilt. The men cheered as she went to retrieve them. Nadja, who was standing by Olek, waved away her turn, too embarrassed to try again.

"What are the stakes?" he asked.

"When I win, you have to ... dance for me," she answered. A small blush threatened her at the admission.

"I would do that anyway," he answered with an unashamed shrug.

"No clothes," she added boldly.

"If you miss, you wear no clothes, too," he said, instantly taken with the idea. "And we both dance."

Pia turned red, but she knew she wouldn't miss. "Fine."

"Agreed," he said. Zoran saw a little tremor rack up her body.

Olena was looking at her expectantly, holding out the knives.

"We need a blindfold," Zoran called. Miraculously, the call was quickly answered as one was passed over the front to Zoran. Zoran crossed over to Pia and tied it around her head. Leaning into her ear, he said, "Perhaps we should keep this blindfold. It might be fun."

Pia blushed profusely. Zoran smacked her hard on her backside and the men laughed. Quietly he backed up. Pia took a deep breath trying to remember where the post was. Luckily, she'd angled her foot when Zoran tied the blindfold on.

"Make your throw!" Zoran called.

Pia lifted her arm, taking aim. Holding her breath, she threw, hearing the blade land on wood.

Zoran grinned. He was proud of her skill. The blade pulled slightly to the right but hit a solid mark.

Pia threw the second and third time. Each blade landed in the post. Suddenly, a loud cheering came up over the crowd.

Zoran grinned as she stiffened. He'd motioned the men to noise.

Pia lifted the blade, trying to concentrate over the shouts. She threw. The fourth hit, though it wasn't as deep as the others.

"Oooo," the men in unison shouted.

"Zoran!" came a sudden panicked shout. "Olek! Yusef!"

Pia frowned, recognizing Prince Ualan's voice. Zoran motioned to Agro to keep the men at the field. He ran toward his brother's call, drawing the sword from his waist as he moved. Yusef nodded to one of the men, who instantly tossed his good hand a blade. Olek was right behind them.

Pia tore the blindfold from her head. Seeing the men running toward the forest she took off after them, knife gripped in her hand. Olena and Nadja soon followed her.

Twelve light blond Var warriors pursued Prince Ualan from the trees, over the forest path. Their bodies grew with fur as they shifted with the vicious, snarling features of wild cats. He dragged Morrigan with one arm. She was unconscious, a dart sticking out from her throat.

Ualan was forced to shift to Draig, using his arm to deflect the enemy's blows as he fought them off with his free arm. He tried to protect Morrigan, her feet trailing in the dirt. Soon the Princes were by his side, shifting into Draig as they fought against the Var. The one armed Yusef bravely hacked forward with his sword, giving Ualan time to get Morrigan to safety.

Ualan dropped his wife behind them on the ground as easily as he could so that he could join the fight against the attackers. Pia didn't hesitate as she ran swiftly to help the men, throwing her blade into one of the creature's throat. As Zoran swung his arm, she ducked beneath him, grabbing the knife from his belt.

Nadja stiffened in fear to see human cats fighting human dragons. Shaking herself at Olena's call, she darted forward to the fallen Morrigan. With Olena's help, they pulled the woman from the fray to safety.

Soon the Var were retreating in the forest. Pia crossed over to one of the fallen men and took the two blades she'd used from their unmoving throats. Ualan nodded his thanks at her. Zoran turned to his wife in pride of her bravery and skill, shifting back. She hadn't hesitated to protect the family.

Ualan turned, smelling Morrigan's trail as he took off down the path, Yusef and Olek were behind him. Zoran hung back, looking at his wife. Not bothering to clean his sword, he sheathed it.

"You did well," he said.

Pia's eyes lit up at the compliment.

"Do we give chase?" she asked, motioning to where the Vars retreated.

"No," he answered. "Let them go for now."

Pia crossed over to him and, wiping his blade on her pant leg, she looked deeply into his eyes as she slid it back into place. She let her fingers linger on his firm waist.

"You owe me a dance, wife." He grinned. He looked meaningfully at her blade. "That one missed the post."

Her eyes narrowed. "I demand a re-throw, I--"

"Tsk, tsk," Zoran answered, his eyes flashing. "Distractions don't count. I want my dance."

"Let's go check on Rigan," Pia said, shooting him a dangerous glare. She was thrilled by the answering promise in his eyes.

Zoran laughed to himself. His wife didn't lose gracefully.

"Yes, and after we can go find that blindfold," he whispered.

As Zoran and Pia approached, Nadja was kneeling by Morrigan and looking at Prince Ualan. The dart was still in Morrigan's neck. Pia frowned in worry. Nadja sighed heavily and whispered, "Let me think. I need to concentrate."

Pia glanced at Zoran, moving quietly closer to his strength.

"Give me your knife," Nadja said to Pia. Pia instantly handed it over. Taking a deep breath, Nadja cut into Morrigan's throat where the dart embedded into the skin. Instantly, green began to drip and ooze from the wound.

Soon, she had the star tipped points of the dart out of the woman's neck. Nadja dropped the blade and continued to bleed the poison.

Pia turned to Zoran to whisper, "Why would they target Morrigan and not your brother?"

Zoran didn't answer. Nadja's words stopped him.

"It's as I thought. I've seen this kind of poison before. Usually jealous old lovers do it for revenge. If you had torn the dart out of the skin, it would have released a poison into the blood stream. She would have lived but you never would have been able to touch her again. It's ironic really. That way it's the current lover that poisons the woman, sealing their fate. You should get her to a doctor."

Nadja stood, warily trying to edge away from them. Her round eyes looked over each of the brothers before turning her eyes to the forest.

"I would say that whoever poisoned her didn't want you to be with her," Nadja said to Ualan, before turning and running away. Olek was right behind her.

Olena stood, watching the woman. Her eyes narrowed. Solemnly, she said, "She didn't know about the Draig."

Ualan picked up his wife. The others followed as he carried Morrigan to the medical ward. No one said a word.

Chapter Twenty

"Why do they attack the Princesses?" Yusef asked with a frown. Olena stood by his side, her face unmoving. Nadja and Olek hadn't joined them, but Zoran and Pia stood next to Ualan. Morrigan was on the hospital bed, having been checked by the doctors and given some medicine to help along her recovery.

Pia thought of Zoran's tender hand on her stomach when he mentioned the possibility of her pregnancy. During the night, while he slept, his hand had found hold on her lower abdomen and she'd lain awake wondering at the naturally slow circles of his twitching fingers on her skin. It hadn't been hard to conclude what he'd been dreaming about. With sudden insight, she whispered, "Because without us you will have no sons. Your line will end."

Zoran stiffened at her soft words and looked at her, his eyes searching.

Pia's lips stiffened. She was very aware that further talk into pregnancy would be better handled when they were alone. Taking a deep breath, she continued, "It makes perfect sense. I've seen you all fight. Especially with all four of you banded together, you would be a formidable opponent. You expect the attack. We're new here and it would be assumed that we had no clear idea of the dangers. Plus, we're women. Men ... ah, no offense to anyone here ... men, especially those from warrior classes, often misjudge women as unworthy opponents."

The Princes listened closely to her words, giving away none of their thoughts. Zoran watched his wife's face, never having seen the serious militant strategist look coming from her.

Pia gazed up at her husband. Her features were pulled with concentration. "If you were to destroy an enemy, Zoran, would you attack their weakness or their strength?"

"Only a fool would choose to fight a strength if a weakness was to be had," Ualan said, nodding to the woman's insight.

"Only they have obviously underestimated the strength of our women," Zoran added. Pia actually turned the slightest shade of pink. Again he was amazed. If the conversation weren't so dire, he'd have thrown her over his shoulder and carted her off to his bed.

"What better way to end this age old feud than to wipe out the leaders before they are born?" Yusef said. He frowned, unconsciously drawing Olena under the protection of his good arm.

"For, if we were to die," Ualan added. "There would be an heir that could sometime rise against them. If they make sure that our line is ended, when we die there will be no one to avenge us. With no King or protection, our people will be left without defense. Everything will be in chaos."

"It's imperative that we discover who is spying for the Var," Yusef said. Whoever had stabbed him knew the back passages well enough to escape through them.

"Spy?" Pia questioned, blinking. She turned to frown at Zoran. "You said nothing of a spy!"

Zoran sighed. He hadn't thought of it when she was interrogating him. It had been hard enough to think when she was torturing his body in such wondrous ways.

"Olena," Pia said. "You remember that servant at the festival, don't you? The one who spilled his pitcher? It has to be him. He was no more fit to be a servant than I am."

Olena shook her head, barely recalling anything but her husband from that night.

"What are you talking about?" Zoran demanded, turning to grab her arms and study her eyes.

"There are too many servants in the kingdom," Ualan mused. "For festivals many come to help. It would take forever to locate them all just to find this one."

"No," Pia said. "He was at the coronation. The spy would be here in the palace kitchens. I remember watching him fumble with some plates. He only carried two unlike the other servants who carried four or more. It has to be him. He was graceless serving. Yet there was something different to his walk and his hand had a sword callous along the ridge. I would almost bet my life he is your man."

Morrigan, who was pale but alive, said through her hoarse voice, "I recorded that night on my camera."

Everyone turned to look at her.

Sheepishly, she admitted, "I'm an undercover reporter for an intergalactic newspaper chip."

Ualan stiffened but didn't stop her from speaking.

"I was supposed to write a story about the royal weddings," she continued softly. Turning to Ualan, she said, "My camera will have recorded part of that night. Maybe Pia's servant can be found on the relay."

"It's worth a shot," Yusef said.

"I'll go find it," Ualan said. He went from the hospital room, his arms stiff. It was silent until he got back. When he did, he handed a small eyepiece and an emerald to Morrigan.

"Can you make it work so we can all see?" Yusef asked.

Morrigan nodded. "I think so."

She requested some saline and wetted the lens before sticking it into her eye. Slipping the emerald on her finger so it could react with her nervous system, she turned the stone. A light shone from her eyes, darkening as she blinked. They watched in amazement as they saw a picture of the Breeding Festival floating on the air.

Coming around to stand across from Morrigan, they eyed the round picture.

"Can you see it?" she asked.

"Yes," Ualan said.

"All right, just let me leaf through these," she murmured. Morrigan closed her eye and the picture disappeared. Pia saw her turn bright red and wondered about it.

"Morrigan," Ualan began.

Morrigan blinked in surprise and a flash of Ualan's naked backside came up bigger than life before his brothers.

"Oh," Morrigan panicked. Zoran and Yusef laughed heartily. Morrigan's cheeks turned a bright, mortified red and she squeezed her eyes tight to block the image out.

Wryly, Ualan stated, "I had no idea I looked that good from behind."

He was rewarded with punches from his teasing brothers.

"Here," Morrigan said, getting back to business as she swallowed over her embarrassment. A screen of the festival came up. "I can't play sound, but you should see the picture moving like a silent movie."

They watched in silence. Then suddenly, Pia pointed, and said, "There, stop, that's him."

Morrigan froze the picture.

"Yeah," Olena said, leaning forward to get a closer look at the corner of the frame. "I remember him. Now that you mention it, he was rather strange."

"He has the coloring of a Var," Yusef said.

"But not the scent of one," Zoran said. "Do you think he has found a way to mask his smell?"

"He wears the tunic of the kitchen staff," Yusef said. "We will find him and question him. If he's Draig, it will be easy for him to prove it. If he's Var, he'll come up with an excuse not to shift."

Ualan nodded. Yusef and Zoran left, their women by their sides.

Once the couples were alone in the hall, Pia glanced at Zoran. Her body shook with a terrible sense at Morrigan's confession. She knew her scars were gone, but she couldn't help thinking she would rather not be publicly known. Quietly, she asked Olena, "Did you know Rigan was writing a story about us?"

Olena shook her head. "She said she *was* not *is*."

Zoran and Yusef exchanged looks. They didn't much care for their private lives to be made known to the entire galaxy. The Qurilixen, by tradition, were a secretive race that kept to themselves. However, they also knew Ualan would feel the same way and would undoubtedly talk his wife out of writing such a story.

* * * *

Pia's blond servant was apprehended almost immediately upon the Prince Zoran and Prince Yusef entering the palace kitchens. Zoran's nose picked up the Var smell beneath an all too potent scent of Draig. They found him hiding behind one of the oversized brick ovens, ducking from his work.

The soldier must have known that he was found out, because he tried to run. It was no use. Yusef was standing in the doorway and with a swing of his good arm he punched the man square in the jaw, laying him out on the floor.

The Draig servants blinked in surprise at the sudden attack. However, as they witnessed the lazy man sprawled on the floor, they cheered without knowing his treachery.

As a fellow worker, the indolent Var spy wasn't well liked in the kitchen.

The royal family was relieved as news was spread of the spy's capture. Olek escorted the Var to the lower prisons where he would be questioned by Agro. Zoran had no doubt that the beefy giant would discover much from the man. When Agro chose to shift, he could be most persuasive.

* * * *

"I'm very impressed by your knowledge," Zoran admitted to his wife.

Pia flushed, turning to look at him. He quickly told her all that had happened--the capture of the spy, his impending interrogation in the lower prisons. When he finished, Pia was nodding her head, her eyes drifting over his body.

"I got you a present," Zoran said. A smile fanned over his lips.

Pia furrowed her brow, and asked, "Another set of knives?"

"No," Zoran said carefully moving across to the couch were she sat. Reaching behind his back, he pulled the blindfold out from behind him. "This."

Pia flushed. Biting her lips, she backed away. "I don't think we can."

Zoran's look disagreed.

"Zoran."

This time he stopped, frowning. "What is it?"

"I'm ... tender," she answered delicately.

"From the fight?" he questioned, growing worried by the way she said it.

"No."

"From...?" Zoran's brow rose and she swore she saw a swelling of masculine pride at the idea that it was his lovemaking that caused her soreness.

"Ah," Pia flushed, her cheeks flaming. "You're going to make me say it, aren't you?"

"Pia," he whispered, unable to help his chuckle. "I'm your husband, you can tell me anything."

"I'm female tender," she answered.

"You wish to love a female?" he frowned, not believing the words, but not understanding her.

"No!" she said, nearing mortification. She'd really never discussed this with anyone, aside from the nurse on the medical base. She couldn't even remember the technical word the old, burly woman had for it. Lifting her hands to motion toward her chest, she didn't touch herself, as she tried to explain, "I'm sore. You know, women once a month get ... sore."

Zoran's eyes narrowed and to Pia's horror, he sniffed at her. The blindfold dropped from his fingers to the floor. Shaking his head, he said, "You are not on your Breeding time."

"I'm not saying I'm pregnant," Pia shot, a look of utter horror coming to her face. Zoran frowned at the way the statement came from her lips. Pia was too embarrassed to notice. "I'm going to ... get ... all bloodied."

He wanted to laugh at her description of it. For the Draig, the woman's Breeding time was almost regarded as sacred. The pheromones the women's body sent off drove husbands mad with lust and the need to procreate. It turned them into true beasts. And from what he'd been told, although women were not made to conceive at such a time, it didn't stop the effect. When she was in such a state, Draig seed could stay within the woman, waiting inside her until her new cycle, causing a greater chance for a belated pregnancy.

"So?" he shrugged reaching forward to kiss her.

"It's gross."

"It's normal," Zoran said, kissing her protesting lips.

Pia instantly began to melt. Then, catching herself, she pulled away.

"Is this because you do not want my children?" Zoran asked, letting her go. When she couldn't answer fast enough, he stood. His gaze hardened, seeming almost to crack within its depths. "If it's what you wish, wife. I'll leave you alone."

Pia gasped at his sudden anger. Zoran didn't give her time to explain. He turned and stormed away, heading out the front door.

Pia sat, staring after him, her mouth hanging open, stunned to silence.

* * * *

Zoran didn't come home that night. Pia stayed up until her eyes felt so leaden she couldn't lift them. He didn't come home the next day either.

Pia, bored out of her mind and needing an excuse to leave the house, went to search out the other Princesses. Olena and Nadja weren't answering their doors. Knowing Morrigan was more than likely recovering, she left her alone. She walked outside. The practice field had a few men on it running laps, but no Zoran or his brothers. Frowning, she turned to go inside. Queen Mede was coming out the front gate.

"Mede," Pia said, smiling.

"I was looking for you," the Queen admitted. "One of the men said they thought you went this way."

"What's happening?"

"Nadja and Olena were attacked last night," the Queen said.

"The Var?" Pia asked instantly.

"No, Nadja's father." A light frown came across Mede's features.

"Are they...?"

Mede shook her head in denial. "No, they're fine."

Pia nodded.

"You were right about King Attor's motives. Agro interrogated the prisoner and confirmed it. He seeks to kill Morrigan, Nadja, and you. It seems that he's taken a liking to Olena, though. That's why he attacked Yusef," Mede said. "The man gave Agro directions to Attor's hidden camp. The trackers go there even now to confirm it."

Pia didn't need to ask the tactics Agro had to used to get that much from the spy.

"They go tonight, then, if he's where they think?" Pia asked.

The Queen nodded.

"I would go with them," Pia admitted.

"Zoran has forbidden it," Mede answered. "Come, let's go back inside. It isn't safe out here."

Pia wasn't worried, but she didn't feel like fighting with Mede over it.

Walking inside, they passed the guard in silence. When they were far enough away to speak in private, Pia stated bluntly, "I have some daughter questions."

Mede was surprised, actually stopping mid-stride with her mouth falling slightly apart. Clearing her throat, a deep pleasure came over her face. Reaching to boldly touch Pia's cheek, she was pleased when the woman didn't flinch and pull away.

"And I would have mother answers for you Pia," she answered, her Qurilixen accent rolling softly. She drew her hand away. "What is it?"

"I know nothing of being a wife."

"You seem to be doing well enough," Mede answered. "There's no 'way' to being a wife, you just are."

"I know nothing of being a woman," Pia elaborated.

"Oh." Mede pressed her lips together. "You mean you and my son haven't...?"

Pia flushed, but she was too serious to let embarrassment stop her. "Yes, we've come together. What I mean, is that I know nothing about this Breeding time, as Zoran called it." Pia shrugged. "I've always referred to it as getting bloodied."

With much effort, Mede managed not to laugh. Pia made is sound as if she got into a fight each month and lost. Having been raised on a male dominated planet, and raising only sons herself, Mede had no idea how to have such a conversation.

"What is it you would know?" Mede asked carefully.

"Zoran wants sons."

"As do all men," the Queen answered with a nod.

"How do I get them?" Pia asked.

This time Mede did grin. She took up her arm and began guiding her down the red passageway. "Oh, Pia, what do you think you've been doing with my son?"

"So when he leaks, that makes sons?" Pia asked, nodding her head as if she understood. "He hinted as much. I wasn't sure as to the how."

"Basically, he becomes even more a part of you, growing inside you," Mede answered.

"And then when he grows in me, he'll go to another until I am ... until it's removed?" she asked. She'd heard that many married men cheated on their wives when they were pregnant.

The Queen merely laughed. "No, it would be impossible."

Pia was confused again.

"Once mated, they do not go to other women--ever. He couldn't even if he wanted to. You would know right away. Besides, if he wanted to, you would know that too. He doesn't desire anyone else, rest assured," Mede said.

"How do you mean I would know? I can't read his thoughts," Pia replied.

"Qurilixen men are given a crystal when they are born. It's their guiding light. When you were paired by the crystal, your lives became joined in such a way that can never be taken back. When he took you to his tent, it was his choice. When you stayed, that was yours. You exchanged part of your souls. By crushing the crystal, you assured that the exchange would never be reversed. There will be no other in his bed or his heart. When a Draig man looks at his wife, all he sees and feels is for her. Very beautiful, isn't it?"

Pia nodded, though she didn't really understand. Surely, the Queen merely spoke in metaphors. She stopped walking to look up at a particularly bold statue of a Draig in human form.

"Do you understand what that means for him and for you?" the Queen asked, her eyes shifting to a subtle gold at her words.

Pia shook her head, her wide eyes staring out carefully, not moving from her spot before the statue.

"It means his crystal is broken. It means he put his every chance at happiness in you. He gave his life to you. There will never be anyone else for him so long as he lives. That's a long time for our people, and for you. By giving you his life, he shortened his and extended yours so your fates could remain together. If you were to choose to leave him, he would be alone for the rest of his days." Mede stopped, letting her words sink in.

Pia trembled. Her heart fluttered dangerously in her chest.

Mede continued, "When you feel as if you can sense him inside you that's what I speak of. It's very real. Soon, when you are bonded completely, you will be able to hear his thoughts in your head. You'll sense his troubles. You'll hear him call you from across the palace. You'll know every moment he wants you, when he's sick, when he's hiding something from you in an effort to protect you. And it will be the same for him with you."

"So if he thought I didn't want his children..." Pia began.

Mede's face paled. She looked as if she might be sick. "Why would he think that?"

"I ... might have ... led him," she began. "I was frightened by the prospect."

"Do you want them?" Mede asked.

"Yes, but, I don't know. I'm scared. What if I do something wrong with it? Or forget to ... do whatever it is you do with them," she said.

"That's why you have family," the Queen said, smiling in understanding. "Every woman is scared, especially with the first. But, I guarantee, there's nothing more rewarding than seeing your husband's face in your child's."

Pia nodded. With a family nearby, it wouldn't be so bad. How hard could it be?

"If Zoran believes you feel this way," Mede said, "he'll be hurt beyond measure. To tell a Draig husband that you have no wish to give him a child, is like telling them you have no wish for their love."

Tears came into Pia's normally strong gaze. She thought of her old wounds. Somehow, she hadn't thought about them for awhile. They no longer mattered. Voicing her last suspicion, a fear that nagged at the back of her mind since Zoran first mentioned he could give her strong sons the night of the Breeding festival, Pia asked weakly, "And if I can't give him sons? What will he do then?"

"Do you have reason to think such a thing?" Mede asked.

"I was injured once, pretty severely," Pia admitted. A tear slipped down her face. "The doctors who took care of me said there was a chance that I may not function as a woman in such a way."

"Let's find out then, shall we?" the Queen answered. "Come on, we'll ask the medic to take a look."

Chapter Twenty-one

Draig trackers soon had the position of King Attor's campsite confirmed. The news came that night that the men were off to battle with King Attor and his Var warriors. Pia respected Zoran's wishes and didn't follow him into battle. If what Queen Mede had said was true, then she had a lot of thinking to do.

Pia hardly slept, waking up from small naps every hour or so. The men were gone all night. Mede stayed with her most of the evening, never once mentioning a fear for her husband. Once she admitted that worry was a lot every woman must bear--worry for husbands and sons. But they were all fine warriors and to voice such concerns would be to dishonor them.

Pia said nothing, having faith that Zoran would come home to her. The next morning, he did.

Remembering what the Queen had told her, she smiled at him as he walked into the door and acted as if he'd just came home from a day training the men. She stayed on the couch, where she'd been silently staring at the fire, lost in a world of thought.

Quietly, she said, "I knew you would meet with victory."

Zoran's eye lit with pleasure at the compliment. He nodded, filled with pride by her words.

"Now, tell me what happened," she griped with a pout forming on her lips, "since you forbade my going with you. It's not fair that you get all the fun."

"It was a small encampment of Var. King Attor is dead. We tried to arrest him according to our treaty and he called his troops to battle. Attor's son will take the throne. Olek is speaking to the new Var King, negotiating a peace," Zoran obliged. He carried his sword to the exercise room, placing it in its place. Then, stretching his arms over his head, he yawned.

Pia stood, following him into the exercise room. She clutched the blindfold behind her back, twisting it between her fingers.

"It will be slow going, but peace can be achieved," Zoran said, feeling her behind him. "Some of the older nobles will protest on both sides. However, in the end, they would bow to the decision of their leaders."

"They have wise leaders," Pia said. "Aggravating, but wise."

"Only because our women make us so." Zoran laughed. He moved toward the bathroom. Throwing off his shirt, he soon stood naked before the hot spring. Pia trailed behind him, her lips curling as she saw his very firm backside. He again stretched out his arms, causing the muscles to ripple over his back in gentle, undulating waves.

"If our battles have ended," Zoran said. "I might be out of a job."

"Oh, I don't know about that," Pia said. She stepped up behind him. He tensed as her fingers walked up the middle of his back, pressing lightly along his spine to his neck. Then, lifting the blindfold, she placed it over his eyes. "I might have use for you."

Zoran grinned. "What use is that?"

Pia merely hummed to herself, as she slid out of her clothes. Then, running her hands over his body, she moved to stand in front of him. Zoran shivered at her light touches but didn't reach for her.

Pia loved looking at her warrior husband. She loved watching him move. She loved feeling his texture. She loved him.

"Well, you did promise to take me hunting and camping," she began, circling his nipples in absent trails.

"And so I shall," he said. Pia licked her lips to watch his mouth move.

"And you do owe me a naked dance."

"You shall have as many as you desire," he murmured, using his senses to lean down to her to find her lips.

Pia let him kiss her, her hands moving down his arms. When he pulled away, she whispered, "Let us go camping very soon. We can dance naked under the stars."

His mouth cocked to the side. He didn't pull away from her lips or remove the blindfold. "Why soon? The best hunting isn't for many months."

She worked her fingers down to his wrists. "If you say so, but I would recommend you changing your mind."

"And why would that be?" Zoran asked, tempted to taste her lips once again.

"Because in several months you'll have to carry me up the mountain," she whispered. She drew his hand forward to her stomach. "The doctor said you grow in me."

Zoran's hands lifted to push back the blindfold. A hesitant smile came to his face.

"Are you saying...?"

"I'm saying, stubborn man, that I love you," Pia answered. Her eyes dipped ever so shyly. He wasn't supposed to have taken the mask off until after she told him. She didn't have time for embarrassment as he lifted her off the ground. Her feet dangled off the floor and she wrapped her arms around his thick neck for support.

His body pressed into hers as he stared deeply into her eyes. A wide grin of pure happiness spread over his features, as he whispered in awe, "I love you, too, wife."

Pia let him kiss her. A well of emotion sprung up between them, connecting them. There were no more boundaries, no more fears, no more doubt.

Pia pulled back. Still dangling, she said, "You got that I'm pregnant, right?"

Zoran only grinned, looking like he'd conquered the world.

Pia smiled naughtily back. With a stiff jerk, she pulled the blindfold back over his eyes. "Now, blind dragon, feel your way into the bath."

Zoran chuckled. He lowered her to the ground, only to press her into his arousal. "I would much rather feel my way into something else."

Pia's laughter rang out over their home.

"You've felt yourself into my heart, Zoran," Pia whispered. She took his face in her hands, holding him against her. "And I'm afraid there's no escaping. You are my prisoner."

Zoran kissed her, hard and sure, maddening their bodies with love and passion. "As you are mine, love, as you are mine."

There was nothing left to be said as he swept her into his arms, blindly kissing her and never intending to stop.

Epilogue

Almost nine months later...

The halls of the Draig Palace were rampant with hysterical men. Ualan, Zoran, Yusef, and Olek all paced a narrow stream down the halls length, only to turn and find their way back. Whenever a scream sounded, piercing the air, they would freeze. Their wide eyes would turn to the medical ward. And, in the following silence, they would curse their damned tradition of kicking fathers out of the delivery room.

Hearing Pia calling his name, Zoran tried to break down the door, only to be subdued by his brothers. The pacing resumed once more, this time joined by the curses of the four men. Hours and many laps later, the gaunt, frightened warriors were allowed to go inside the medical ward.

A nurse came forward, holding out a strong, proud son to Ualan--a beast of a child with his mother's dark hair and his father's brown eyes. A doctor brought forth an even larger boy, handing the baby to Yusef. The child had hair of red flames and gray eyes that sparkled with mischief. Olek's son, a tiny lad, was swaddled in Queen Mede's arms. The queen gave the boy to his anxious father who couldn't stop grinning.

Zoran, standing tall above his brothers, eager to hold his son, looked over at Pia on the bed. She smiled dreamily at him, her hand twitching for him to come to her. Zoran thought she'd never looked so beautiful.

The doctor stepped forward and handed him the tiniest bundle yet. Zoran blinked in surprise. Pia had given him a very healthy, bald little girl. As his daughter's eyes opened, it was his own light brown staring out from her mother's perfect face.

Going to their wives, the Princes held the babies to their chests, grinning and fawning like fools. The Princesses just smiled sleepily, marveling at how four strong Draig warriors could be brought low by helpless little infants.

THE END

Be sure to check out the next installment in Michelle M Pillow's Futuristic Series! See what happens in the lives of the Dragon Lords' enemy Princes in, *Lords of the Var*, coming to print Summer 2006. For more information or a complete listing of all books in the futuristic saga, please visit Michelle M Pillow's website (www.michellepillow.com).

You met their father in Dragon Lords...
"To be ruled by a woman is to be ruled by weakness and Kingdoms are only as strong as their rulers. A King must stand alone, beholden to none." --King Attor of the Var

Now come meet the sons...
The Var Princes were raised by a hard man who put no stock in love—especially love with one woman. Brought up to never take a life mate, these men will do everything in their power to live up to the dead King Attor's expectations and never fall in love.

A sneak peak at
LORDS OF THE VAR 1: THE SAVAGE KING
By Michelle M. Pillow
COMING IN PRINT SUMMER 2006 FROM NCP!

Kirill watched the door to his bedroom open. He'd been sitting in the dark, trying to relieve the stress headache that built behind his eyes for the last week. The pain started at the base of his skull and radiated up to his temples until he could hardly see straight.

A heavy responsibility had been thrust on his shoulders, a responsibility he really hadn't prepared himself for--the welfare of the Var people. King Attor had not left him in a good position. He'd rallied the people to the brink of war, convinced them that the Draig were their enemy, and even went so far as to attack the Draig royal family.

Kirill would see peace in the land. However, he knew the facts didn't bode well for it.

The Draig had a long list of grievances against King Attor and the Var kingdom. Before his death, Attor had ordered an attack on one of the four Draig Princes, all of which ended horribly for the Var. Prince Yusef was stabbed in the back, a most cowardly embarrassment for the Var guard who did it. If he hadn't been executed in the Draig prisons, he would've been ostracized from the Var community. Luckily, Prince Yusef survived or else they'd already be at battle.

Attor had also arranged for the kidnapping of Yusef's new bride. Princess Olena had been rescued or else that too would've led to war. The old King had tried to poison Princess Morrigan, the future Queen, on two separate occasions. She too lived. And those were only the offenses that Kirill knew about in the few weeks before Attor's death. He could just imagine what he didn't know.

Kirill sighed, feeling very tired. He'd known since birth that the day would come when he'd be expected to step up and lead the Var as their new King. He just hadn't expected it to be for another hundred or so years. His father had been a hard man, who he'd foolishly come to look at as invincible.

"Here kitty, kitty, kitty." His lovely houseguest's whisper drew his complete attention from his heavy thoughts.

Ulyssa bent over like she expected him to answer to the insulting call. He dropped his fingers from his temple into his lap and a quizzical smile came to his lips. As he watched her, he wasn't sure if he was angered or amused by her words.

"Are you in here, you little furball?" she said, a little louder.

She wore his clothes. Never had the outfit looked sexier.

His jaw tightened in masculine interest, as he unabashedly looked her over. All too well did he remember the softness of her body against his and the gentle, offering pleasure of her sweet lips. She'd made soft whimpering noises when he touched her--yielding, purring sounds in the back of her throat. Even with the aid of nef, he was surprised by how easily and confidently she melted into him. The Var were wild, passionate people and were drawn to the same qualities in others. He suspected she'd be an untamed lover.

Too bad she'd belonged to his father first. In his mind, that made her completely untouchable--though none would dare question his claim if he were to bring her to his bed. Technically, by Var law, she belonged to him until he chose to release her. For an insane moment, he thought about keeping her as a lover. He knew he wouldn't, but the thought was entertaining.

Kirill's grin deepened. Ulyssa strode across his home to the bathroom door with an irritated scowl. It was obvious she didn't see him in the darkened corner, watching her. He detected her engaging smell from across the room--the smell of a woman's desire. It stirred his blood, making his limbs heavy with desire. And, for the first time since his father's death, his headache relieved itself.

"Hum, maybe I'm looking too high. I'm sure there has to be a little cat door here somewhere."

His slight smile fell at her words. It was easy to detect the mocking in her.

"Where's your little kitty door, huh?" Ulyssa whispered to herself, her blue gaze searching around in the dark.

Kirill grimaced in further displeasure. He watched her open the door to his weapons cabinet. Her eyes rounded. She nodded in appreciation before closing the door and continuing her search for an exit.

She stopped at a narrow window by his kitchen doorway. Her neck craned to the side, as she tried to see out over the distance. Kirill knew she looked at the forest. From under her breath, he heard her vehement whisper, "Where exactly did you little fur balls bring me? Ugh, I need to get out of this flea trap, even if I have to fight every one of you cowardly felines to do it. I've fought species twice as big and three times as frightening. A couple little kitty cats don't scare me."

If this insolent woman wanted to play tough, oh, he'd play. Curling gracefully forward, Kirill shifted before his hands even touched the ground. He let one thick paw land silently on the floor, followed by a second. Short black fur rippled over his tanned flesh, blending him into the shadows. His clothes fell from his body and he lowered his head as he crept forward. A low sound of warning started in the back of his throat. He was livid.

Ulyssa froze, hearing the growl behind her. She really hadn't expected anyone to be in the room or else she never would've ranted like she had. Biting her lip, her eyes automatically scanned for a weapon as she turned.

Seeing the oversized panther stalking her, its body low against the ground as if she were its prey, she gasped. "Oh, whoa, easy there big fella. Are you one of them or are you just a pet?"

Ulyssa had fought all kinds of alien species and yet somehow her training hadn't prepared her to face a wild animal like this one. She could see the tempered speed in the panther's streamlined body. Steeling her nerves, she looked him in the eyes and reached out the back of her hand. "Are you in there, Var ... warrior ... man? Can you hear me?"

The animal roared, loud and long, brandishing his deadly fangs. She jolted back in surprise. His jaw snapped shut, as if he would bite her. His beastly yellow-green eyes narrowed in warning.

Ulyssa lost all bravado as she backed into a wall. Her heart let loose, hammering in her chest. Adrenaline rushed through her veins, making her shake. Her breath came out in ragged pants. She was terrified, too frightened to scream.

The animal crept closer. To her shame, she felt tears threaten to fill her eyes. Some agent she turned out to be! Her programming for this planet didn't include animal combat. Weren't you supposed to cower before wild animals and let them have dominance? Or was it the other way around? For the life of her, she couldn't remember. It's not like they had many wild animals left running around Earth these days. Those they did have were in locked conservatories, kept away from human interference, and left to their own devices.

The panther roared, bringing her attention back to the

trouble at hand. Ulyssa recoiled, lifting her arms to protect her chest and face as she pressed into the stone wall. A dark blue banner waved near her nose as she turned her head away. The image of a styled panther fluttered before her. She whimpered, closing her eyes. Her body tensed, bracing for the initial attack. Silence followed and she couldn't move.

"Shhh," a gentle whisper soothed. "I didn't think you'd be so scared of me."

Don't miss out on collecting these exciting Harmony™ titles for your collection:

Clone Wars: Armageddon by Kaitlyn O'Connor (Futuristic Romance) Trade Paper 1-58608-775-4
Living in a world devastated by one disaster after another, it's natural for people to look for a target to blame for their woes, and Lena thinks little of it when new rumors begin to circulate about a government conspiracy. She soon discovers, though, that the government may or may not be conspiring against its citizens, but someone certainly is. Morris, her adoptive father, isn't Morris anymore, and the mirror image of herself that comes to kill her most definitely isn't a long lost identical twin.

The Devil's Concubine by Jaide Fox (Fantasy Romance) Trade Paper 1-58608-776-2
A great contest was announced to decide who would win the hand of Princess Aliya, accounted the most fair young maiden in the land. The ruler of every kingdom was invited--every kingdom that is save those of the unnaturals. When King Talin, ruler of the tribe of Golden Falcons learned of the slight, he was enraged. He had no desire to take a mere man child as his bride, but he would allow the insult to go unchallenged.

Zhang Dynasty: Seduction of the Phoenix by Michelle M. Pillow (Futuristic Romance) Trade Paper 1-58608-777-0
A prince raised in honor and tradition, a woman raised with nothing at all. She wants to steal their most sacred treasure. He'll do anything to protect it, even if it means marrying a thief.

Warriors of the Darkness by Mandy M. Roth (Paranormal Romance) Trade Paper 1-58608-778-9
In place where time and space have no boundaries, ancient enemies would like nothing more than to eradicate them both, just when they've found each other.

COMING in APRIL:

Labyrinth of the Beast by Desiree Acuna (Erotic Fantasy Romance) Trade Paper 1-58608-782-7

Conclave of Shadows by Julia Keaton (Historical Romance) Trade Paper 1-58608-780-0

Printed in the United States
69133LVS00002B/1-120